Pirates, at last!

"Man the Boarding Party to starboard," yells the Captain. "Get the nets across! All hands to the Boarding Party!"

I gets to my feet and stumbles down the ladder, numb with terror. Got to find Jaimy.

The men are grabbing cutlasses from the rack. The nets and hooks are already across to the pirate ship. Our Marines are up in the rigging, firing down at the pirates below, keeping them away from the netting. I sees Jaimy up at the front of the mob by the rail, waiting for the order, cutlass in hand. The men are howling like demons. I grabs a cutlass and it's heavy in me hand and I knows I'll never use it but . . .

Jaimy, you fool, I want to shout. *Wait! You're only a boy! Let the others do it!*

"Away the Boarding Party!"

Jaimy is the first one across the net and I sobs and blindly follows. . . .

Bloody Jack

PART I

An Orphan, Cast Out in the Storm,
Body and Soul Most Lightly Connected,
A Tiny Spark on the Winds of Chance Borne,
To the Fancies of Fortune Subjected.

Prologue

My name is Jacky Faber and in London I was born, but, no, I wasn't born with that name. Well, the Faber part, yes, the Jacky part, no, but they call me Jacky now and it's fine with me. They also call me Jack-o and Jock and the Jackeroe, too, and, aye, it's true I've been called Bloody Jack a few times, but that wasn't *all* my fault. Mostly, though, they just call me Jacky.

That wasn't my name, though, back on That Dark Day when my poor dad died of the pestilence and the men dragged him out of our rooms and down the stairs, his poor head hanging between his shoulders and his poor feet bouncin' on the stairs, and me all sobbin' and blubberin' and Mum no help, she bein' sick, too, and my little sister, as well.

Back then my name was Mary.

London, 1797

"We'll be back for the rest of the lot in a few days," allows one of the men, and he's right 'cause me mum and me sister both goes off the next day and the men come

1

back and takes me mum and puts her in the cart, her legs all danglin' over the side and not covered up proper, but it's Muck that comes and picks up me poor little sister and throws her all limp over his shoulder. I din't know 'im as Muck then, but I do later, and it's Muck what takes me out all bawlin' to the street and sets me on the curb.

"There, there, Missy, there, there. Old Muck'll see ye soon," says he, leavin' me in me tears and grief as he puts Penny in his wheelbarrow and heads off down the street. "Inside of a week, I suspects."

There's the sound of sweepin' behind me and the door slams shut.

I runs and runs, just out of me head with terror, and I keeps on runnin' till I starts heavin' and gaspin' and chokin' and I can't run no more and I falls down in an alley, the cobblestones all hard against me knees and cold against me face. I crawls on me hands and knees up in a dark doorway, and I puts me thumb in me mouth and I sucks on it real hard, with me tears runnin' down me face and on me thumb and in me mouth all salty and dirty, but I don't care, I just wants to die, just die is all. I curls up huggin' me knees to me chest, hopin' I'll go real fast so's to be in Heaven with Dad and Mum and Penny, and I'm prayin' to God, like I been taught, for Jesus to come take me in his lovin' arms and say that I've been a good girl, there, there, but He don't come, no, He don't. What comes is nighttime and a gang of kids what grabs me and strips off all me clothes.

"Ain't she the fine one, then—she's got drawers, even!" says the one what pulls me dress off over me head and me underdrawers off over me feet, and who in her mercy throws her filthy old shift at me nakedness and tells me to put it on. Shakin', I does what she says 'cause I don't know what else to do even though it stinks and it's way too big for me and me clothes is way too small for her but she puts 'em on anyways.

"Look at me," says the girl what stole me clothes. "I'm ready for the bleedin' Derby, I am!"

"Let's go," comes a voice from the end of the alley.

"Stoof it, Charlie," says the girl what stole me clothes. "Oi'm not yet done with me *toi-let*."

The others laugh and lark about in the dark and cast wild shadows on the walls about me, and then they heads off down the alley. The girl what stole me clothes looks back at me cowerin' and weepin' in the doorway.

"Well, come on, then. And quit yer snivelin'. It'll do ye no good."

I snuffles and gets up.

Bloody Jack

Bloody Jack

Being an Account of
the Curious Adventures
of Mary "Jacky" Faber,
Ship's Boy

L. A. Meyer

Harcourt, Inc.

Orlando   Austin   New York   San Diego   London

Requests for permission to make copies of any part of the work
should be submitted online at www.harcourt.com/contact or
mailed to the following address: Permissions Department,
Harcourt, Inc., 6277 Sea Harbor Drive, Orlando, Florida 32887-6777.

www.HarcourtBooks.com

First Harcourt paperback edition 2004

The Library of Congress has cataloged the hardcover edition as follows:
Meyer, L. A. (Louis A.), 1942—
Bloody Jack: being an account of the curious adventures
of Mary "Jacky" Faber, ship's boy/L. A. Meyer
p. cm.
Summary: Reduced to begging and thievery in the streets of London,
a thirteen-year-old orphan disguises herself as a boy and connives her way
onto a British warship set for high sea adventure in search of pirates.
[1. Orphans—Fiction. 2. Seafaring life—Fiction. 3. Sea stories.
4. Pirates—Fiction. 5. Sex role—Fiction.] I. Title.
PZ7.M9795Bl 2002
[Fic]—dc21 2002000759
ISBN 978-0-15-216731-8
ISBN 987-0-15-205085-6 pb

Text set in Minion
Display set in Pabst
Designed by Cathy Riggs

J L N P Q O M K I
Printed in the United States of America

As always,
for Annetje

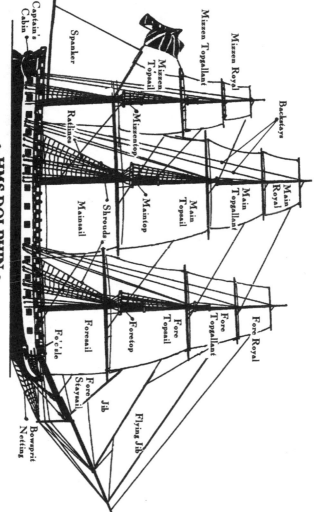

~ HMS DOLPHIN ~

Captain's Cabin
Spanker
Mizzen Topgallant
Mizzen Royal
Mizzen Topsail
Mizzentop
Reflines
Backstays
Main Royal
Main Topgallant
Main Topsail
Maintop
Shrouds
Mainsail
Mizzen
Main
Fore Royal
Fore Topgallant
Fore Topsail
Foretop
Foresail
Fo'c'sle
Fore Staysail
Jib
Flying Jib
Bowsprit
Netting

Chapter 1

Rooster Charlie allows as how today he's goin' to see Dr. Graves himself, the bloke what sends Muck around to pick up dead orphans for the di-seck-shun and for the good of science and all, to see if Charlie his ownself can get paid for his body *before* he goes croakers so's he can have the pleasure of it himself, like.

Me and the others laugh and jeer and say, "Charlie, you ain't got the bollocks. He'll prolly open you up right there, without so much as a by-your-leave." But Charlie, he hikes up his pants and gives his vest a pat and off he goes to sell his body. The pat is for his shiv, which he keeps tucked next to his ribs.

I've been with Charlie and the gang for four, maybe five, years since That Dark Day when me world was changed forever, but I can't be sure, the seasons run into each other so—we shivers and dies of the cold in the winter and sweats and dies of the pestilence in the summer, so it's all one. It's been close a couple of times, but I ain't dead yet.

We begs mostly, *please Mum please Mum please Mum,* over and over and we steals a bit and we gets by, just. There's only six of us right now 'cause Emily died last winter. I woke up next to her stiff body in the morning in our kip and I took her shift, which is too big but which I wears over me other shift, that givin' me two things I own besides me immortal soul. We tried takin' poor naked dead Emily down to the river and floatin' her off with the proper words and all, but she's stiff and hard to move and Muck caught us at it and stole her away. He gives us a curse for tryin' to get her away and for takin' her shift, too, that which he could have sold to the ragman.

Charlie is the leader of our gang and is called the Rooster 'cause his last name is Brewster, and him being such a cocky little banty, it seems natural, like. He's small, but he's smart and quick. Charlie's hair is straight and red and hangs to one side like a cock's comb. He's got britches that were once white and a once-white shirt and a bright blue vest over that, and he looks right fine, he does. A flash cove is our Rooster Charlie.

Besides him there's Polly and Judy and Nancy, and Hugh the Grand, him what is big and strong like an ox but what is a bit slow in the head. Charlie is fond of pattin' him on his broad back and sayin', "Our Hughie is our muscle and our tower of strength in this world of strife and trouble," and every time he does it, Hughie blushes all red and rocks his head side to side and grins his big dumb grin in his gladness. Charlie takes care of us, and with his cheek and his bravado and his shiv and our Hughie, the other gangs keep their distance.

Since I'm the smallest, I get called Little Mary, even though I ain't near to bein' the youngest no more.

The gang is always changin', as we loses some and we brings some in. Like the girl what stole me clothes before, whose name is Betty, was stole herself awhile back as two of the women from Missus Tuttle's lit upon our little band to find a replacement for their servant girl who had died. They picked Betty and allowed as they was gonna make a fine lady out of her, *Isn't that right, Bessie, just like us.* So they takes our Betty off, and Charlie says that he'll give it two days and then he'd go see her and if she wanted to come back, he'd steal her back, but after the two days he goes to see, and, no, she didn't want t' come back, she wanted to stay and be a fine lady. And I din't get me clothes back, either, even though they prolly would still have fit.

"Whyn't all us girls go off to Missus Tuttle's to be fine ladies," says I, thinkin' maybe there'd be food there and beds and stuff, but then Charlie tells me to shut my silly girly gob, as what do I know about anything in the world. Then he tells us what goes on at Missus Tuttle's, but I don't believe him, not for a minute. Disgustin', it is. "Such a mind you have, Charlie, to be thinkin' of such."

"Mary, bless you, you'll find out soon enough," says Charlie.

Our kip is up under the Blackfriars Bridge, just where the bridge meets the road real sharp so there's a cave under there, like. We got some straw from the stables on the sly, a little bit at a time, so at night we all burrows in and sleeps in a pile for warmth and comfort. When it rains, trickles of water come down through the black stones, but we knows where they'll be comin' now, so we keeps away. Can't keep away the damp from the river, though. I think that's what took Emily off, the damp and cold from the river. In the night the lights from the city lamps bounce off the waves, and on foggy nights horns sound low and mournful back and forth. It's ships makin' their way to someplace else, and I want to be going somewheres else, too.

Other gangs would like to have our kip, but with Hugh the Grand shakin' his big fists and bellowin' and Charlie wavin' his shiv and the rest of us throwin' rocks, we manages to chase them off and keep our home, at least for the time bein'.

At night, when we're all in a pile, we talks and makes up stories about what we're goin' to be if we grows up. Like Charlie says, he'll be a soldier and all and trade his shiv for a great gleamin' sword and fine red uniform and won't all the fine ladies love him and we girls all says we loves him right now but he says that don't count, us bein' worthless drabs and all and he gets jabbed in the ribs for his cheek.

Hughie allows as how he'd like to be a horse handler 'cause horse handlers have to be big and strong, which he is, and he likes horses and even likes the smell of 'em. We all hold our noses and say *phew,* but he don't care, he likes 'em, is all. There's lots of horses here in Cheapside 'cause of all the markets and fairs.

Judy's of a practical turn of mind, too, as she wants to go into service and be a maid for a fine lady, but first she's got to get big enough to be useful to some such fine lady and not just eat her out of house and home. Polly, she just wants to marry a good man and raise up babies. Nancy says she wants to get married, too, and maybe she and her man would have a tavern where there'd be lots of good things to eat and drink, but they'd keep scum like Muck out, it bein' a respectable place, like.

I say I want to be the captain of a fine ship and sail around the world and see the Cathay Cat and the Bengal Rat and gaze upon the Kangaroo, which is what I heard some sailors singin' about over at Benbow's Tavern one day and it sounded right fine to me, them all happy and singin' and carefree, it seemed. I'll get rich and famous and spend all me money takin' care of poor miserable orphans, and I get handfuls of straw thrown at me for me sentiments.

"'Cut out the middleman!' says I to the worthy doctor. 'Pay me now only *half* what ye'd be payin' Muck for me earthly remains and I promises to come and lie down on yer doorstep every time I feels sick and liable to die. I'd even carry a note to the effect that if I perished somewheres else, my body was to be delivered to the Honorable Doctor without delay!'" says Charlie, having returned from the anatomist's full of gruesome stories of bloody tables and knives and things put up in jars.

"And Muck himself is there ascowlin' at the notion of his bein' cut out of the bargain, but the doctor says no, it was against his ethics to conduct negotiations with a live body, even though he was sure I was possessed of an admirable spleen."

We're all gigglin' and snortin', and Charlie goes on with, "I owns I got a right fine spleen and if Your Honor would pay me now, I'd be sure to keep it in special prime condition for his later use and joy. Massage it up twice a week to keep it nice and soft and all." Charlie shakes his head sadly, swinging his red mop.

"His Honor would have none of it, and he has Muck put his foul hands on me to toss me out, spleen and all."

"And for that," says Charlie, "I resolves to abuse me spleen most terrible."

We all gets a howl out of Charlie's prancin' around and telling of the stomachs that are blown up and dried like the blowfish we see in the fish market, and other guts tanned and pickled and preserved. But then he tells of seeing a baby's hand floating in some juice and that shuts up my laughing right quick.

I knows me sister Penny is put up in jars, and I suspects that someday I will be, too.

Chapter 2

I'm thinkin' I'm maybe twelve years old now, but it's hard to tell 'cause time slips by out here on the streets. That would be about right, though, figuring I was about eight when I was turned out an orphan into the storm of life, me bein' so happy with Mum takin' care of Penny and me, and our dad teachin' us to read, him bein' a teacher what had come to London with Mum, who was a deacon's daughter from a poor church in the north country, to take up a teaching post, but the post fell through and he had to fall back on letter writin' for the people what couldn't do it for themselves. It was enough to get along on till somethin' better come along, but what come along was Death and nothin' better.

Maybe I'm thirteen. I don't know. I'm still so damned *small*.

Because I was taught to read by me dad, I do the readin' for the gang. It's me special trick, like, different from the beggin' and the thievin' and the runnin' from the coppers and the throwin' of rocks and such which all of us do. Doin' the readin' keeps me sharp in the practice of it, and by soundin' out the words, I keeps pickin' up new ones. I don't always know what the meanin' is, but I usually gets it worked out.

When the printers on Fleet Street puts up the news sheets and broadsides on the walls outside their shops, we all goes over and I climbs up on Hugh the Grand's shoulders and I reads what's put up there. The people what gather about can't read for their ownselves and they likes it when I does it for 'em, and when Polly and Nancy and Judy scampers about with their hands out, well, sometimes the people puts in a penny.

There's wanted posters, too, for bold and darin' highwaymen, and there's news of the brewin' war with Napoléon, who's out kickin' up trouble in the high Germanies, and everyone shakes their heads and says we'll be back in it soon. Charlie 'specially likes the broadsides, which are songs written out making fun of something or somebody or some big thing that happened. He quick learns the words by heart and then goes out on the street and sings 'em, caperin' about, and some people likes it and again we girls pass the cups around and maybe we get a penny or two, and then we can get a meat pie to share, which is a great and rare and wonderful thing.

There's cartoons what are put up, too. Men and women drawn with big fat eggs for bodies and little sticks for arms and legs, and big awful faces with big lips and noses, and words come out of their mouths in bubbles and I read them, too. "Like, see this cove here is saying the Tory members are nothing but a bunch of baboons, and this here baboon over to the side is saying that he doesn't see the resemblance and his mum is much offended," but the words from the baboon is comin' out of his bum instead of out his mouth, and everyone gets a good laugh and Hugh the Grand shakes with the laughin' even tho' I knows he ain't got no notion of what's funny about it, and for me it's like gettin' a ride on a big old dumb horse when Hughie laughs.

I says to Charlie a couple of times, "Charlie, how come we don't do the readin's all the time, it's a good trick and there's plenty of different print shops and we always gets some pennies when we does it? We could even set up in letter writin' and make even more and not have to do the beggin'. Why not, Charlie?"

But Charlie just shakes his head and says, "Mary, we got to have a lot of irons in the fire, not just one thing, 'cause if that one thing plays out, why, where would we be then?"

I nods me head, but I ain't satisfied with the answer.

"Please Mum, please Mum, please Mum," says I, stickin' out me hand. I've been put to the beggin' on this corner today and I'm workin' a lady and a little girl what has just come out of a bakery shop and have bags of sweet smellin' stuff. "Please Mum, please Mum, please Mum. *Please.*"

The girl pipes up with, "Can't we give her a penny, Mother?" The girl is all dressed in white with ribbons and looks like she's been scrubbed pink. "She's awfully dirty and she looks cold."

"No, dear," says the mother. "Your dear uncle John gave you those pennies to buy yourself something special, and I don't want you to waste them." *Evil old sow.*

"I'm going to give one to her, anyhow," says the

sainted girl firmly, and she pulls out a purse all covered in bright thread. She reaches in and pulls out a penny and plants it in me outstretched fist, careful not to touch any part of me grimy self. It's all I can do not to snatch the purse and run.

"Bless you, Miss," says I.

The lady grabs the girl's arm and starts on up the street. "You are just throwing your pennies away. I'm sure her father is right around the corner waiting to take your penny to drink. I am *very* displeased with you."

Somethin' happens in me head and I says, "No, Mum, you've got it all wrong. I ain't got no Dad or no Mum neither and—"

"Come, Dear," says the woman, nervouslike. I follows 'em down the street and I knows she's lookin' for a constable but I just can't help it and I clutches the penny in me fist as I runs after 'em and I'm chokin' up and the tears are startin' out of me eyes and runnin' down me chin and I shouts, "Me mum was just like you, she just died is all, it warn't her fault, she just died like me dad died and me sister died and Emily died and…"

I stops in the middle of the street and throws down the penny. It rings against the cobblestones and I lets out a howl and I hopes that a horse comes by and stomps on me head 'cause I hates the beggin' and I'm scared of the stealin' and I just want Jesus to come and put me out of my misery, but instead it's Charlie what comes and puts his arm around me and says, "C'mon now, Mary, it's awright, it's awright. Hush now, hush. Ye just got to remember it's, 'Please Mum, Please Mum,' over and over. Ye can't get personal, they don't like it. Hush now."

"But me mum was a lady," I blubbers, all snotted up and teary.

Charlie bends down and picks up the penny. "I know, Mary, I know. I reckon ye just wasn't cut out for the beggin'."

Charlie buys a meat pie with the penny and sticks it in his vest pocket, and we heads back to our kip, it startin' to get dark and all. We'll divide up the pie when we all gets back in the kip, along with whatever else the others have managed to scrounge up. Charlie's got a good way of dividin' up the stuff we get. He says he learned it from a man who was once in prison, and what Charlie does is he takes his shiv and cuts up whatever's there into pieces as alike in size as he can judge it. Then he turns his back so he can't see the pieces and one of us points at a piece and then Charlie calls out one of our names and that one gets that piece, and so on till it's all shared out and fair.

We're almost there and I'm quieted down now and I asks again, "Charlie, why don't we just do the readin' thing? We always makes money at it. I hates the beggin' so."

Charlie is quiet for a while and then he says, "Awright, Mary, I'll be tellin' ye straight. Yer the bright penny, anyways, and ye'll see the wisdom of me thinkin'."

Charlie stops in the gloom and takes me by the shoulder and turns me around and looks me in me eyes. "It's 'cause I don't want ye stolen, is why."

I looks up at him and he puffs up and goes on.

"Now, suppose we stands up in front of the broadsides and newspapers and such every day, and awright, we'll make money, I'll grant ye that; prolly enough to get by on, but…"

And here he stops and looks hard at me again. "It won't go without notice, don't ye see?" And he shakes me shoulder.

"Some bigger and meaner gang will see that yer little trick is a good quick way t' turn a penny and they'll be off wi' ye in a minute. I'll try to stop 'em, but all I gots is me shiv and Hughie. They've got bigger and tougher coves runnin' those gangs. Some are full growed and I couldn't stop 'em. Like Pigger O'Toole and Dirty Henry. Ye want to be with *them*? That's why I only runs the readin' game ever' few days so's nobody'd notice ye and why I'm always on the outer edge of the crowd keepin' me eye peeled for some cove checkin' ye out. That's why I told Hughie that if anyone ever makes a grab for ye that he's to hold on to ye and run away and hide, not stand and fight like he'd want."

Charlie stops to see if I'm gettin' this. I am.

"And if a big and nasty gang don't get ye, then one of the printers'd see that ye could be of some use to him and without the bother of an apprentice, 'cause no girl's ever an apprentice in the trades, and he'd take ye and use ye for setting words for a while and then he'd take ye and use ye for other things when ye got older and then he'd throw ye out. Or his wife would. Is that what ye want, Mary?"

I looks down all meek and says, "No, I don't want that."

Charlie puts his arm around me shoulders, and I puts me arm around his waist and presses me face against his vest. I likes it when he does that, puttin' his arm around me, I mean, and I get to be close to him and all.

We go back to the kip.

Dashin' highwaymen and funny drawin's ain't the only things out in front of the printers' shops—there's also the posters for the Newgate hangin's, which I don't find fun at all 'cause Charlie one time told us about the hangin' of Mary Townsend a year or so back and how she was only thirteen and condemned for stealin' bread or somesuch. When she was dropped on the gallows, she wouldn't die 'cause she didn't weigh enough to break her neck when she come to the end of the rope; she just dangled there kickin' and chokin' for the longest time till the merciful hangman took the rope in his hands and jumped down on her thin shoulders with his heavy boots, which snapped her neck and stopped her chokin' and kickin' for good and ever, and I'm so sick when I hears this that I pukes up the nothin' in my belly and I runs off and don't sleep right for three nights and I never get the thought of poor Mary Townsend completely out of my mind, ever, and I have a weird awful sense that it's goin' to happen to *me* someday, too. I don't know why, but I do. It keeps comin' to me in dreams or when me mind wanders, and I dreads it and I shakes when it comes over me.

So when the others go off to work the crowd at Newgate on Mondays, which is the hangin' day—unless it's a holiday like Christmas, in which case the poor wretches are hanged the Saturday before so as not to upset the joy of the day—I won't go with 'em; I stays in the kip. I've seen the awful horrid things hangin' in the cages at the edge of the city, all black and dried out and stinkin' wi' the birds pickin' at 'em.

Along with the posters in front of the printers is advertisements for extra good viewin' windows for rent by the day in the Newgate courtyard, so's the toffs can have a party with their friends and watch the hangin's, and when a young girl is bein' hanged, the price goes up. Ten pounds, sometimes.

I am sick to me heart over such hateful things in the world, and I prays for deliverance.

Chapter 3

Muck sits at the table outside the Bell and Boar drinkin' his pint and soppin' his bread in the stew what sits steamin' all glorious in front of his fat gut while we try to coax a penny out of him, but the swine says no, it wouldn't be good business practice to feed us. Ah no. He shakes his head sorrowful, like he can't help the way things are.

"It'd be like starvin' a goose before y' kills it, which is counter t' yer best interests, see? Only it's like backwards with orphans 'cause ye certain don't want t' *feed* yer orphans—they might not die, and where would we be then?"

"Back t' robbin' graves direct, like the rest of the ghouls, I suspects," says Charlie, standin' there with his arms folded across his scrawny chest. He fetches a black look from Muck. Charlie looks back at Muck with just as black a look. *Charlie, be careful,* I thinks to meself. *Muck may be stupid, but he's dangerous, too, and remember our motto, Charlie,* Keep Yer Head Down and Yer Backside Covered, *and ye ain't doin' that, Charlie, ye aint doin' that at all. Yer stickin' yer neck out.*

"Shut yer jaw, gallows bait," says Muck, lookin' all dark and threatenin' at Charlie, "or I'll have ye in me barrow before ye thinks maybe it's time."

"Sod off, Muck," says Charlie, and he saunters off down the street to wait for us to finish working the crowd. I'm glad Charlie has left, but I wish he hadn't said those things to Muck.

Muck leans back in his chair and wipes his hands on his coat. The table he sits at has been set up in the street outside the tavern's door to catch the cool of the day. He sucks at his teeth to get the morsels out and sighs in the warmth of the day and allows as how he wishes it were winter 'cause the orphans die more regular in winter, mostly from the cold and not from disgustin' diseases like in summer, diseases which maybe a poor working man could catch from their corpses when he's tossin' 'em in his barrow. Nay, in winter, it's one here and one there, and they're easier to keep 'cause of the coolness. Stack 'em up like cordwood, y' can.

"Sure, and in the summer ye might have a fine pestilence which mows 'em down like wheat in a field, but then ye have too many of 'em at once and the surgeons can't use 'em all and they starts to stenchin' and me meself has to haul 'em out to the lime pits at me own expense, mind ye, and not even a thank ye fer me troubles," he says, all wounded.

It was a warmish winter and the spring was warm and dry, mostly, and the summer has been cool and we orphans ain't dyin' at a clip that pleases Muck and his patrons. Loud and long are Muck's complaints and beatin' of breast. We orphans usually aims to please and promises to die real soon if he'd just give us a penny, but it don't work, it never does. Inside us we're happy with the state of our health, and we pictures in our minds the anatomical surgeons sittin' all sad at their empty tables a'tappin' their knives and askin' the merciful heavens for a fresh orphan and not gettin' one today.

Muck goes around mournful-like, liftin' our shifts and countin' our ribs, which is easy to count 'cause they stands right out for the countin', and he asks if we been havin' the runs and such and looks powerful downcast when we says no.

Polly asks him why the doctors like us orphans better than the grown-up dead people, which they could get all they want from Newgate, and Muck says, "Why bless yer heart, dear, it's 'cause yer so light and small. The good doctor can flip ye over on the table wi' two fingers when he needs t' empty out yer other side, not like a full-growed corpse what weighs maybe fourteen stone. And ye've got the same guts as a grown-up, mostly."

Polly's eyes well up with tears at the thought of her own dear self bein' parceled out on the table. Polly is our best beggar 'cause she's got these huge blue eyes that brim up and spill over at the slightest thought in her lovely head of the meanness or sadness in the world. And she is lovely, too, under all the dirt, with her pink skin and cherry cheeks and cupid lips and loose curls makin' a dirty gold frame for her dirty little face. She's wondrous good, too, at the piteous cryin' and when she puts her hands together like she's a little angel prayin' and lets go the waterworks, she gets me and the other girls all in a fine howl and you'd think it'd all melt the heart of a statue and we'd get tons of money, but we don't. Hearts of stone are all we got round here and they're evil cheap, but if any of us can wring a penny out of 'em, it's Polly. I betcha Charlie don't want *her* stole, neither.

"And another thing," says Muck, all like a schoolteacher teachin' the young ones about sweetness and light and dancin' around the maypole and such, "another thing the doctors like about orphans aside from their fine compactness is they ain't got no ugly yellow fat to wallow through on their way to the prime organs."

Muck takes his stick and lifts up Judy's shift. "Look at that," he says fondly. "Not an ounce of fat, bless her. See, right there's the edge of her liver, just waiting to be popped out, and this bump here is bound to be her appendimox and…"

Now Judy is cryin', too, and so's Nancy, and I gives up on this street for today and gathers up the girls to head off after Charlie.

"I'd despise it if I had to go back to the actual grave robbin'," Muck says gloomily, puttin' on an air like it's beneath him in his present state of Purveyor to the Holy Order of Anatomical Surgeons.

"It's dirty work and I don't like it," he allows. Plus he knows he'd get hanged for it if he got caught, which would serve the beast right, and I feels that way even though I hates hangings.

Chapter 4

Me immortal soul took a beatin' today as I steals a whole loaf of bread. The beggin's been real bad lately and we ain't et in two days and Nancy is poorly, and I seen the bread come out of the oven and put on the coolin' board outside the bakery and I loses me mind with the smell of it sittin' there all steamin' and callin' out to me, and I grabs it and runs.

I'm runnin' down the street in mortal terror and there's shouts behind me, but I runs faster and I'm seein' the gallows and the rope and Mary Townsend and the hangman jumpin' on me shoulders till me neck snaps and me gullet is stretched, and I'm blind with fear but I keeps on runnin' till me breath is tearin' holes in me chest and finally I lies down in the gutter with me arms wrapped around the bread and waits for them to come and wrap the noose around me neck and haul me up.

But nobody comes with the noose nor without it, so I gets up and heads back to the kip, me breath comin' in gulps and me immortal soul in tatters.

The others is already back, as it's gettin' to be dark, and they stare in wonder at the grand loaf, everyone 'cept Charlie, who ain't here. Polly has got a bit of cheese at the beggin' and we're all lookin' forward to a feast, but where's Charlie? We waits but he still don't show.

It's almost pure dark now and Hugh says, "Mary, go out and find 'im. Likely he's down at Lambert's. That's where I saw 'im last."

Out I scrambles, hopin' to find Charlie right off 'cause I know I bought meself some more time in purgatory with the stealin' of that bread and I wants to at least get to the pleasure of eatin' it as some small payback for me poor damned soul. I ain't worried about the bread bein' et while I'm gone, 'cause we have our rules, and I ain't worried about the dark streets 'cause I knows 'em like a rat knows his rat hole, but I am worried about Charlie. He's usually back at the kip to count our heads before dark.

I crosses Earl Street and heads up Water Street and over to Broad, but Charlie ain't at Lambert's and he ain't at The Plow and Stars and he ain't at The Soldier's Joy. I look across the evening sky and there's the dome of Saint Paul's, but I know he ain't off in that direction 'cause that's Bellycut George and his gang's turf and we never, never go there at night, so I heads across Ludgate to check out Benbow's, but nothin'. I've been lookin' a long time and I'm thinkin' I'll go back to the kip to see if he's come back whilst I was gone, and so I cuts down through Slipburn Alley. It's right dim in there 'cause the buildings come together overhead, and as I'm goin' through I trips over somethin' and sprawls headlong onto the cobbles. There's sticky and gooey stuff all over the cobbles and on me hands and on me knees and on me shift and I don't know what to think, and then I look.

What I tripped over was Charlie, and Charlie's dead.

I lifts up Charlie's head, but the back of it is a bloody mush in me fingers and I know he's gone and the tears well up and I starts makin' high keenin' wails. I hugs him to me and rocks back and forth and say, *Ah, Charlie, Charlie,* over and over and over. I'm cryin' for poor Charlie dead in me arms, and I puts me face on his and keens some more. *Who done ye, Charlie, ah who done ye and who stopped yer dancin' and jokin' and foolin' for good and ever? Not another street kid, 'cause every street kid knew ye and yer shiv and would have taken it after they did ye, but here it is gleamin' all wicked in me hand. Who then, Charlie?*

I runs me hand up Charlie's chest and opens each button as I go up. When all the buttons are undone, I pulls off Charlie's vest, sobbin' all the while.

Ah, Charlie, you was a good one, you was. You looked out for us in your way and took care of us in your way and always shared even though you didn't have to and was always happy in spite of all. And takin' your clothes is prolly a sin, too, and I don't mean no disrespect, Charlie, but I got to do it. I got to get away.

I slips Charlie's shirt over his ruined head as gentle as I can and then loosens the cord on his trousers and pulls them off. His legs flop all limp and slide on the stones and I remembers how they used to dance and caper and now they don't do nothin'.

Goodbye, Charlie. I close his dead eyes and kiss his dead cheek. *You was my darlin'.*

Leavin' the alley, I sees a horse trough in the gloom and I commences to washin' Charlie's clothes what was dirtied by his dyin'. After I gets most of the blood and dirt off, I takes off me two shifts and rolls 'em up. I puts Charlie's clothes on wet, grateful it's a warm night. I puts the shiv in next to me ribs like Charlie always done and I sticks me old shifts under me arm and gets ready to head off, but then I hears a noise and jumps back quick in a doorway. I peers out and there's Muck wheelin' his barrow toward the alley and toward all what's left of Rooster Charlie.

How long will it be 'fore it's me that Muck is coming after?

I'm lookin' down through the grate at the shapes below and I counts three, no, four of them huddled down there. Three girls, one boy.

"*Psst!* Toby!"

The shapes start in alarm. I'm startin' to shiver from the wet clothes, in spite of the warmth of the night. I hisses down through the grating, "It's me, Mary, from Rooster Charlie's gang."

Toby gets up and walks toward me, his face striped white and black from the moonlight and the shadow of the grate. "What's up, then."

"Charlie's been done," I says, as even as I can.

"Wot? The Rooster done! It can't be!" wails one of the girls.

"Who done it?" asks Toby.

"Dunno," says I. "Prolly Muck." Then I tells him what happened at the Bell and Boar and in Slipburn Alley.

Toby lets loose a string of low curses and while he's doin' it I says, "I want you to take over our gang, Toby."

I lets that sink in a bit and then plows on. "I don't want 'em picked up by Scroggs or Jimmy Ducks or Dirty Henry or any of those. I takes you for a decent sort, Toby, the sort'll look after 'em a bit. Like Charlie done."

"I ain't nobody's mother," says Toby. "And I ain't—"

"Our gang lost two today, so there's Judy and Polly and Nancy and Hugh the Grand, with your bunch that makes eight, a good-sized group, and we got a better kip than this. More privatelike, where coves can't piss down on ye like here."

I'm talkin' fast, tryin' to make the deal. "Be right comfy with the bunch of you snugged up in there."

"What about Hugh?"

"He'll follow your lead. He's slow, but he's strong and loyal. You kin be the brains and he'll be the brawn. It worked for Charlie."

"You're not goin' back, then."

"No, I got to go. You tell 'em I died with Charlie...no, tell 'em I went to sea and will come back rich and famous. That'll give 'em a laugh. Tell Hughie I hopes he gets to be a hostler. That way he'll know you came from me with my blessin'. They got a loaf of bread and some cheese. They'll share it with you."

"You think it'll still be there?" says Toby all doubtful.

"I know it'll be there 'cause that's the way we done things. So it's done, then?"

"Awright, it's done," says he. "Come, me girls, let's go see your new sisters and brother." The girls get up all excited by the happenings and the thought of some bread and cheese. They gathers up their rags.

"And, Toby," says I, "don't let Hughie go after Muck. Ye'll have to calm him down 'cause he loved Charlie like we all did. Tell him if Muck is onto makin' his own corpses, it won't be long 'fore Muck does the Newgate Jig his own damned self."

"That's one hangin' I won't miss," says Toby with feelin'.

"Luck, Toby."

"Luck, Mary. Sorry about Charlie."

"Aye."

That's the last time anyone on this earth ever calls me Mary.

Chapter 5

God is a tricky cove, all right, as I didn't mean for Charlie to die so's I could be delivered, but that's what He come up with. I'd like to think of Charlie up in heaven, his red mop shinin' in the celestial light, crackin' up the archangels and such with his japes, and meetin' up with Mum and Dad and Penny and all the others I've known who've died, but I don't know. I don't know nothin'.

'Cept now I knows to be careful what I prays for as it might be granted. In the future I'll pray like "God, deliver me from this, if you please, but don't be killin' Charlie in the doin' of it."

But what's done is done.

The first thing I do after I leaves Toby and his bunch is to take out me shiv and hack off me hair, grabbin' handfuls and sawin' away, leavin' it in clumps in the gutter along me way. I cuts it as close to me head as I can get it. I figures I'll follow the Thames down towards the sea as no one knows me face down there and it is a good a place as any to make a new start. I hears that's where the navy ships are and maybe I'll find a way to make meself useful and so get to keep body and immortal soul together for a bit longer.

That night I walks till me clothes dry out and then I kips in a dooryard, cold and hungry and miserable.

Charlie, why'd y' have to go and mouth off to Muck like that? If you hadn'a done it we'd still be like we was, the Rooster Charlie Gang against the world, but you did it and now yer dead and gone 'cause of it and nothin's ever gonna be like it was. Yer dead, Charlie, and that's it and that's all, but I still can't believe even though I seen you lyin' there all still all quiet all dead.

I wipes me nose and me eyes on me sleeve and curls up into a tighter ball.

Y' know, Charlie, it's stupid, but I sort of thought that we would get together someday when I got older, like gents and ladies get together, like. At least for a little while before ye went off to be a brave soldier. At least for a little while we'd walk along, ye all cocky and fine and me beside y' with me arm through yers, even though I know I'll never be a lady. I sort of thought that, I did. But, no. Nothin' now.

In the mornin' it begins to rain and I'm wet again. I walks on and don't scare up no food this day, neither, and I knows that body and soul might start to separate themselves soon if I don't get some right quick. I lie down on a bed of stones in a dark alley when night comes and the cobblestones bite me skin where me bones poke through and I'm thinkin' that I ain't never slept alone before and I don't like it. I misses the feel and smell of the others in our cozy kip when we were in for the night. Yes, and the whisperin' and gigglin' and snugglin' up together. I could go back. I could get along with Toby.

No. I've got to go on. I'll come back someday, I will. *Stop yer cryin'. Stop it now.*

I'm keepin' close to the river on me way to the sea, as I won't get lost that way and I'm used to the river 'cause of our old kip bein' so close to it and all, and it gives me some comfort somehow.

I'm workin' me way down a street on the outskirts of the city, tryin' to escape notice and to look like a simple lad out runnin' an errand for his mum and up to no mischief, Officer, honest I ain't, when a man in front of a tavern calls out to me, "Here, boy, hold me horse," and passes the reins of the beast to me. Me and the horse stands there for a couple of hours, each of us real suspicious of the other, whilst the cove inside eats and drinks his fill, and when he comes out aburpin' and pattin' his gut I puts on a look like I've been real sharp in the performance of me duties and he gives me a penny.

When he gets on the horse and leaves, I heads into the same tavern and for me penny I gets a bowl of stew and a bit of bread, which is something wonderful. I licks the bowl clean, tucks the bread in me vest for later, wipes me mouth on me sleeve, and heads out.

It's easier bein' a boy, I reflects.

It's easier bein' a boy, 'cause nobody bothers with you. Like, I couldn't have gone into that tavern yesterday as a girl 'cause they would have shouted, "Get out of here, you filthy girl," while they didn't say anything when I went in as a filthy boy. My filthy penny was as good as anyone else's.

It's easier bein' a boy, 'cause no one remarks upon me bein' alone. Lots of boys are alone but girls never are. The girls gets scooped up into beggin' and stealin' gangs, or workhouses, or worse. True, on my journey south I was eyed by some gentlemen of the street who thought as they would look better in me vest than me, but a flash of me shiv put some caution in 'em and that was that.

It's easier bein' a boy, 'cause when someone needs somethin' done like holdin' a horse, they'll always pick a boy 'cause they think the dumbest boy will be better at it than the brightest girl, which is stupid, but there you are.

It's easier bein' a boy, 'cause I don't have to look out for no one but me. I'm feelin' a great sense of freedom, like a weight's been lifted from me shoulders, as I'm dartin' me way down to the docks. I'm feelin' a little ashamed for feelin' so light, too, what with Charlie dead and me leavin' the others and all, but that's the way it is.

I slips between two loose boards into a stable that's all closed up for the night, and I burrows in the warm and sweet smellin' hay.

I decide my name will be Jack.

Chapter 6

There's a great bustle and fuss down at the set of piers that I chances on where the Thames starts to really widen out and look like open sea, and me mouth is hangin' open and me eyes are wide with the spectacle of it all. Ships like these never got up the river as far as our kip, only dirty old barges and scows. These ships are huge and beautiful and there's hundreds of 'em and their poles what stick up are impossible high and there's a right forest of 'em. It's a blue and glorious summer's day and there's flags snappin' in the breeze and men in grand uniforms struttin' about and sailors with great long pigtails coilin' rope and runnin' up the poles and doin' other sailor things.

There's men on the dock shoutin' and cursin' and groanin' under the loads they're carryin' on one of the ships, and I works me way over in that direction to see what I can get up to. I ain't et since that stew awhile ago and me belly is in its usual spot, plastered up flat against me backbone, and while that ain't an out-of-the-ordinary thing for me, I wouldn't mind seein' me condition bettered. Body and soul will be kickin' up and thinkin' of partin' soon if I don't get somethin' down me neck fast.

I see that the ship is called the *Dolphin,* from the name carved on its fat end. The name has a couple of fishes carved to either side of it, and both the fishes and the name are painted a shiny gold. The pointy end of the ship has a carvin' of a lady who's mostly comin' out of her dress, which is also painted with a lot of gold and some red. And a lot of skin color.

Towards the middle of the boat there's a board laid across to the dock where the workers are carrying the stuff onto the ship and there's a gang of street boys on the dock hangin' about.

"Hey, Mate, wot's the word?" says I, lowerin' my voice all hearty and boylike to one of the boys, and he tells me the ship is takin' on six ship's boys for the comin' voyage and they're leavin' today and what would they want with a scrubby runt like me?

I contains meself and don't tell him to sod off but instead worms me way to the front of the mob. I spies a likely piling next to the water. Hookin' me toes in the ropes what are tied round it, I climbs to the top, nimble-like, and sits down to better catch the proceedin's but not before I have to put me toe in the eye of someone who tries to climb up after me. "Find yer own perch, Mate," I says. Serves him right, too, 'cause it's the boy what called me a runt and he should watch his mouth.

I looks over to the ship and sees an officer dressed in a fine blue uniform, all decked out with gold and ribbons and sword and buckles. He's standin' all straight and grim next to a portly gent who's dressed in a black suit of clothes and who don't look military at all 'cause he ain't wearin' a fancy hat like the other bloke, and he's got these little round glasses set on his nose. And there's a little cove in a dusty suit sittin' at a table set up there and every time one of the beasts of burden goes by with his load, this bloke writes somethin' down in his pile of paper. Fillin' out the group is this fearsome lookin' sailor what's got a piece of heavy knotted rope in his hand and a mean and nasty look in his eye. He's got muscles like a horse and looks to have a brain to match.

I thinks to meself about the thought of goin' to sea: I sure as hell ain't got no prospects here, and it's just as dead you get from starvation, muggin', or bein' stepped on by a horse, as you get from drownin', which is, of course, the seagoin' option. And I hears that they'd feed us, even. I'll believe *that* when I sees it. True, I'd have a bit of trouble passin' as a boy, but I ain't had no trouble so far and I been at it for a week or so. And if they finds me out, I'm sure they'd just put me off somewhere and where they'd put me off might be a finer place than this. Maybe a place with oranges. I ain't never had an orange. I catches a whiff of somethin' they might be cookin' downstairs on the boat and that settles it. Trial by belly, case closed. I'll give it a try.

"Awright," calls out the evil one with the knotted rope to the mob of us, "what kin any of yiz do?"

Do? I wonders. What do we *do?* We all look around at each other. What does he think, we're all bloody runaway apprentices with trades? Missin' sons of royal houses? What we *do* is scavenge, beg, and steal—ain't it plain?

Some of the brighter ones furrow their brows and look deep into their heads to see if they had any hidden virtues that might please His Majesty's Royal Navy, and most come up empty, but not all.

"Sir, I can splice a line!" shouts a thin-faced boy, and he's motioned aboard.

The crowd then announces that they *all* can splice a line, by God, but now it don't wash. The mob murders the lucky line-splicer with their eyes as he makes his way up the gangplank, and then another boy calls out, "I'm strong fer me size, Sir, take me!" Another tops him with, "I'm strong as two of him!" Still another says that he don't eat much, and finally all the others chime in with their qualities and the place is a bedlam of shoutin'.

Shoutin' which comes to a quick end when the cove with the rope waves it at 'em and shouts with a voice to wake the dead, "Pipe down, ye whoreson guttersnipes, or I'll come over there and show ye what me nobby's for!"

The mob pipes down.

I gets me resolve together and me feet under me and I stands up on the top of the piling and puts me fists on me hips to show I know no fear.

"Sir!" I yells with all me might. "I can read!"

Well, that puts a right stopper in the boys' gobs. "What the hell's the good of that?" they mutters, and, "Bleedin' little schoolboy he is. Bloody cheek, it is."

But the officer on the ship looks over at the well-rounded cove and cocks a bored eyebrow. "What say, Mr. Tilden?"

Mr. Tilden, who looks like he'd rather be doin' a plate of sausages than doin' this, looks at me and says, "Is that so, boy? Then what's the name of this ship?"

"The *Dolphin*, Sir!" says I, joyfully pointin' to the name. "It's writ right back there on the arse end of the boat, Sir, with the fishies!" The mob grumbles in common hatred of me.

"And what does that say, boy?" He points to a huge sign painted on the wall of a building.

"Ships' Chandler, Sir! H. M. Wilson and Sons!" I says, less sure this time.

"And what does it mean, boy?"

"Why, Sir," says I, sweatin' now, "that's where Mister Wilson and his boys makes chandles for ships." I smiles hopefully and with all me charm, but there's some snorts of laughter from the ship.

"If you're such a grand scholar, boy, then why do you want to go to sea? You could apprentice to a printer. You could study to be a teacher. Why the hard life of a sailor?"

I places me hand over me thumpin' heart and says, "Oh, Sir, all me life I have longed for a life on the rollin' sea. It's in me blood, like, and can't be denied. I wants to see the Cathay Cat and the Bombay Rat and gaze upon the Kangaroo and all the other wonders of the world!"

The pack of boys is now booin' and hootin' and throwin' things at me, but the fat man looks at the officer and gives a short nod.

"Very well, boy, you can come aboard," says the officer, and I slides down the pilin' with me heart in me throat and suffers a few kicks and threats and jabs on me way to the plank but I don't care, 'cause I'm bein' delivered and goin' to sea.

As I cross the plank I look down into the dark water and give a bit of a shiver. Then I calms meself and goes on.

A girl what's born for hangin' ain't likely to be drowned.

———

"What's your name, boy?" says the weedy little man at the table, his pen ready.

"Jack, Sir," says I, as steady as I can. "Jacky Faber."

"Age?"

I thinks fast. A wrong answer could get me tossed back off. I thinks I'm twelve, maybe even thirteen, but that's too old for a boy of me size. Ten, maybe. But what if they won't take boys that young?

"Ten, Sir," I says, and he looks up at me without sayin' nothin'.

"Ten and a half," I says quickly, "almost eleven."

"All right," he says, writing in his book. "You are now written into the record of this ship and, as such, you are now bound by all the rules that pertain to members of the Royal Navy. Should you wilfully disobey any of those rules or the Articles of War, you will be punished by imprisonment, flogging, or hanging. Do you understand?"

"Yessir." I quavers. *Is there no place in this world without a handy gallows?*

"Good. You'll be the schoolteacher's boy. Mr. Tilden?"

Mr. Tilden turns to me and tells me to stay out of the way until we get under way. He says he'll send for me later and hopes that I will be a good boy.

I promise that I will be, that I'll be *ever* so good, and thank you, Sir, for takin' me, and off he goes in the direction of the glorious smells that are coming up from below.

I takes meself over to the side of the ship so's I can be out of the way and not be noticed and so's I can watch the proceedin's on the dock. The boys is still makin' a commotion, tryin' to get picked to be taken aboard. The boy what said he could splice a line comes up next to me and says his name's Davy and I say mine's Jacky and ain't it prime that we got picked to go, and we looks each other over and knows from the dirt and rags that we comes from the same kind of place. Under the dirt he's got light brown hair and a thin face and he seems like a decent bloke and I asks him if he really can splice a line and he says yes, if it's a little one. He's picked up some seaman lingo at a tavern where he used to beg and sometimes do chores. We both look out over the crowd, mates now.

Three more boys are picked and they hustle aboard. Guess they only needs five. The clerk signs them in and they wander about till they spies us at the rail and joins us. They be Benjy and Tink and Willy. Benjy and Tink seem like decent coves, but Willy, he bein' the one that said he was strong enough for two, he gets it in his head that he's gonna be the boss boy of all of us and figures to set things up right away and hauls off and hits me hard in the shoulder, me bein' the smallest and a good place to start. I don't want to fight, but I know I can't let him mess me about or I'll endure it forever, so I tightens me lips against me teeth in case I take a shot to the mouth and gives him a hard two-hand shove in his chest, which almost knocks him off his feet. I lets out a string of Cheapside's choicest curses, which settles things between us. It's all bluff but I'm glad it worked, and I'm glad the others sees this and knows I ain't to be pushed around.

"Here, here," says Davy. "They won't put up with fightin' on a king's ship, they won't." He points down the hatch at the hulkin' black cannons lyin' down below.

"They'll put you across one of them brutes, pull down yer pants, and switch yer bottom till it bleeds."

Davy seems to have picked up a lot of seaman's lore at his tavern, and I takes him at his word. I resolves again to be ever so good as I can't have me pants pulled down and be switched, which sounds right cruel even if I was a boy and not in fear of bein' found out and tossed overboard, or, at the least, put ashore in a strange land full of cannibals. I want to be good, anyways, as it's me nature and I'm thinkin' I could be right content here, as they might feed me and it smells awful good whatever it is, comin' up from down below, and everythin's so *clean*. I ain't never seen anythin' as clean as this place. The deck under me feet is fairly gleaming, scraped down so's it's almost white, and I feels it's a shame me dirty toes is standin' on its loveliness, smearin' it up, like. All the gear is put away just so, and there's new paint on everythin', smellin' clean and fresh.

Then a terrible thought hits me. I looks around frantic and thinks *What about the call of nature, you twit?* In the streets it was just get over a sewer ditch and hike up yer shift and there y' go. This will have to be solved straightaway, thinks I with a sinkin' heart, as I feels the call right now and sorely regrets havin' that last big drink at the trough.

"Hey, Davy," I says, all bluff and hearty and offhand, "where does a cove take a leak in this ark?"

"Damned if I know," says Davy, carelessly, but he saunters over to a sailor what is curlin' rope into a coil on the deck.

"Beggin' yer pardon, Sir," says he to the sailor, "but where might a lad shake the dew off the lily on yer fine barky?" Davy's got a bit of a lip on him, I notices. The sailor looks up at him.

"Y'could go piss in yer hat," he growls pleasantly, "if ye had one." He keeps on coilin' the rope, all unconcerned, but then he says, "Or ye could go down to the head, which is next deck down, all the way aft." He jerks his thumb towards the back of the boat.

We all winds our way down a ladder and gets to the next level, which is where the big guns are, and we walks back. We gets there to find the head, a curved room that has a bench in the back curve with holes in it for the sittin'-down business and a metal trough along the side for the stand-up business. I looks down one of the holes and sees the water of the harbor below.

"Aha!" says Davy. "Belly up t' the bar, mates," and he steps up to the trough and fiddles with the front of his pants, and the others join him. I goes to the end of the trough a little way from the others and fiddles with the front of me own pants, keepin' me hands coverin' anything I might be doin', which is nothin', but the boys don't notice 'cause they're too busy makin' crude jokes.

Then they're all fidgetin' and shakin' and I do the same as don't I know how boys relieve themselves after havin' lived with two of 'em for the past four or five years in right-tight quarters?

And then we're all walkin' out, but I hangs back and lets 'em get ahead, and then runs back in and quickly drops me drawers and gets on one of the holes in the

43

bench and lets go. The job done, I pulls up me pants and pats meself on the back for a cool bit of trickery.

When I leaves the head, I find the others have gone off somewheres, so I goes back to me station by the rail. The mob of disappointed boys is gone, but there's a man and a boy standin' on the dock by the plank. The man has his hand on the boy's shoulder and the boy has his head down and is lookin' powerful grim. This would be the sixth boy, I figures. It looks like it was already set up for this lad to come aboard, not picked up like the rest of us. He ain't dressed fine, but he looks clean, which'll set him apart from us, I'll wager.

At last the boy straightens up and shakes his father's hand. He turns and comes up the gangway and does the usual signin' in with the clerk. The boy has a bundle with him, and I suspects it's a blanket and a coat. A bleedin' prince, I thinks. All I got is what I got on and my little bundle of shifts. I hopes we're goin' somewheres warm.

The boy turns from the table and walks away lookin' lost, so I leaves me post as they're pullin' up the plank anyways, and sidles up to him, friendlylike. Close up I see he's a tall, thin lad with dark hair that is actually combed, and he's doin' a lot of gulpin' and blinkin' of the eyes.

"Cheer up, Mate," I says, showin' me teeth and givin' him a light poke in the ribs with me elbow. "Welcome aboard the good ship *Dolphin,* and what might you be called?"

"Uh…James," he says, soundin' not too sure. "James Fletcher."

"Awright, Jaimy, then. I'm Jacky. Let's go see if Jaimy

and Jacky can scare up somethin' to eat. I heard a rumor that they might even feed us; can ye believe it?"

Jaimy looks puzzled. "I suppose they shall," says he, and I'm sure he never thought otherwise. "What else would we do if they didn't feed us?"

"Why, beg, steal, and scavenge, like always," I says, "pick up what falls through the cracks, like."

He looks at me funny, but at least he ain't blinkin' away tears no more. We heads in the direction of the food as a shrill pipin' starts up.

We tumbles down the stairs where there's a great millin' about of men and I sees huge cauldrons set up at the end of a big room and sailors sittin' about with great gobs of meat on tin plates and they're chompin' away and me mind goes dizzy with the smell and me knees go weak with the thought that I might get some, too. I goes up to the cook what's dealin' out the heavenly meat and just looks at him not knowin' what to say or do and he says, "Where's yer mess kit, boy?" and I says, "I ain't got one, Yer Honor," and he mumbles, "Better git a mess kit, boy," and he reaches over and gets a shingle lyin' by and plops a great hunk of steamin' meat on it as well as a biscuit and says, "Half ration for ship's boys."

I says, "Oh, bless you, Sir, bless you," and takes meself off, delirious with joy, and heads for a spot at a table.

I gets the biscuit down me neck before I even gets to the bench and as soon as I'm down I attacks the meat, crammin' its loveliness against me lips and chewin' the fat and grindin' the gristle and suckin' up the hot salty juice and swallowin' as fast as I can and if I could have snorted it up me nose to get it down any faster I would have. At last it's done and I licks the shingle and licks my fingers and wipes me mouth on me sleeve and then I licks me sleeve. *Lord!*

I now takes time to look about and notice that Jaimy and me has been joined by the other boys and they're eatin' just as ravenous as I did, lookin' 'round furtive to make sure no one's thinkin' of grabbin' their grub. I see, too, that Jaimy's got a tin mess kit, prolly bought for him by his father. *Must be nice,* says I to meself, thinkin' back to how homesick he looked when he first come on board and how homesick I was when I was tossed out in the street on That Dark Day with me mum and dad dead and me sister goin' to be put up in jars. *Try that for a serious dose of the homesickness, my fine young fellow.*

Jaimy ain't eatin' his dinner with any relish at all, just pickin' at it and wrinklin' his nose.

I gets the feelin' that the nose wrinklin' is part from what he's eatin' and part from the squalid nature of us boys sittin' next to 'im. I sees as how we could be a hard blow to an untrained nose. *Cheer up, lad,* thinks I, happy in me full belly and in me filth and squalor, *I've always found the nose to be a most forgivin' organ. It sets up a powerful protest right off, but it quits when it knows it's beat.*

"Better eat it, boy. It ain't gonna change none. Same thing, day after day," says a sailor sittin' across from us. "Ain't that right, Snag?"

"Right you be, Mate," says the sailor named Snag, who seems to have but one tooth in his head but who still seems to be able to chew up his ration right smart with that one tusk. "Don't never change. Old Horse come to his sad end in a poor sailor's gob."

That's awright with me, I thinks, *just keep bringin' him on.* He and the other men tap their biscuits on the table, and worms and weevils falls out of some of 'em. If there was any of 'em in *my* biscuit, they'll have to take their chances in me gut. They won't be the first bugs I ever et, neither.

Jaimy eats the meat and biscuit, slowly.

The talk around the table is that we're goin' out to look for pirates, there ain't bein' a proper war goin' on right now, but I don't care if we're goin' out to run around in circles and dance ring around rosie as long as they keep feedin' me that lovely pork. Or beef. Or horse, or whatever it was.

"'Scuse me, Sir," I says to the sailor what had spoken and seemed like a nice sort compared to the usual run of cutthroat I'd seen on the ship so far and might answer some questions without givin' me the back of his hand. "But do they always feed us so early? It's only early in the afternoon. And where're we supposed to kip and what…"

The sailor holds up a hand. "First of all, you don't be callin' me 'Sir.' You be callin' me Delaney, Foretopman, Rated Able, and if we can stand the sight of each other in a few weeks, you can call me Liam. You say 'Sir' to the men in the fancy uniforms, and you don't say anythin' to them at all unless they talk at you first, and when you have to talk to them, you look down at the deck and put your right knuckle to your forehead and say, 'Beggin' your pardon, Sir.' And you never lifts your hand to them or you'll be flogged or hanged. Second of all, we're gettin' fed early 'cause we're sailin' with the tide, which is soon, and it's likely to be chancy out there and they wants us fed so's we can work through the night if we have to. Which we prolly will."

I thanks him for his kindly advice.

"And thirdly, any questions about your place on this bark, you ask the Bo'sun. He's the one wi' the cudgel. The nobby. *And* he's the one what handles The Cat. He ain't an officer, but it wouldn't hurt for you green hands to call him 'Sir' for a while. He won't mind."

Just then there's a long piercin' warblin' whistle and all the men jumps to their feet and heads off.

"That's it, then," says Liam Delaney. "We're off to sea."

PART II

While the Winds Do Blow,
And Enemies Abide,
Music and Friends Hath Charms,
To Set Our Sorrows Aside.

Chapter 7

We are all salty sea sailors now, havin' survived our first days at sea, if only just barely.

The first day out was glorious, as we rode the tide out to the mouth of the harbor, our sails goin' up and our banners a'spankin' and people wavin' from the shore and us boys not knowin' what to do yet so we just watches in wonderment and stays out of the way. Some of the hands is way up in the riggin' lettin' out sails and some is on deck haulin' on ropes, and the officers are shoutin' all sorts of strange orders like it's another language altogether. I'm marvelin' about the newness of it all and the smell of the air, which don't smell like sewers or rubbish or horses or anything like the city. Sea monsters or cannibals or pirates may get me in the end, but at least Muck won't, and if I watches meself, maybe I won't get hanged after all. It's all just grand, I thinks.

At least I thinks that till we clears the calm waters of the harbor and hits the open ocean and the ship leans sickeningly on its side and I slips and falls down and the boat stays like that for a while till there's more bawlin' of orders and it lurches over to the other side. I can feel the roll of the waves under the boat and the wonder to me is that this ship can be moved about so easy by the wind and weather when it must weigh a million pounds at least and carries tons of men and food and cannons and cannon-balls and powder and such. It's like a city block in London suddenly comes loose from the earth and starts oozin' around. It ain't natural-like, and it makes me all queasy. For the first time in my life I ain't thinkin' about eatin'.

When everything calms down and night falls, I catches the Bo'sun's eye and fearfully asks him where we're sup-posed to go for the night, and he motions us downstairs to the gun deck where sailors are puttin' up their ham-mocks, but no hammocks for us, no. We're to sleep in a pile between two of the massive guns, and I hear Jaimy draw in his breath sharply beside me and I knows he don't like it, but it looks like home to me and the other boys. There's even a pile of old blankets and I dives in, grateful to be lyin' down 'cause me stomach feels better that way, and the others join me. Jaimy, too, in spite of the squalid nature of the rest of us, and I manages to wriggle up next to him. I don't know why I wants to, but I do and I gets it done.

So we're lyin' there and we get into talkin' about where we come from, and Davy and Tink and Benjy are just like me from the streets but from the other side of the city and we know a lot of people in common, 'specially Muck, and we all spits when we hears the name of Muck. Willy, the big one who tried to face me down when we first stepped on this ark but who seems all right now that he sees there ain't gonna be no bully runnin' our bunch, is from a farm where he slept in a barn with the animals and had to work terrible hard ever' day. But this year the farmer what kept him give him the boot 'cause his own kids was gettin' big enough to help on the farm, so here he is. He was glad to get off the farm to become a salty sea sailor 'cause he really didn't like it much, the dirt and the hard labor and all.

"Seafarin' looks to be hard labor, too," says Tink. Tink's a medium-sized lad with dark curly hair and a pleasant look about him. We'll get along.

"I know, I know," says Willy, like he's thought about all this real deep. "When there's a battle or storm or such, ye work like bloomin' 'ell, but when the battle's done and the storm's over, ye set down wi' yer mates to a cup o' tea or grog, if ye're still alive, and if ye ain't, well, at least ye ain't rakin' no manure. It ain't constantlike, y' see. I hates constant work. Work that never gets done."

"Least you got to eat constant," says Davy, and some of us grunt in agreement.

"Wot I likes most is," says Willy, endin' what is prolly the longest speech of his life, "is that the ship ain't got no manure."

We don't ask where Jaimy comes from, 'cause we already knows he's a nob, at least compared to us, and he don't offer nothin' in the way of his past life. It prolly saddens him to think of it. It don't matter none, I thinks, we're all just ship's boys now.

"Shaddap, ye little twits," comes a growl out of one of the hammocks swingin' overhead, "before I comes down and puts the bashin' on yiz." Already sounds of snorin' is issuin' from the men overhead.

So, with the roll of the waves beneath me, I sleeps.

———

The next day the wind and seas gets even rougher and the boat adds some new moves in its dance through the waves, which are now like mountains, and we goes up and down and now sideways and over and I don't get up for three days, 'cept to crawl to the head to spew up the vile juice in me gut through one of the holes, then I crawls back to the kip and gets sick again but this time I don't make it to the head and I has to clean it up, which makes me sicker yet. I'm makin' me usual deals with God and hopes that Jesus will come take me in His lovin' arms, but once again He don't come and on the next day Jaimy brings me some food and I eats it and keeps it down, and on the next day I am up and I never gets sea-sick again.

I am ready to do my duty.

Chapter 8

We ain't been out a week and we're all still green and hardly over the seasickness when Sunday rolls around and it's announced that we will have a Captain's Inspection and Church. It is on this fine day that I have me first real scare in the way of the discovery of me female nature. The problem with the head warn't nothin' compared to this.

It seems that every Sunday, if it ain't blowing a gale, the Captain comes round and peers at everything and everybody to make sure all is up to snuff, and then we rigs for Church. The Captain's name is Captain Locke, but we're just supposed to call him Sir if he ever talks directly to us, which ain't likely.

So Sunday mornin' the ship is all in a stew about gettin' ready for the dread Inspection. All the decks are double cleaned and the copper and brass is polished and the men comb their hair and put on their best outfits, which is white trousers and blue tops with a flap on the back and blue caps and a blue neckerchief with a fancy knot on it at the neck. The midshipmen have on their black trousers and black jackets with white shirts and black neckerchiefs, and the officers put on their best uniforms, which are all blue with gold piping and big cockaded hats with more gold on them, too, and everyone looks just fine. 'Cept us ship's boys, of course.

Finally, when everything's done and everyone's standing stiffly at their divisions, the Captain comes around, followed by the First Mate, Lieutenant Haywood, and by the Bo'sun, who don't look happy. Every time the Captain looks at a cannon or a bucket or a seaman and then says something to Mr. Haywood or the Bo'sun, you just know that some poor sailor's gonna pay.

The Captain inspects the division next to us and says something sharp to the midshipman in charge of that division, Mr. Wemple, fourteen years old if he's a day, and Mr. Wemple turns bright red but keeps his head up 'cause hangin' your head ain't allowed in officers, even if they want to do it and I can tell Mr. Wemple really wants to do it and crawl away and hide but instead he says, "Yes, Sir, beggin' your pardon, Sir, I'll see to it right away, Sir."

I dares to steal a look at Captain Locke out of the corner of me eye. He's got the grandest uniform of any of the officers, with a jacket of the deepest blue velvet and shiny gold buttons and gold swabs on his shoulders and pants just the creamiest white with nary a spot on 'em. He's got gray hair under his fine cockaded hat and a long nose and the fiercest eyes under his craggy brows and a mouth that looks like it could snap an unlucky ship's boy in half. I starts quiverin' to be standin' so close to such a man, a man who could have me poor self pitched over the side and suffer nothin' for it.

The Captain leaves Mr. Wemple in his despair and walks by us. We boys ain't been assigned to divisions yet so we're just standing in our kip between the two cannons, our blankets and gear in a pile behind us. We're tryin' to look military and stand up straight and all with our fists down to our sides and we hopes the Captain goes right by us, being not worthy of notice, but it don't happen.

He turns and puts his baleful eye upon us and our kip. We cringes.

"Good God!" he roars, and I about wets me pants. "These boys are filthy and this is a sty! Take them out and hose them off *right now*! I'll not have them at Church looking like this! They are an abomination!"

He's got a voice like thunder and damnation and he seems right steamed about our natural squalor, and I'm tremblin' away, shakin' on me pins and tryin' not to faint from fear when he looks at me and his gaze goes over me shorn head and his eyes widen.

"And carbolic soap, too!" he shouts. "This one has lice, by God! *Lice!* And on *my* ship!"

Well, of course I have nits, thinks I through all my fear and confusion. *It's summer, ain't it?*

The Bo'sun herds us out directly, himself in no fine mood, thinkin' that we're the ones to blame for his low standin' in the Captain's eyes and I reckons he's right, but right now I'm not thinkin' of the Bo'sun's station in life, I'm thinkin' of how I'm gonna be discovered in the most humiliatin' way, all starkers out there on the deck to the hoots and cries of all till they puts me overboard. I've heard they have put girls over the side as they're supposed to be bad luck and I hopes they at least gives me a barrel to cling to and, *Oh, dear God, please.*

We go in a miserable lot out to the deck where there's a long canvas hose hung on a rack on the bulkhead. I look at the others: Davy, Benjy, Tink, and Willy just look scared as they doff their shirts and drop their pants. Jaimy looks humiliated beyond all thought and I am terrified beyond all hope.

I hears some men down below pushin' on the pump and it's makin' its whooshin' noise and the hose is startin' to swell and thicken. Then I notice that Davy is holding his hands down to his lower belly with his shoulders hunched against what he knows is the comin' blast of cold water. The others are doin' the same.

Quick as I can I whips off me vest and shirt and rolls 'em up with me shiv inside and throws 'em aside and that don't matter none 'cause from the waist up me and the boys are all the same. Then I drops me pants and quick gets me hands up in front like I'm freezin' like Davy and then the water hits me from behind and I *am* freezin'. I squeals just like the others and then someone gives me a piece of soap, somethin' I ain't never seen since That Dark Day, and I takes it and rubs it around and gets up some suds and that covers me up in the right spot and it don't matter that me tail is showing, 'cause me buttocks is just as thin and starved as the rest.

The Bo'sun sprays us off one last time to get rid of the soap and warns us to stay clean or next time he'll tie a line around our ankles and keelhaul us and won't that scrub our nasty little hides clean, bouncin' along the barnacle-covered bottom of the ship till we're pulled up on the other side, maybe drownded, maybe dead, maybe not, but bloody and clean for certain.

I grabs me bundle of clothes, holds it in front of me as if for warmth, and runs to a rope locker and gets on me pants. Then I walks back out and, more slowly, put on my shirt and vest.

I am not yet undone.

Then we have Church. They set up this box thing all covered with fancy rope work on the front edge of the quarterdeck, which is a raised deck at the rear end of the ship. The quarterdeck is where the Officer of the Watch stands, lookin' up at the set of the sails and givin' orders to the sailor at the huge wheel that steers the ship. That's also where the Captain and Master and wheelman are found during a fight. Me, too, I finds out later.

We all stand down below on the main deck. The weedy little clerk what was on the dock the first day turns out to be a preacher, too, and after a few songs and some prayers, he gets up behind the box and tells us what rascals we all are, and how Jesus wants us to turn to the right path, and I think as how I always turn to the path that will most likely get me out of a scrape and I hopes that's the path he means.

Then we have some more prayers, which are powerful deep and solemn, and then some more songs. I finds I knows some of the words from when my mother used to sing 'em, like "Praise God from Whom All Blessings Flow," so I sings them.

Then after the preacher steps down, the Captain steps

up and reads the Articles of War, which lays out all the crimes we could be up to and how they're all punishable by death. Grim stuff, and I 'specially don't like the sound of some of them 'cause I think I could be guilty of them, and then I thinks of poor Mary Townsend and the hangman on her shoulders and I thinks it'd be the Bo'sun on *my* shoulders and then I tries not to think of that no more.

Chapter 9

THE *DOLPHIN*

"Sir, HMS *Dolphin* is a forty-four-gun frigate and a man-of-war in His Britannic Majesty's Royal Navy! She is two hundred and four feet in length and is forty-three feet wide at the beam. She carries twenty twenty-four-pound guns on either side and two nine-pound guns forward and two aft! She can carry provisions for four hundred and seventy-five men for one full year, and her present complement is four hundred and five officers and men! HMS *Dolphin* is commanded by Captain Stephen Locke, Sir! God Save the Ship, God Save the Service, and God Save the King!"

I have been told to memorize this.

MY DUTIES

I am ready to do my duty, but I finds out it ain't just one duty, it's a lot of 'em, each accordin' to the situation. What the ship is doin', like.

If it's just regular sailin', I helps out Mr. Tilden, the Professor, whose job it is to teach the midshipmen—which are apprentice officers—like, in readin' and arithmetic and science and the classics, whatever they are. In helpin' Professor Tilly, as everyone is soon callin' him, but not to his face, I sets up the table in the morning with the writin' slabs and chalks and gets the midshipmen somethin' when they wants it durin' class, like water and such, and I cleans up after they leaves, and they generally leaves a mess, the pigs.

The Professor tells me another of my jobs is to clean up me... *my* way of speaking. He says a lad what can... *who* can read as well as me shouldn't talk like a guttersnipe, so I resolve to clean up my mouth. I find it's almost easy to talk in the right way, as that's the way we did it in our rooms before That Dark Day, and I only picked up the other way of talking later with the gang, who I hope are all right, guttersnipes or not. I notice, though, that I fall back into the street way of talkin' and thinkin' if I'm excited or fearful, which is a lot of the time. Which way will win out when I grow to be a lady—*if* I grow to be a lady—I don't know.

I also have other chores, like helpin' with the morning scrubbin' of the decks, which is almost fun, all of us grindin' down the decks with the holystones and sand and makin' them gleam all white and new, and cleanin' the head, which ain't fun at all. Then, too, Benjy and I, being smallest, got to crawl down in the big cooking cauldrons after the feedings to clean them out with scrapers and it's powerful suffocatin' work, since we're headin' south and it gets warmer every day. But we manage to pick up a bit of extra grub from the cook for our trouble, so it ain't so bad.

If we Beat to Quarters, which means we're gettin' ready to fight or practice at it, then I've got to do the beatin'. On the drum, that is, which I keep in the kip, and which I must run to as fast as I can when I hear the alarm. The other boys are all powder monkeys, which means they run back and forth durin' a battle carrying heavy sacks of gunpowder to the guns. Being the smallest, I get the drum, which is fine with me. I put on the drum with leather straps what go 'round my shoulders so that the drum hangs at my waist and then beat upon it with these two sticks, which sets up a fine *rum-tum-tum* and tells all the men to get to their battle stations. The Bo'sun Mate's pipin' and his club help get them there, too. Whilst I'm doin' all this whackin' at the drum, I'm headin' for the quarterdeck where the Captain and First Mate and Master stand bellowin' out orders. Then I'm to stand in front of the Captain and, though I dread bein' so close to such awful majesty, I've got to look up at his face, and if he says, "Fire!" I've got to beat on the drum again as loud as I can so's the gunners'll know. Dreadful scary stuff, but I like it, in a way. There's a show-off part of my nature that comes out when I'm in the center of things, and I know I must try to control it for the sake of The Deception, but sometimes it runs away with me.

In all the other special happenin's, like pullin' up the anchor and gettin' the ship under way, I stay on the bridge, but when the call, "Away, the Boarding Party!" goes out, I'm to drop the drum and with every other man on the ship, 'cept for the Captain, wheelman, and Master, grab a cutlass from the rack and get ready to jump across to the enemy ship that we're pullin' up next to and take her by force of arms.

I'm hopin' we meets a timid sort of enemy.

THE WATCHES

In addition to everyone's daily duties, we stand watches, one in three, which means that one third of the entire crew—officers and men and boys—is up on deck throughout the day and night, ready to fight or handle what else might come along till the rest of the crew is rousted out of their hammocks or from their daily work to help 'em. I don't mean people like Tilly or the doctor or the deacon, no, they get to sleep through the night, the sods, I mean the regular officers and seamen. And ship's boys.

The Captain don't stand watches, neither, but his cabin's right below the quarterdeck and there's a shiny brass speakin' tube right next to the wheel that goes down to above his sleepin' head, and if the Officer of the Watch calls down to him with somethin' on his mind, the Captain is up on the deck in a moment, his nightgown and nightcap blowin' in the wind. The Officer of the Watch had better have a good reason to call him, though, as the Captain's mood don't improve with bein' awakened out of a sound sleep, I've noticed.

The watches rotate, like one night I'll have the Evenin' Watch, which is eight o'clock in the evenin' to midnight, and the next night I'll have the Midwatch, which is midnight to four in the mornin', and the next night it'll be the Four to Eight in the mornin'. I stand my watches back by the quarterdeck and my job is usually fetchin' coffee and food for the Officer of the Watch and wakin' up people and runnin' any errands that need to be run.

Jaimy and I are in the same watch section, I made sure of that with a little cajolin' of the Master-at-Arms who's in charge of who's in what watches, and sometimes we meet and talk and sometimes we just sit there and watch the stars wheeling about the heavens. I like that a lot, I do.

THE MIDSHIPMEN

The midshipmen are a sorry lot. There are ten of them and they are some of them the sons of Royal Navy officers that the Captain has taken on as a favor to teach them the ways of the Service and the sea, and they are some of them the sons of rich men who have bought their sons a place aboard. One such is Midshipman Bliffil, and he is the reason they are a sorry lot, as from the first day out he has bullied them without mercy, and their spirits suffer. He is the oldest of them and he's big and not bad to look upon, handsome even, if not for the cruelty in his eyes and the sneer that's always on his lips except when he's toadyin' up to the officers. He is brutal as a sledgehammer, and I'm afraid of him and I try to steer clear of him. Bliffil rides them all, but he 'specially torments Mr. Jenkins, the one next senior to him. Poor Mr. Jenkins seems helpless before him.

To us, though—ship's boy or Able-bodied Seaman— the midshipmen are officers and they command divisions throughout the ship, and we must knuckle our brows to them and obey their every command, even though some of them are not yet twelve. If they hit us, we must take it, and not even raise a hand in our own defense.

MY SEA DAD

All the ship's boys and all the midshipmen get with an experienced sailor to teach them the things they need to know, like how to splice a line (Davy *didn't* know, the liar) and how to tie the knots and how to sew and mend and row and sail the small boats we have aboard. These sailors ain't exactly told to do this teachin', it's more chancy than that. Like if a man is the sort that likes to teach what he knows, well, us young ones can sense that and we drift together. The Royal Navy smiles on this way of teachin' 'cause it figures that if we're around long enough we might grow up into Able-bodied Seamen and be able to replace the poor sod what's just had his head blown off and ain't able bodied no more.

In my usual connivin' way, I seeks out Liam, the sailor from Ireland who was nice to me that first day, and he seems willin'.

"Liam Delaney, a name that won't shame me," he sings as he guides my clumsy fingers over the rough rope— "*Line,* Jacky, *line.* It's line when it's runnin' loose, it's rope when it's coiled up and put away. Makes perfect sense"— showin' me how to separate the strands with a marline-spike and how to weave them together in a splice or a bight. I get it, but I'm better with the needle and thread.

Liam is tall and strong and he has a lilty way of talkin'. His hair is as black as the coal. He plays the pennywhistle and has given me one and is teachin' me to play it, but I'll never be able to play it as good as him.

"Black Irish, I am," he says proudly. "My ancestor was some poor Spanish sailor, one of the many what washed ashore after the Armada was beat and wrecked and our Irish girls took them to their hearts and their beds, bless 'em, and here I am today." Some of the sailors hangin' about smirk, like they'd like to offer a comment on Irish girls and their beds, but a look from Liam warns them off. He's known as a willin' and fearsome fighter.

"Ah, yes," he says wistfully, "we Irish have always been kind to strangers, we have, and not always for the better for us."

THE OFFICERS AND MEN

The Captain is Captain Locke and the First Mate is Lieutenant Haywood and the Second Mate is Lieutenant Lawrence. The Sailing Master is Mr. Greenshaw and the Gunner's Mate is Mr. Stanford. Beyond that I don't know right now as there are many more officers and mates but I can't even name them as they have very little to do with me. We've even got Marines with their grand bright red uniforms, who stand about stiffly guardin' things and sweatin' in the heat in their high collars.

There are four hundred and five seamen and boys aboard and they are a mixed bunch. Most are English, of course, with a lot of Scots and Irish and Welsh and Americans thrown in, but there are also some Italians and Portuguese and even some black men, the first I'd ever seen.

They don't look at all like the cartoons of 'em in the newspapers back in London. I suppose I must have been starin' at the one with the fierce tattoos all over his chest and arms and face, tattoos that were raised like bumps, and he caught me at it and so he growls and bares his teeth at me, teeth which I'm shocked to see are sharpened to points, and I yelps and runs away, but I hear him laughin' as I leaves:

"Be careful when you stare at the lion, boy. He may charm you and eat you."

Most of the men aboard are good-natured, some silent, some solemn, and some free and easy. But some are scary, too, of course, there being so many men aboard and some are bound to be bad ones. One man 'specially gives me pause and makes me nervous. He's named Sloat, Bill Sloat, and I noticed him early on 'cause he always seemed to be lookin' hard at me, which seemed to me strange, as being a ship's boy I'm certainly of no account and not worth noticin'. But I'd be walkin' along and I'd turn a corner and there he'd be, smirkin' at me and sayin' things like, "Well, and if it's not our little Jacky," and, "Ain't you a fine little sailor boy then, Jacky." I thought at first that he was just bein' friendly, but no, I don't think that's it at all.

Sloat has long greasy black hair and a black beard with red in it and dead white skin, and you can be sure he was there at our hosin' down. I don't like him and neither do the other boys. He stares at them, too, but he keeps his evil eye 'specially on me, and when I find it fallin' on me, it takes all of the joy out of whatever I'm doin' and I slink away and hide. I think he knows that I'm in fear of him, and I think he likes it.

I tell Liam about him and Liam scowls and says that I'm to keep away from the likes of him and to stay out of dark corners and out-of-the-way places.

"Up in the riggin' in the sunlight is the safe place for a ship's boy, not crawlin' around down in the dark hold. You listen to your old sea dad, now."

Liam don't know it but I've already done some crawlin' around belowdecks, and I've found a few secret places where I can practice my whistle as it's not allowed above decks except on Sunday and how can I learn otherwise? And I got to have a place to wash up and do other stuff out of sight. I've got a right-little chamber pot rigged up so I don't have to use the head, but I still go to the head sometimes when I know there's no one in there and go up to the trough as if I'm properly rigged out to use it, and I wait till I hear someone trompin' in and then do the shake-and-wiggle action the boys do and cinch my pants and leave, havin' furthered The Deception.

I find I like bein' clean, and I keep after the others to hold up their end so we won't have a repeat of the hose-down humiliation. I don't miss the lice, either, even though I never ate 'em, like some did. Almost never.

It's not all work-and-learnin' on the ship. Us boys spend a lot of time climbing in the riggin', daring each other to go higher and higher and swingin' out over the abyss, the ship's deck so small down below. I think we're not yelled at 'cause they want us to get used to the scary heights for when it's our turn in later years to man the top. And if we fall to the deck or go over the side, well, what's one ship's boy, more or less?

There's singin' and dancin', too, on Sundays after Church and Inspection, with the great louts stompin' about and roarin' out songs. Liam plays the squeeze box, too, and is much admired for his skill.

It's official now. We're off to the coast of North Africa to fight the Barbary pirates and protect fair England's merchant fleet, which sounds grand to me, but I am somewhat fearful of being there off the coast of the Barbary lands, 'cause if I'm discovered and put off into one of their ports, wouldn't I be made a slave right off?

Chapter 10

We ship's boys are all tight pals now. We lay about in the foretop together as much as we can, when our jobs are done and we're not on watch and we're not racin' around the rigging like demented monkeys. The foretop is a platform built high in the foremast, which is the mast in front, where the foretopmen climb up to when they got to change the sails. There is a little platform built on the mainmast, which on the *Dolphin* is the highest mast, and that's called the main top and then high above that is another, smaller platform called the crow's nest, and that's where the lookout stands, gazing out over the sea, looking for pirates and such.

Not for us, though, we stick to the foretop, which is big enough for the six of us and is our second kip, a club, like, where we're generally not bothered, being hidden by the sails billowing all around us. The officers and midshipmen usually stick to the rear of the ship, so we're out of their sight and hearing, which is good, 'cause if they saw us lazing about they'd sure find something for us to do.

We sprawl about in the sun and talk. The boys talk about how brave they're going to be when we come upon some luckless pirate. Jaimy especially talks fierce about how he'll be the first across, and he waves a pretend sword and allows as how he'll be made an officer 'cause of his bravery, and Davy stands up with his pretend sword and they joyfully hack at each other. I reserve judgement on how brave I'll be in a fight, 'cause I don't think I'll be brave at all and I'm just hoping I don't disgrace myself.

Today after our duties, I'm sitting down with me shiv in my lap and I'm carving a rooster's head on the hilt of it in remembrance of Charlie whose shiv it was original. I borrowed the carving gouge from Liam, and I'm making the outline. I figure I'll rub some colors in later when I get 'em. We start talking about our old gangs and I'm tellin' 'em about Charlie and Hughie and the girls, when Tink pipes up with, "Me and me gang had a run in wi' Charlie Rooster's crew once...I recalls a really big bloke and a bunch of girls throwin' rocks and red-haired Charlie, of course, but I don't recall *you*. Funny, that." Tink peers at me, curiouslike.

"That's 'cause I was up on Blackfriar's Bridge with a big rock ready to drop on your stupid head if you got any closer to our kip," says I, "and it would've been good riddance to the likes of you—and I wish I had done it."

Tink grins his good-natured grin. "You're right. It was at a bridge." He leans back against the mast and smiles up into the sun. "And now we's mates. Ain't it strange?"

Stranger than you know, lad.

Jaimy has loosened up considerable since he first came on board all stiff and horrified by the likes of us. He's one of us now, but there's chinks in his knowing about life and the lives of others. Like now we're all talking about our past lives and I'm talking about Charlie and the gang and then I tells about That Dark Day when me family died and how Muck come for me sister and I'm startin' to choke up a bit and then Jaimy up and says he don't believe a word of it.

"Ah, you're all having me on," he says, resentfullike. He don't like being made fun of.

"Nay, it's true, Jaimy," says Benjy. "Muck was one o' them what come and got the dead uns and sold 'em to the doctors."

But Jaimy's still sittin' there not believin' it, and for some reason I loses me head and gets all hot and I'm quick up on me hands and knees facing him and me eyes are wellin' up and I says, "Of course you ain't believin' it when all ye ever did then was ride in yer damn fancy coach and stare out at the kids in the street with their hands out to ye, and if ye ever did wonder where they come from, yer high-and-fine mum'd tell you they all come from the fancy houses, aye, and all their mums tarts and all their dads villains and drunkards, too, right?"

I jumps up to go and sticks me shiv and me carvin' tool in me vest.

"Come on, Jacky, it ain't his fault," says Davy.

"Yes, it is. He's a bleedin' toff what don't know nothin'!"

Jaimy's face is red and he looks at me mad and I glares back at him. "Watch your mouth, Jack," he says through his teeth. He clenches his fists.

"Piss off, *James*," says I through me own teeth. "I bet ye thought the street scum could go to fine orphanages and such anytime they wanted. They couldn't, *James*, 'cause there ain't no orphanages! There's only Muck and sickness and cold and starvin' and shame and brothels and the gallows!"

The tears are runnin' down me face for real now, and I turns and grabs a shroud and wraps me legs around it and slides down to the deck. Then I goes down to one of me hidey-holes way below deck and curls up and hugs me knees and looks off in the dark.

I wonder about these moods that have been coming over me lately when ever'thing's going along just fine. Why'd I have to light into Jaimy like that? It really wasn't his fault. I do know I'm going to have to control myself more or I'm going to be found out and The Deception will be over and I'll be put off to be a slave to some awful sultan and I know I cry much too much for a boy and I resolve to stop.

Saucy sea sailors don't cry.

Later we're all back up there in the foretop, with me a little shamefaced. Jaimy punches me in my arm and I punch him in his and all is forgiven and forgotten, and in the warmth of all this forgiveness we decide to set up a secret society, the Brotherhood of the Ship's Boys of His Majesty's Ship the *Dolphin*.

We make up secret handshakes and signs so we'll be able to recognize each other when we're locked in dark dungeons and pirate castles and such. We decide on the number three as our secret number, and we swear mighty oaths to stand up and protect each other and to never tell the secrets to others on pain of death. We swear never to forget each other when we are far flung across the face of the earth and famous in legend and song.

Davy says we must put a mark upon ourselves to prove the Brotherhood or it don't count for much, and we have to agree. For starters we each takes out our knives and nicks our left thumb to draw blood and then puts all our thumbs together so that we are blood brothers just like the savages, but Tink don't think it's enough for such a dread Brotherhood as ours and why don't we cut off our right earlobes and sew 'em all in a packet and send it overboard with a note to Neptune, which makes me sick but I say nothing, and Davy pipes up with, "Why don't we all get the same tattoo when we go ashore?"

Everyone thinks that's a great idea, 'cept me, but I don't say nothin' 'cause I don't want to stand out and who knows when we'll go ashore again. A worry in the future is better than a mangled ear right now.

They all fall to deciding what sort of tattoo to get and where to put it and Willy says, "Why not get a naked dancin' girl like Big Morty has on his arm which 'e can make dance by flexin' 'is muscle? We could get it done on our right butt cheek."

The others admit that would be prime but maybe we ought to have somethin' a bit more nauticallike. I agree with all my heart, thinking about how I'd have some real explainin' to do if I grow up to be a lady and get married and on my wedding night my husband discovers a naked dancing girl tattooed on my tail. Course, I'd rather not get a tattoo at all.

We decide to leave what and where till we're ashore and can see what can be had. We solemnly adjourns the meeting of the Brotherhood and decide to meet at the bowsprit for a bit of a splash, a baptism of our new Brotherhood, so we slide down the shroud lines like the salty sailors we are and do not climb down the rope ladder like pathetic landsmen.

We make it to the bowsprit without being waylaid by any who might think the *Dolphin* might be better served by us doing some actual work. The bowsprit is the pointy thing on the front of the ship that has a narrow gangplank running out on it and has one of the fore-and-aft sails hooked on its end. There's a net rigged under the bowsprit to catch any sailor who might fall off the gangway in heavy weather.

The net might have been rigged for that serious purpose, but it ain't what we use it for. When the ship hits gentle rolling swells, like it's doing right now, the bowsprit dips down toward the wave and the net goes under the water a bit. We doff our shirts and climb down in the netting and try to stifle our squeals as the water surges up to meet us. The water hits us powerful hard, but the net holds us safe.

We're getting near Gilbraltar now and the water is turning a clear blue and dolphins, the most amazing things, come up close to us in the net. They look at us with their bright little eyes and they seem almost to be laughing at us and our ship, which is named for 'em but which ain't near as fast. We laugh at them and each other as we plow through the foam, the dolphins larking about and jumping clean out of the water and not working hard at all to keep up with us. We 'specially hoot and jeer at Davy since the shameless monkey has taken off his pants as well as his shirt, but the other boys don't follow his lead as they are already soaked, which is lucky for me 'cause now I don't have to make up some lame excuse and leave.

When we come back on deck and put our shirts on, Bill Sloat is there and he's looking at me, smiling.

Chapter 11

Mr. Tilden holds the class for the midshipmen at a long table set up in the gun room, which is where the officers eat, all 'cept the Captain, who eats his own fine dinners in his own fine cabin. After the officers are done with their breakfast, but before the midshipmen come in, Tilly gives us ship's boys some instruction, him being an American and democratic in his ways. Also, I think he's doing an experiment, like, to see what can be done with rabble such as us. He gives us some science and arithmetic and navigation, and he gives us new words to learn. Today's words were *consolation, solace,* and *balm*. I think he picks 'em out of the air.

Tilly wants all us boys to learn to read and talk right 'cause he says that will take us far in the world and make us the equal of any man, no matter what his birth. That's Tilly's American nature coming out, I guess, but I don't know how true it is. We'll see.

Since I can read better than any of them, from my days as a professional reader on Hugh the Grand's shoulders, I'm to help tutor the others. This makes them hate me in a good-natured sort of way, but it pleases me.

Willy is hopeless in the way of reading, but he tries and maybe someday he'll be able to write his name. I'm still on the alphabet with him and Benjy. Benjy don't seem to care too much for this kind of schooling, as he just sits there all dreamy and looking out the hatchway at the light while I'm trying to teach him something. He's good at the seamanship, though, so he'll do all right. He just wants to be a sailor, after all. Yesterday in the foretop he said he figures his dad must have been a Swedish sailor, 'cause of his really blond hair, or maybe a Finn or a Dane. He don't know, and his mum didn't know, either, on account of her occupation. Davy and Tink look down and away when they hear this, so I know they're thinking of their mums. Barmaids, chambermaids, milkmaids, maids all and all dead. Benjy says he don't hold it against his mum none for what she done, as she loved him and tried to do her best for him while she lived. Things got real quiet in the foretop for a while.

Davy and Tink are bright enough but both are scamps what can't sit still. They've each of 'em already been stretched bare-assed over a cannon and switched for devilment, where they cried and howled like babies and promised never to do it again, which ain't likely. They are beyond the alphabet and on to simple words.

Jaimy doesn't really need any help in reading, but I tutor him, anyway, just 'cause it makes him mad, and 'cause I like to be around him, mad or not. He can write a fairer hand than me and can talk better, so I'm learning from him, too, and that makes it better for his precious pride.

After the boys and Tilly leave, I set up the table for the midshipmen. It ain't my favorite part of the day, since I'll have to be around when the awful Mr. Bliffil bullies the others and makes them hate themselves. I can see the shame in their faces and I don't like it. Bliffil is one of those blokes who can be happy only when he's making someone else miserable.

The midshipmen straggle in and grumpily sit down and toss their books on the table in front of them. I try to stay out of sight back in the shadows, wishing Tilly would get here soon. I want this to be over so I can get back outside and practice my flute and my sewing and be with my mates.

Bliffil saunters in last, cuffs the backs of a few heads, pushes Mr. Eakins out of his chair and sits down in it. He looks blearily around the table, his hair uncombed, his shirt open and dirty. I wouldn't be surprised if he was stealing the rum ration from some of the smaller midshipmen and then terrorizing them into silence. As if he knows what I'm thinking, his gaze falls upon me.

"Come here, boy," Bliffil says to me.

"Sir?" I says, fearfully. I go over to the table. I know that this is not going to turn out well and I starts tremblin'.

He opens one of the books in front of him and says, "Read this." He shoves the book over in front of me, and hope rises in me breast. Maybe he's heard I can help with readin' and maybe I can help him and maybe this'll soften his hard heart.

"'Of arms and the man I sing,'" reads I, "'Who, forced by fate, and haughty Juno's unrelenting hate...'"

I don't get to go on 'cause Bliffil's hand whips out and

the back of it catches me across the mouth. Shocked, I raises me hand t' me lips. He warn't lookin' for help, I knows now, he just wanted to shame me. I can tell by the look in his eye that he despises me for knowin' the words.

"Don't you raise your hand to me!" he hisses, and I puts me hands down to me side.

"I…I'm sorry, Sir," I whispers. "I just sounds 'em out. I don't know what they means. It's a trick, like."

"What does this mean?" he says, pointing to another passage.

"I don't know, Sir."

The inside of my lip is cut and I can taste the blood.

"And this?"

"I don't know, Sir."

"You insolent little snot," he hisses, and he leans out to hit me again. I closes me eyes and waits for it with me arms held down tight to my sides.

His next blow catches me on my ear and it knocks me down.

"Get up," he orders. I get up, me ear ringin' and the room spinnin' around.

"What does this mean?"

"I don't know, Sir."

"Going to cry, snot?"

"No, Sir," even though I already am.

"We'll see about that." His hand cocks back again. I squeezes me eyes shut and cringes.

"Ma…ma…maybe the boy has had enough, Mr. Bliffil."

I pops open a cautious eyelid. It was Mr. Jenkins what spoke.

Bliffil slowly turns to face Mr. Jenkins, the look on his face that of total amazement. "Wot!" cries Bliffil. Mr. Jenkins has now gone white in the face and stares down at his tablet. "The Jellyfish opens its noise hole and tells *me* when enough is enough! Bloody cheek I call it and I won't have it, by God!"

Bliffil grabs Mr. Jenkins by the neck and forces his head down to the tablet and rubs his face on it. When he lets go and Mr. Jenkins raises his head, his face is splotched with the white of the chalk and the red of the shame. There is no fight in his eyes, nothing but humiliation. He looks to be fighting back tears.

Then Tilly finally comes roaring in with, "Gentlemen, gentlemen, compose yourselves! We continue today with…" And I am able to fall back into the shadows and nurse my lip.

I decides then and there to never go into the midshipmen class again without Tilly being there.

Chapter 12

We have long since gone through the Strait of Gibraltar, which was the most amazing thing with the great rock itself and the salutes from the port and the gay dolphins playing at our bows. I wish we could have gone into the port to look about, but, no, we are off to the coast of North Africa, where we will search for pirates. It's getting really hot. We have been having nearly daily drills with the big guns, and the boys get worked right hard as they run the sacks of powder to the gun crews. They doff their shirts, and their chests fairly gleam with sweat. I doff my shirt and pound my drum and sweat with the rest of them.

My shirt, however, is not my problem as you could still play a tune on my ribs had you the proper hammers and musical training. No, the problem is with my pants. They are getting tight across the rear. When first I put on poor Charlie's pants, there was room enough to spare and I had to roll up the cuffs several times to keep them from flopping around my feet. What with the three full meals a day that I've been getting and what we've been cajoling out of the cook, my haunches have filled out and are getting right round, which is not good in the furthering of The Deception. I've got a little taller, too. I only roll up the cuffs once now.

But I am some skilled in the sewing now and I resolve to make new pants. Baggy ones. I go to see Liam and he tells me I'm to go see the clerk, Deacon Dunne, down in ship's stores, and draw some cloth and thread against my wages, and off I go.

Deacon Dunne casts a wary eye on me. "Jack Faber, is it?"

"Aye, Sir."

"Two yards of white duck?"

"Aye, Sir."

"This essentially uses up your pay so far. What with the mess kit you were issued when you came on board lacking one. That's charged against your name, too."

"I know, Sir," says I, still marveling that I get paid at all.

Deacon Dunne nods to his assistant clerk who goes to get the cloth and thread. "Have you been reading your Bible, Jack?" he asks, drilling me with his gaze.

"Oh yes, Sir," say I, and put on a face of all honest innocence, "and I find it a great consolation and solace. A balm, even."

He looks at me doubtfully, but he delivers the goods.

I am good at the sewing and I am prideful about it. I can sew a straight seam and I can cut the shapes out of the whole cloth and see how it's all going to come together and and how it's going to fit and hang. The boys are not good at the sewing. Willy is too clumsy with the needle and Davy and Tink and Benjy lack the patience and Jaimy considers it beneath him. We'll see when his clothes turn to rags on him just how far beneath him it is, the snob.

Within a day and a half I have a new pair of trousers. They have a drawstring at the waist, lots of room in the butt, and wide cuffs so I can roll the legs up above my knees for the deck washing and such.

I also have some cloth left over, so I make myself a pair of underdrawers, the first I've had since That Dark Day. Then an idea comes to me, an idea so wonderful in its cunning and boldness that I am grinning and giggling as I carry it out. I take a piece of the remaining scraps of cloth and roll it up into a sort of soft tube. Then I fold another piece up to make a soft round pad. I sew the tube onto the pad and then take the two of them together and sew them in the front of my drawers, so that if anyone is ever checking out the front of my pants for evidence of male equipment, I won't be found lacking.

I am well rigged out.

The north coast of Africa is all dull, barren brown rock broken up by patches of sandy desert with dunes that come all the way down to the edge of the sea. The sand whips up into clouds that reach all the way out to us sometimes and we can taste the grit in our mouths. We chase what we think to be pirates, but they always slip away from us, dodging into tiny harbors or running into waters too shallow for us to go. It makes the crew mad, 'cause they're hungry for plunder and prizes. But not me. I don't care if we ever catch a pirate.

The seas roll by and the months do, too, and I do my duties and loll about in the foretop under the sun with the boys, and I practice my pennywhistle and do my sewing and study my lessons and grow lazy and sleek. I have seen Morocco and I have seen Tripoli. Egypt, too. All from five miles out. I marvel at how far I have come since the days in the streets and I dream of how far I might yet go.

So sail on, *Dolphin,* I say, weave your way in this watery world and keep on sheltering this poor orphan girl as long as you can.

I have four tunes by heart now: "The Tenpenny Bit," which was the easiest one, the one Liam showed me first, and "Dicey Riley," and "The Pigtown Jig," all of which are good for the dancing, which I can now do a bit of. Liam showed me the heel-and-toe action of the feet and I caught on right fast. The Scots on board say I should dance with my arms folded in front of me, and the English say one hand on the belly and the other on the small of the back, and the Irish say it must be done with the hands held rigidly to the sides, but it's all one—it's the feet what do the work, anyway.

I know a slow and sad song, too, and it's my favorite, called "Down by the Sally Gardens." Like most of the slow tunes, it's about a poor and trusting girl who is led astray by her false true lover, who asks her to go riding with him and she goes with the scoundrel only to have a knife thrust in her dear and lovin' and trustin' heart and her heart's blood does flow and she's tossed in a lonesome grave with only the wild birds to mourn. But it's a lovely tune, anyway, and the whistle has a way of sounding sad and far away on the slow songs, even when it's right up against your lips.

I caught on right fast to the dancing and playing because I have this thing in me that loves to show off and be in the center of things. I try to fight it 'cause I know it's dangerous to The Deception, but I don't always succeed.

A month or so after I made my pants, I wheedled some more cloth out of Deacon Dunne with the promise that I'd learn some Scripture by heart. This time I got a bit of blue cloth as well as the white and a length of white piping, and I made me a shirt. It's white with a drawstring on the bottom and a blue flap on the back, and I stitched the white piping around the outside edge of the blue flap, about an inch in, and then above that, on the bottom edge, I stitched in HMS *DOLPHIN* in white thread.

The whole outfit looks smart as new paint, and I prance about in it in front of the boys, who hoot and holler and swear they'd never be caught dead in such a rig, and the next time we Beat to Quarters for exercising the great guns, I wear my uniform. The officers dress up for Quarters and battle, I think, so why not me?

When we first started doing the gunnery drills, we did them without firing the guns. We did them just to see how fast we could all get on station. It was a hopeless mess at first with everyone running into each other, but after a few weeks it all got worked out and everyone got to their spot lightning fast, even when the drill was in the middle of the night and everyone had to pile out of their hammocks in the dark. The Captain was satisfied, and the next drill, we knew we would really be firing the guns. I was all excited, but the first time the Captain yelled "*Fire!*" and I hit the drum, the tremendous crash of the full broadside sent me tumbling to the deck and my nose ended up between the Captain's black and shiny boots.

"Looks like the crew still needs a bit a work, Mr. Haywood," says the Captain to the First Mate, both of 'em lookin' down their long noses at me lyin' there in disgrace.

"Afraid so, Sir," says Mr. Haywood. At least the Captain don't kick me as I get up all red and shamefaced.

But I'm used to the sound now, and today after we'd had a number of rolling broadsides (each gun fires in turn as the target comes into its range) and gun number twelve (Jaimy's gun, hooray!) blows the target barrel to pieces, the Captain looks satisfied with the performance of his crew, and we secure from Quarters. I go to leave the quarterdeck, but the Captain stops me.

"What is your name, boy?" he asks, claspin' his hands behind him and rockin' back on his heels and peering at me quiverin' down below.

"Faber, Sir," I quavers, thinkin' I'm gonna catch it for somethin', I don't know what but… "Jack Faber, ship's boy," I manages to gurgle.

Please, Sir, no switches, please.

"Well, Faber. You are well decked out. Where did you get the uniform?"

"I made it, Sir."

"Good work, then. It's good to see spirit and initiative in the low ranks. Especially in the lowest of ranks," he says, and then calls, "Mr. Haywood."

"Sir?" says the First Mate, coming over to also tower over me.

"The boy has made this uniform for himself. Issue out enough cloth for him to make uniforms for the ship's boys. How many are there?" he asks me.

"Six, Sir."

"Very well," says the Captain. "Cloth for six uniforms. They will make very presentable sideboys when we make port. Make it so, Mr. Haywood."

"Begging your pardon, Sir," says Mr. Haywood, looking at me as he would at an annoying kind of bug, "but the midshipmen usually are the..."

"Make it so, Mr. Haywood," says the Captain evenly. "Our fine midshipmen will have to deal with it."

So, for my troubles, I have received a commission from Lord Captain himself. Furthermore, I now know how our Captain feels toward our middies, and I tuck that away in a corner of my mind.

Chapter 13

"Hold still, Davy, I mean it," says I, crossly. To drive home my point I bring my fist up with the measuring tape in measuring the inside of his leg for the trousers and gives him a whack where he don't want to be whacked. He howls and grabs himself and allows that he always thought I was one of the sods the Professor was talkin' about today, and this was proof in front of God and everybody.

Mr. Tilden's words for today were *buggery, sodomy,* and *pederasty.*

"I give you these words only to protect you from the sin, the Sin That Dare Not Speak Its Name," he said, his mouth set primly, and then he commenced to tell us, in detail, what the words meant. "Now, you boys don't get caught in any situation like that. A pure mind in a pure body. Stay away from dark places. It's a hanging offense, you know."

Our mouths are hanging open speechless. Then the boys roar up and say they'd die before some cove did *that* to them. I am struck dumb. I am completely amazed and disgusted.

I may yet be hanged, thinks I, but it will not be for *that*.

"So watch yerself, sodomite," says Davy, as I again bring my tape to bear, and I, of course, have to follow that with a burst of my best and vilest curses to keep up my standing as a true lad.

It's funny about Davy and me—we look so much alike, sandy hair and pointy noses and chins, we could be brother and sister. Which is probably why we fight so much. More than once the others have said, "Why don't you two just shut up?" or "Stop with the bickerin' or we'll drop you both over the side."

We are up in the foretop and I am measuring the boys for their new uniforms and they are fidgeting around more than usual. I think they're a little resentful that I caught the eye of the Captain. Let 'em be jealous, thinks I, there's more than one way to promotion and pay, not just in the brave swinging of swords and in the hacking and hewing of your fellow man.

The cloth for the uniforms is in a neat pile in our kip, waiting to be measured and cut up. I went and got it this morning with Benjy 'cause he wanted to see what was down there. He stood gawking at all the cloth and ribbons and other fine things on the shelves in the small stores room, while I dealt with the Deacon.

"So. Eighteen yards of white duck, three yards of blue, fifteen feet of white piping, spool of white thread, spool of blue thread, two needles, one piece chalk. Is that correct, Faber?" Deacon Dunne looks over the top of his spectacles at me.

"Yes, Sir, it is."

Deacon Dunne checks a ledger and scrawls some figures on his slate. Then he looks at me with suspicion. "For your last foray into sartorial splendor you needed three yards white duck, one half yard blue, and thirty inches of piping in total. Am I again correct?"

"Yes, Sir. As I recall."

"Well, then, according to simple arithmetic, you are trying to swindle His Majesty out of four yards of cloth and thirty inches of piping, because you already have a uniform and we only need cloth for five."

"The Captain said six, Sir."

"Cloth for five uniforms," says the Deacon, firmly. He writes in his ledger.

"It isn't fair, Sir," I says. "I already paid for mine and it isn't fair." I sulks for a moment. "Shall I tell the Captain you've changed his order, then?"

Instantly, I regrets my cheek.

"Shall you relieve yourself of your pants and bend across that bench while I give you several dozen, *then*?" hisses the Deacon, holding aloft his metal yardstick, which would be a very serviceable switch. "Shall I, *then*, you insolent young pup?"

"Oh no, Sir!" I bleats, falling to my knees and hanging my head and cursing myself for my stupidity. Out of the corner of my eye I see Benjy lookin' wary and easin' away from the bench I may be stretched across, as he don't want to be included. I clasps me hands 'neath me chin and looks up at the Deacon with me best street-orphan-supplicatin'-teary-eyed look and cries, "Beggin' yer pardon, Sir! I didn't mean it! Please, Sir, no switches. Five uniforms it is, Sir!"

"You should have seen our brave Jack down on his knees before the Deacon," crows Benjy when we're back up aloft. He falls to his own knees and mimics my craven performance. "Please, Sir, please don't make me drop me drawers and bend over that horrid bench, Sir!" My so-called mates are all laughing and rolling around holding their sides.

"Pleadin' for his life over a simple switchin', he was!" Benjy plows on. "Like he was bein' lashed to the grating for a proper lashin' with the Cat-O'-Nine-Tails like poor Miller last week. And a bloody mess he was, but *he* didn't cry out, no he didn't, he took it till he passed out, he did."

Yes, he did, and I had to beat the drum for it, when the call went out for All Hands to Witness Punishment, and I had to watch 'cause I had to know when the flogging was about to start so as to start the drumroll, and when to stop it when it was done, and it was all I could do to keep from throwing up on my drumhead.

The lads all jeer and hoot at me for my cowardice, but I don't care 'cause I seen Davy and Tink get theirs before and they howled and cried and begged for mercy, just like me. I'd rather beg my way out of a beating than actually take it. If that makes me a coward, then so be it. I never was very brave, anyhow.

The Deacon let me out of the switching and he credited me back the cost of my uniform, so it all worked out.

'Cept now I got to learn another fifty lines of Scripture. I'll be a bleedin' preacher, I will, before I get off this barky.

I don't hold it against the boys, though, all their teasing and stuff, 'cause they don't know about The Deception and all.

Maybe I would be braver if I was an actual boy and wasn't so worried about discovery.

THE DECEPTION

I've done some thinking on why I've been getting away with The Deception so far.

In the first place, men and boys are used to thinking of females as all pink and white and powdered up. I, however, am tanned brown as a nut, at least the parts of me that show, which is my face, neck, arms, and legs to my knees. I've been rolling my pants up over my knees 'cause it's hot. My shins are just as scratched and scabbed as any of the boys.

In the second place, I read a lot. I always have a book in the kip and I have one next to me right now in the foretop, *An Account of a Voyage to the South Seas* by a Captain Cook, and girls ain't expected to be scholars. They're never sent to school, at least the poor ones ain't, and the rich ones only sometimes. So someone sees a person reading a book, they think *boy.*

Third, as I have just shown, I can curse as well as any sailor. The fact that I don't know what most of what I say really *means* don't seem to matter.

Fourth, I keep my hair cut as close to my head as I can

get it. The lads are all letting their hair grow into the long pigtails like the other swabs, but not me.

Fifth, I have a thin sharp face. I'm not at all round-faced and girlish, and my lips are thin, not pouty like Polly's and Judy's and Nancy's and Emily's before she died, back in London. They all looked like girls from the day they were born and could never have passed as a boy for a minute, but not me. What that means for how I'll look as a lady, I don't know. Will anyone fancy me? There's a mirror that's hung up at the foot of the foremast, for the men to use for shaving, and I stare at my face in it for a long time. Is there anything in this face for a boy to admire? Davy once pointed me out to another sailor, who was looking for me to assign to a work detail, as "that rat-faced little runt over there." *Rat-faced?* It's true my nose is more pointed than most, and if I put the palms of my hands to my face it is rather thin, sort of like an axe blade. But *rat-faced?* Is it because I'm so plain that I'm getting away with The Deception? I don't know. Would Jaimy fancy me if he knew? I hope so, but maybe...I don't know.

I like the sewing. Its simple nature, the same thing over and over, soothes my mind. Plus, when I'm finally put off the ship, which must happen some day, I'll have something I can do to pay my way. Maybe playing the whistle, too, with a cup in front of me. I wonder how Arabs feel about girls playing pennywhistles on street corners.

I've done now with measuring Davy and Tink and Willy, and now I'm doing Benjy. While I'm putting the tape to him, I'm thinking about yesterday and how it was Sunday and we had the singing and dancing in the afternoon. It was going to be my first time playing the whistle in front of the crew, and I'm dreadful scared and nervous, but Liam says to just go out and do it, lad, and Snag says, "Lets have a tune, Jack-o," and so I goes out and begins "The Tenpenny Bit" 'cause it's the easiest. I don't play it good at first, but then I warms up and it starts to sound good and Sanderson gets up and starts dancin' and soon some others and Liam joins in with his concertina, and it's all grand. Then they clap and whistle when we're done with that tune, and I loves the clappin' and we plays the other dance tunes I know and others are playing fifes and whistles and even a fiddle, and I puts down me whistle and starts to dance a jig in the Irish fashion and there's more whistlin' and clappin' and singin' and more songs and more dancin' and when it's over and I heads for the passageway to the kip, all sweaty and flushed and happy, Sloat grabs me by the arm and pulls me aside in the dimness.

"Ain't you just every man's darlin' now, Jacky?" he whispers, his breath hot on my cheek. "Darlin' Sportin' Jacky, the pretty little sailor boy."

I tries to jerk my arm away and run, but he holds me fast. His eyes are wild and feverish and they bore into mine.

"We'll have to set down for a talk some day, won't we, Jacky?" he says. "A nice long talk, just you and me."

With that, he loosens his grip and I runs off, but not before he gives me a slap on my backside.

"Soon, Jacky, soon," he promises, laughin' low.

I gets back to the kip all shaky and breathless and my skin's all crawly and shudders run through me and I wish I could take a bath. I curse myself for all the showin' off. I *must* be more careful or I will dance my own destruction.

I'm measuring Benjy's shoulders and the boys are again bragging about how they pities the poor foolish pirate who dares to take up arms against the Brotherhood. They're waving their pretend swords around, cutting and slashing and parrying and thrusting. Just abaft of the mizzenmast is a rack with hundreds of cutlasses in it, but they are locked through their hilts with a long chain and the Master-at-Arms is the only one with a key. A good thing, too, otherwise the idiots would be hacking at each other for real.

Jaimy's talking about how fine it would be to be an officer on a man-of-war, and the others agree that there's nothin' better in the world than to be a man-of-war's man, officer or seaman, but I speaks up with, "Wouldn't it be far better to have a merchant ship and you could get rich by taking stuff from a place what's got a lot of that stuff and taking it to a place where they *ain't* got a lot of that stuff and would be grateful for it? In doing it you'd be sailing around the world and you'd get your Bombay Rat and your Cathay Cat and you'd see the Kangaroo and have your adventures, instead of swashbuckling about, trying to blow the head off another poor mother's son.

"Wouldn't that be just prime?" I sighs.

They all snort and jeer and tell me I'd just be carrying coals to Newcastle and I say, "If Newcastle wants coals, I'll haul 'em," and they jeer and say, "That's where coals come from, ye twit," and I say, "I don't care if it's fish heads, a cargo is a cargo," and I will increase and prosper, they'll see.

Now I get to measure Jaimy.

Chapter 14

Nothing else matters now, because I am dying.

Everything was going along fine. The uniforms are almost done. I've been staying out of Bliffil's way. I've avoided Sloat's evil eye. The music is a joy to me heart. I love the boys of the Brotherhood. I'm learning lots about navigation and science and arithmetic. I am happy with my station in life. All that doesn't matter now because I'm dyin' of some horrible disease and it will soon all be over.

Two days ago I started to bleed. Down there.

It's lucky I had me drawers on or I'd been discovered right then for sure, taken to the doctor and found out, and then put off on shore amongst the Arabs, to die without a friend. At least here I'll die among me mates.

I thought at first that I had snagged myself on something, but no, that warn't it. I took myself down to the hidey-hole where I takes care of necessary things, and I cleans myself up and washes out my drawers. I rips up the smaller of my two old shifts and takes a strip of it and runs it between my legs and takes another strip and ties it around my back and belly holdin' the first strip in place, and then I pulls the drawers back on wet 'cause I can't have 'em hanging out to dry with the fake cod on it and all. Then I heads back to the light.

This has set up a powerful worry in my head and I been mopin' around all down in the face. I can't think of nothin' else.

"C'mon, Jacky, cheer up," says Davy kindly. "Things could be worse."

Easy for you to say, Mate, when you're not dyin' of some awful plague, your insides turnin' to mush and runnin' out of ye. But I just say that I'm not feelin' good, so sod off and let me alone.

I know it's my insides what are turnin' on me 'cause me belly hurts, too. I've gone down to look through the Professor's books but couldn't find nothin' that spoke to my condition. The Doctor's books are all in Latin, so they're no good, neither.

"Just don't give it to me," says Davy.

Not bloody likely, Mate.

It's the third day of The Problem and I am weary of the worry. I decide what I'll do if it don't stop is wait till I'm weak with the loss of blood and then go see the Doctor and beg to be put off in some decent port 'cause ain't I been good and done my work and all and made the uniforms and never been switched? The Doctor ain't a very warm type and would probably just want to drop me over the side, but it'd be the Captain's call and maybe he'd be kind. It is a plan and I feel better for having a plan.

The talk among the sailors is that we're low on water as it hasn't rained in months and so we'll have to make port soon. That would be good for me, since we wouldn't be going to an Arab port for the water.

I get a scrap of paper from Tilly's desk and a quill and a bottle of ink and go back down belowdecks.

The Last Will and Testament of Mary "Jacky" Faber

I, Mary "Jacky" Faber, Ship's Boy, having died of some terrible and wasting disease, as you well know since you are reading this note which you have found on my lifeless body, give out my worldly things as follows.

To Liam Delaney, Seaman, I give him the love that a grateful daughter gives to her father and I give him back his whistle and thank him for the joy and comfort he has given me.

To Benjamin Hanks, Ship's Boy, I give my uniform and other clothes as he is the one closest to me in size.

To James Fletcher, Ship's Boy, I give my knife and the sure knowledge that once a poor girl loved him. I hope he will think of me fondly, sometimes.

To the other lads of the Brotherhood of Ship's Boys, I give my thanks for their friendship and wish them great good luck in their lives. You now know of my female nature and I hope you will not hold it against me when you think of me in the future.

Even though I am a girl, I would take it most kindly if my remains were treated with some respect and not just thrown overboard with no words said over me. As I have no hammock to be sewn up in, perhaps a bit of canvas could be bought with my remaining pay for that purpose. I want to be buried as a girl, so please put me in my old shift before you put me over the side.

To all my other friends on the dear Dolphin, *I give my everlasting love and affection. Please pray for my Immortal Soul, as it needs it.*

Signed
Mary "Jacky" Faber, deceased

I tuck my Will inside my vest, where it will surely be found when I breathes me last.

Chapter 15

My Problem went away. I am much relieved and my high spirits return.

The thing still bothers me, though. Why did it happen? Why did it go away? Am I cured? Will it happen again? I resolve to do further study. I keep my Will tucked in my vest.

The Professor's words for today are *insidious, surreptitious,* and *disingenuous.* He spells them out and we write them down on our slates and he tells us what they mean. I help Willy write his out. He sits next to me now, on my left, since he always needs help. Tilly is on my right, at the head of the table, and Jaimy is across the table from me. The others are slumped in their chairs half asleep.

"Any questions?" asks Tilly, not expecting a reply. He closes his books, the lesson being over for the day.

"Mr. Tilden," I speaks up, all toady and respectfullike. The lads shoot me looks of pure hatred for holding up their escape back to freedom and the light. "A while back you told us all about those smutty pederasts and sodomites and buggers for our own protection and we *really* appreciates it that you're looking out for our best interests."

I hesitates and then presses on. I've *got* to find out some things. "Now, why don't you teach us the other thing," I continue, trying not to blush, "like the way of a lad with a maid…"

That gets the boys' attention. They whoop and pound on the table. Well spoke, Jack-o! Let's have it, Professor!

"…so that our educations will be complete, like, and we'll profit by it by not going down the way of sin and such."

But the Professor will have none of it.

"Oh, Jack," says he, looking at me all sorrowful, "and I thought you were a good boy." He shakes his head sadly.

I want to say that I've been a very good boy, more than he knows, but he plows on. "You of all people. I hoped that you might be a serious scholar some day. Or a man of letters, or even a man of the cloth." He looks heavenward and heaves a sigh of regret for my lost promise.

"Oh, Mr. Tilden," I say all earnest and wide-eyed, "I ask only to be given guidance down the right path, me a poor ignorant boy what don't know no better and port visits coming up where all the temptations will be laid out before my innocent eyes."

"All I will say to you young dogs is…" The circle of leering young dogs leans in closer. "The right path is the one that leads away from the Sins of the Flesh and toward the Pure Light of Reason and Righteousness!" Tilly is really red now.

"If you could be a bit clearer on the 'Sins of the Flesh,' Sir," says Davy, "the mechanics of it, like."

"Wot? You want me to give you *instructions* in fornication?" Tilly's all swole up like a toad now. I hope he don't take a fit. I can't understand why he's getting so hot about this—he wasn't at all shy in telling us all about those sodomites and such. There seems to be a bit of the Puritan in our Tilly.

"No. I'll have no part in it," he says, setting his mouth in a prim line. "No, you'll have to go to the tarts for your lessons in lechery just like all the bad boys before you who are now roasting in Hell, and you'll get the pox just like them and your noses will fall off and you'll come to the doctor and me, saying how sorry you are and how you'll never do it again and please, Sir, can I have some salts of white mercury, but it'll be too late for that and we'll say it serves you right, you little hounds!"

Tilly gets up all sputtering and spitting and chases us out.

"Keep your minds on your studies and your parts in your pockets or they'll fall off, too!" he says as we tumble out of the room. The anatomy of the female is not his favorite field of study, to be sure.

Is that it, though? Have I got the pox already? If so, how did I get it? I feel my nose to see if it's ready to fall off, but it seems right secure.

The pox? Is that what's wrong?

Chapter 16

TWEEEEEEEWARBLEWARBLEWEEEEEE...

The Bo'sun's pipe cuts all cruel through our sleep at a little past two bells into the predawn of the morning watch. I lurch up out of the pile of us and grab my drum hanging on the carriage of the number-eight gun and sullenly start in to beating it, still half in my sleep, and head for the quarterdeck. I'm standing there yawning, thinking it's another bleedin' drill.

But it ain't. We've got a pirate!

TWEEEEEEWARBLEWARBLETWEEEEEEEEEE...

Amid all the running around and bellowin' of orders I see a ship off to our starboard, much smaller than us, with two masts and big swooping sails rigged fore and aft. It's a corsair and we've managed in the dark to get between him and the shore. The burning hulk of the ship the pirate's just plundered is glowing in the lessening dark. It glows for a while and then winks out. Poor sods, dead or drownded now.

I suspect the pirate was so caught up in the robbin' and the killin' that he didn't notice us sneaking up in the darkness, the *Dolphin* all dark and quiet. He tries furiously to get back towards the safety of the shore, but he can't, 'cause we've got a good stiff breeze from offshore behind us. He'd have to beat up against the wind to give us the slip, and while he was tryin' it, we could fall right down upon him and blow him to pieces. In desperation the pirate tries to outrun us to seaward.

"It won't wash, Sinbad, my lad," says the Captain with grim satisfaction. "Let's have all she'll give us, Mr. Greenshaw."

"Aye, Sir," says the Master, who then bellows through his speaking trumpet, "All topmen aloft to make sail!" Some of the men, the really prime seamen, leave their Quarters stations and leap aloft. I see Liam and Snag among the gang racing up the mizzen rigging, Henderson and Saunders up the after mast. The topmen hurry out onto the booms and loose the furled sails from their lanyards, and the sails belly out in the wind and are pulled taut and hard by the men on the lines on deck. More orders from the Master, and the royals and the topgallants whip out and the *Dolphin* plows forward ever faster in hot pursuit. In spite of my peaceful nature I am excited. A prize!

It's coming to full dawn now, and the pirate has put on all sail in his attempt to shake us. The corsair with its masts raked back looks fast, but we are gaining on it. We can see the men on board scrambling about furiously. They have a line of loaded guns and are aiming them. There's a puff of smoke and then a boom rolls across the water, but their shot goes wide and the ball skips harmlessly across the water.

"Mr. Lawrence," calls out the Captain, "give him a shot

from the starboard chaser, if you please." I don't have to drum for this order, only the times when the Captain says, "On my order."

The Second Mate is stationed forward and aims the long gun on the right side of the fo'c'sle. He puts his eye on the sight and looks down the length of the barrel, a smoking punk in his right hand. Suddenly he brings the ember down to the touch hole and the gun roars and slams backward. A miss.

"Let's have another, Mr. Lawrence," says the Captain, as if he's asking for another biscuit with his tea. Mr. Lawrence's crew reloads at full speed. It's Tink that brings up the bag of powder, which is thrown down the barrel and tamped. The ball is tipped in and then the wad is rammed home to hold the ball in. The Second Mate again aims and fires. This time it hits the pirate and the gun crew sets up a cheer, but the ball only smashes in a cabin wall.

We are getting closer. About fifty yards now. Closer. The pirate fires again and the cannonball whistles over the Captain's head and makes a neat round hole in the mizzen staysail. This is serious now and no longer fun. People are *shooting* at me. I tear me eyes from the pirate and keep them on the Captain. If a ball is gonna come kill me, I don't want to see it on its way to me own dear body. Me legs start in to shakin'.

"Well, enough playing with toys," says the Captain, strolling casually about, as if he were taking a turn round the park on a sunny day instead of being shot at with murderous intent. The Master, too, is standing all cool with his hands behind his back, gazing up at the set of his sails, awaiting the Captain's next move.

"Mr. Greenshaw, when I give the signal, bring the ship to port so that the starboard guns will bear. After the broadside, bring her back on this course."

"Aye, Sir," says the Master. Seeing the Captain and the Master so easy and all should help me quiet the shakin' in me knees, but it don't. Maybe it'll be all right. Maybe the pirates will give up. *Please, God, don't let me disgrace myself.*

"Starboard guns," shouts the Captain through his trumpet to the crews of the big guns below us, "hold steady. Aim your guns but *hold steady.* Fire on my order."

I lifts me quiverin' sticks and waits. The Captain looks at the Master and nods. Mr. Greenshaw speaks in a low voice to the man at the wheel and the ship begins to turn to the left. I waits, me legs all jelly.

The *Dolphin* turns some more. Then further she turns. The wind spills out of some of her sails. Still she turns.

"*Fire!*" bellows the Captain, and I hammer on me drum and there's that awful crash as the guns all roar out as one and the *Dolphin* herself heels over from the blast.

There's a cheer from the crew: The pirate has been hit hard! Some of her guns ports are shattered and her foremast is down! It's broken about a third of the way up and the huge sail is dragging in the water, slowing the corsair down to a crawl. Some of the pirates are swinging axes, desperate to cut the sail away. Some of the pirates are getting into small boats. *That's it,* I prays. *Run away!*

"Hold fire," orders the Captain. "Starboard guns, reload with grape. Aim to clear their decks. Fire only on my order."

With that order, I knows we means to take the corsair, not sink it. We are taking a chance in order to take a prize.

The Master has brought the ship back in direct pursuit of the pirate and we draw even closer. She can't run from us now, but some of the pirates are still puttin' up a fight. I can hear the grapeshot rattlin' down the barrels.

"Same again, Mr. Greenshaw," says the Captain, and again the *Dolphin* swings to port. I watches the Captain and wait.

"*Fire!*" says the Captain, and again I hit the drum and again the guns shout out their terrible bark. The powder smoke whips back across the deck, stingin' me eyes. I sees the pirate has downed men all over its decks. We're drawing closer and closer. I sees red comin' out of their scuppers. *Dear God.*

Then there's a splinterin' crash and I'm up in the air and flat on me back and knocked most out of me senses. The *Dolphin* shudders. Then there's another blast. There's smoke and screamin' and cryin' from down below. The pirate's guns have fired point-blank into our side.

In spite of her injuries the ship pulls up beside the corsair. There's another horrible crash as the pirate gets another broadside into us. Such awful *screaming*.

"Man the Boarding Party to starboard," yells the Captain. "Get the nets across! All hands to the Boarding Party!"

I gets to me feet and stumbles down the ladder, numb with terror. Got to find Jaimy.

The men are grabbing cutlasses from the rack. The nets and hooks are already across to the pirate. Our Marines are up in the rigging, firing down at the pirates below, keeping them away from the netting. I sees Jaimy up at the front of the mob by the rail, waiting for the order, cutlass in hand. The men are howling like demons. I grabs a cutlass and it's heavy in me hand and I knows I'll never use it but...

Jaimy, you fool, I want to shout. *Wait! You're only a boy!. Let the others do it!*

"Away the Boarding Party!"

Jaimy is the first one across the net and I sobs and blindly follows across, tryin' to hold me water and knowin' I ain't gonna be able to, and now I've lost sight of Jaimy and I slips on the deck and falls down 'cause it's covered with blood and there are dead men everywhere and I gets up all smeared with blood and *where's Jaimy* and *there he is* headin' aft and I heads off after him but slips again in the slick blood and falls over a pirate lyin' there without a face but with two primed and cocked pistols in his belt so I drops me cutlass and pulls one out and goes after Jaimy again.

I comes round the after cabin and there he is, lookin' confused, like he don't know what to do, and then next to me the cabin door flies open and this pirate comes out with a chest under his arm and a great curved sword in his fist and he heads for the side but Jaimy is in his path and Jaimy doesn't see him and the pirate raises his sword above his head.

"*Jaimy!*" I screams and Jaimy turns to see his doom and I raises the pistol in both hands and pulls the trigger and the gun bucks in me hands and smoke flies in me face and then the pirate ain't doin' nothin' but kneelin' there bleedin' through a hole in his chest, his life runnin' out of him. Jaimy looks at the pirate and then at me, all stunned.

The pirate drops the chest and it falls to the deck and pops open and gold coins spill out and across the deck, and Mr. Lawrence is there beside me and some other of our men and they scoop up the gold pieces and when they're doin' that, Bliffil comes up from behind the bulkhead where he's been hidin' and sinks his sword into the still kneelin' pirate. The pirate topples over and Bliffil raises his now bloody sword in a great show and howls in triumph. I don't think Mr. Lawrence saw what Bliffil did, but I seen what Bliffil did, and he knows I seen it.

All the pirates are now dead or gone and I turns to go back to the ship. The ships have been made fast together so it's easy to get across this time. Before I go over, I am sick and throws up. I walks on and everythin's all bright and clear but not real somehow.

The men are putting the cutlasses back in the rack. They looks at me walking up, the pistol still in me hand and the blood on me face and arms and hands and on me clothes gettin' all stiff and turnin' brown, and I sees them as if all twinkly and jerky and slow. Real slow. *Bloody Jack,* I hears someone mutter. The Master-at-Arms takes the pistol from my hand, almost gently, and I turns and walks down the passageway. Men are washing the bloody deck with hoses and buckets but I hardly sees 'em, and the reddish foam swirls around my ankles and runs out the scuppers but I hardly feels it. In my dream I hear that many of our men are injured and four of them are dead. It's Martin and Dobbs and Mr. Leigh, the Midshipman in charge of number-six gun, and Benjy.

Benjy's dead, too.

———

I walk by the number-six gun and there he is, pinned to the wall with a jagged splinter in his chest, his own heart's blood spilled down over his shirt. A man bends down and yanks out the splinter and Benjy slips down to the deck like a little rag doll.

I do not scream. I do not cry. I only turns and walks on, down, down to my deepest hidey-hole where I lies down in the dark and pulls my knees to my chin.

Bloody Jack.

Chapter 17

It falls to a sailor's mates to sew him up in his hammock when he's dead and put the cannonball in to make him sink, and since I'm the one handy with the needle, I'm the one what sews Benjy up in a piece of canvas, him being too small for a hammock and him not having one, anyway, while the others stand around crying and grieving. Jaimy goes and gets the ball from the number-six gun and we puts it at Benjy's feet and I sew the canvas up toward his poor face. His eyes are half open and so's his mouth, and I can't stand the thought of him being down in the dark depths with his mouth open, so I sends Tink to get a length of light line and we binds Benjy up so his mouth is closed. Before I sew the canvas all the way up, I reach in and close his eyes with my fingertips. Then I do up the last few stitches and we see Benjy's face no more.

The bodies are laid on boards, which have one end on the ship's rail and the other end held up by the man's friends. The Captain and his officers and all the men not on watch or in sick bay are standing by with their hats in their hands. As the Deacon says the words over each man in turn, the board is lifted and the body slides off the board and into the water.

Benjy is the last. The Deacon lifts his hand in benediction.

"Benjamin Hanks, we commit your body to the sea and your soul to God. Amen."

We lift our end of the board, and all that's left of our mate Benjy slips off into the sea.

It's a cowed and quieted group of ship's boys that meets in the foretop in the coming days, as the Brotherhood mourns the loss of one of its own. There are no more boyish slashings of swords, no more grand boasts, no more dreams of glory. No jokes and japes out of Davy. Tink and Willy, too, just sit about and mope. Jaimy is all gloom as well, and I'm thinking it ain't all about Benjy— he's thinking about the fight, too, and he ain't happy with how he did in it. As for me, I'm the most quiet and mopey of all, not only 'cause I can't get Benjy out of my mind, but also 'cause I'm the only one of us who's actually killed someone, and that weighs heavy on me, too. That, and my bleeding has started again. Perhaps soon I'll be down with Benjy as payment for my deeds.

I get next to Liam a lot in the days after Benjy's death. I say to myself that it's to practice my seamanship and my whistle, but it's really just to be with him as his very presence gives me much comfort. Liam lets me carry on in my sad state all weepy and glum for some days, but then he starts to give me little nudges in the ribs and flicking up my nose with his finger and saying, "Stiff upper lip,

Jack," and I push his hand away and glare all stormy at him. He shakes his head.

"Jacky. You've got to let them go after a while, you know. You grieve for your mates what have passed on for a decent time and then you have to let them be."

"I know," I whimpers, "but..."

"But, nothing. You've got to think of the fine times you had with your mate, not the moment of his perishin'. Every tear you shed now only wets his windin' sheet and disturbs his rest."

I poke my head into Liam's shoulder and then let it rest there for a bit, looking out across the rolling sea and the puffy white clouds scudding along the horizon. Then I head off for the foretop. He's right. I'll let Benjy go. I'll let them all go.

The Brotherhood gathers in a circle and offers up a prayer for Benjy every day for a week after his death, then once every Sunday. It's the best we can do. It's the way of the man-of-war's man, as Liam says, and it has to be that way.

On my pennywhistle I make up a slow, mournful tune, and I call it "The Ship's Boy's Lament." Liam allows that it is very good and that I should teach it to other players as I travel the world, and because of that Benjy will always be remembered, sort of. We are on our way into legend and song.

The repairs on the pirate ship are done, and the *Dolphin* is patched up as best as the ship's carpenter can manage. The former pirate is manned with a small crew, Mr.

Lawrence commanding. I know it is a feather in his cap, and I wish him the joy of it as he seems a decent sort, for an officer. The word is that in recounting the action on the deck of the pirate to the Captain, he gave me credit for capturing the money box when he could have taken that honor for himself. Not that I wanted credit for any of that. Money was the last thing on my mind at the time. At least Bliffil didn't capture any glory with his sham of bravery.

Midshipman Bliffil is part of the prize crew and I am glad to have him off the ship, if only for a short time. The mood in the midshipmen's berth lightens considerably, and we boys venture in there for the first time. We tell them how sorry we are about Mr. Leigh, and we hang about and look at their stuff. The middies ain't really so bad—the younger ones are just boys like us. Mr. Jenkins's got a real flute, the kind you play from the side. He shows me how to blow across the hole to make the sound, but I ain't very good at it.

The morale of the ship is high, for we are officially heading into port to sell the prize, make repairs, and take on water. *And* have our first liberty call, with money in our pockets. We are going to a place called Palma, which sounds wondrously exotic.

So, in spite of ourselves, our boyish high spirits steadily return.

We feel guilty about it, but there you are.

Chapter 18

We're all in a line at the head of the ladder leading down the side of the ship, all the boys decked out in their spanking new uniforms, and I can't stand it, I'm just about to bust with pride seeing how splendid they look. The Captain and the officers are there beside us, too, waiting for the Admiral to come aboard for a meeting with the Captain, and the noble *Dolphin* is all bedecked with flags and buntings and sailors in their best uniforms manning the rails and the tops. We ain't the only King's ship in the harbor, there's the *Endeavor* and the *Surprise* and some others I can't make out from here. Merchant ships, too.

The Bo'sun is at the end of the line of us boys, looking over the side for the coming of the Admiral's gig, his pipe in hand. It's a whistle with just one hole in a bulb on the end that he puts his hand over when he blows it to make it warble. He has drilled us over the past week about how we're supposed to stand and what we're supposed to do when he sounds his whistle, and a slow and painful death has been promised us if we mess it up.

The Captain is pacing around, all covered in blue and gold, and he looks us over and seems to approve, but he looks at me the longest. I stare straight ahead as instructed, not meeting his eyes. *Please don't say anything about the battle, Sir,* I prays. *I am not what I seemed to be.*

He doesn't. Instead he says to Mr. Haywood, "See that this one grows his pigtail so he'll match the others."

Uh, oh.

"Yes, Sir," says Mr. Haywood.

I've had the feeling of late that Mr. Haywood would have preferred that I had been dropped over the side early on in my enlistment on the *Dolphin*. He leans down to me and growls, "Make it so, Faber."

"Aye, Sir."

There's a fuss as the Admiral's boat is seen coming. We get ready and hold our breath, and when a footfall is felt on the gangplank, the Bo'sun whips his pipe to his lips and lets go with a blast and we boys whip up our right hands to our foreheads, hands flat with palms out, middle finger just touching our right eyebrows. The Admiral strides by, wearing more gold than I've ever seen and an enormous hat. He is followed by several more officers. When he gets past us, the Bo'sun stops blowing and we bring our hands down to our sides, smartly, thumbs on the side seams of our pants. The Captain takes off his hat and bows low to the Admiral, and the Admiral bows to the Captain, but not nearly so low. The Captain presents his officers to the Admiral and there's more bowing all around and the Admiral is smiling and saying, "Good show," and I shouldn't wonder 'cause I heard he gets a cut out of our prize money, although I don't see why he should.

Finally, all the officers head down to the Captain's quarters to tear into the wine, brandy, and food that's been laid out, and we're put At Ease, which means we can relax as long as we don't move our right foot from its spot on the deck. That way we can be in position to snap back to attention when the officers come back on deck.

"Lor', look at that," says Willy, looking out over the town of Palma. It don't look like any sort of town we've ever seen. The buildings are low and colored pink and white and there's acres of trees. "I bet those are orange trees. Or bananas. I ain't never had neither."

Neither have I, thinks I, and I can't wait to get ashore. But not for oranges. We fidget and wait.

I know the men are anxious as well. They've been in a state of high hilarity the whole time since we set course for this place. They were barely able to contain themselves during the last Church we had, with the Deacon warning about loose women and vile vessels and evil seductresses and such, and working himself up into a fine froth. I don't think it made much of an impression on the men, though, for all that.

The Professor put his two pence in with the words for yesterday being *debauchery, dissipation,* and *wantonness.* I've a feeling that me and my sisters do not have a high standing in the worlds of religion and learning.

Finally, the Admiral and his toadies come back, considerably cheered and red-faced from their fine luncheon, salutes and bows all around, and they leave.

We are dismissed.

We ship's boys don't ask permission to go ashore, 'cause we know they'd just say no, so we pile into the first boat going ashore and keep our heads down under the gunwales. Nobody notices us in all the excitement, anyway.

Soon we're rolling up the street, bold as brass, the solid ground strange under our feet, salty sea sailors looking for food and drink and fun... and a tattooist. We go past several taverns, which are already filling up with sailors tossing their money on the bar and bellowing for ale and food and music and dancing and dollymops to dance with.

Yesterday we boys got in the Purser's line and two shillings, five pence were put in our outstretched hands, against our part of the prize money. Rich beyond our wildest dreams! Someone in the line behind me said, "Bloody Jack should get a double share for savin' the gold," but I didn't like that and I hurried away.

We ask at one of the taverns and are told there's a good tattooist called Roderigo on up the street and to look for the sign with the needle in the hand. I'm not liking this one bit, but I know when I'm trapped and will have to make the best of it.

On the way there we pass a brothel and one of the women leans out the window, showing a large expanse of white powdered chest, and says, "Oh, look at the pretty little sailor boys. They're all dressed alike. Oh, come look, Seraphina!" Another woman appears and coos over us and asks us in. She pouts when we push on. Jaimy's face is brick red.

We spot the tattooist's sign, and then the tattooist. Roderigo is sitting on a stool in front of his shop, wearing no shirt, and pants that only come down to his knees. Every inch of his skin that he could reach with his needle is covered with tattoos. The walls of the tiny shop are decorated with drawings of the tattoos that he does. We shyly sidle up.

Roderigo eyes us hungrily.

"You come to Roderigo for the tattoo, eh? You come to the right place. I am the Master. I am known from Bristol to Borneo, from Canada to Timbuktu. I trust no one with my own skin but me. You should trust no other with your skin, too. Guaranteed, my young friends, no mistakes, no fading, no infection. What will you have from the skill of Roderigo?"

Roderigo has a tattoo of a dreadful snake with dripping fangs coming out of the waistband of his trousers and curling over his hairy belly and Tink is of the opinion that it would be *just* the thing and I about faint dead away, but it costs too much and we decide we have to have something more nauticallike, anyway. We finally settle on a small anchor with a little rope around it and HMS *Dolphin* underneath in small letters. This is only two pence, and so within our means.

Then we lay to deciding where the tattoo is to be and Davy says, "On the back of the hand, of course," but Jaimy says that he is going to be an officer and officers aren't allowed to have tattoos, not ones that show, anyway, but Davy says that Jaimy can have his wherever he wants it—on his nose for all he cares—but he's going to have his on the back of his hand, by God, by Neptune, and by all the heathen gods, so there.

I can see this is going nowhere and pipes up that all the tattoos got to be in the same place on each of us or it ain't a Brotherhood thing, and it's got to be hidden and secret from everyone 'cept us so's we can swear secret oaths on our tattoos and reveal them only to each other when we're down in dungeons and stuff and hideously disfigured so we couldn't be recognized any other way, and it makes sense to them and we decide on the right hipbone up front just before it meets the belly.

Before they can change their minds I go up to Roderigo and jam the two pence in his fist and pull down the top of my pants a few inches to expose my hipbone and say, "Put it there."

Roderigo pockets the coins and takes out a needle and a bottle of ink and sets to. It hurts like hell, but I've been hurt worse. He makes a few jabs with the needle and then dabs the bloody dots with the ink. Soon the dark blue anchor starts to appear. Even though I'm biting my lip, I have to admire his skill and speed. In fifteen minutes he's done.

"Don't wash it for a while," he says, turning next to Davy, who ain't acting all so brave now that he's seen me get the needle. As all eyes are on Davy, I slip away unnoticed and go back to the brothel we saw on the way up the street, 'cause now I know there's a woman there who speaks English.

She says her name is Mrs. Roundtree and ain't I a little young for this sort of thing, but she leads on into a little room and I follows the cloud of perfume that follows her and says, "No, Ma'am, I just want to talk," and she looks at me funnylike and sits down on the bed.

"Sit down, then, lad. It'll still cost ye a shillin'."

"Yes, Ma'am," I say, and pull out one of my shillings

and give it to her. I sit down in a chair with a frilly thing around it and begin. "I've got this friend and she's a girl and she's got somethin' wrong with her and she don't know who to—"

Mrs. Roundtree gets up and comes over to me, pulls me to my feet, and gives me a few pokes here and there and then grins.

"Well, now, Miss, shall we have some tea? We've got a lot of ground to cover."

I come back out into the bright light of the day having got me an education for sure. I find I ain't dying, which is a great relief to me, and I find out about *all* the other things, like the way of a man with a maid, and babies and how they're made and born. All pretty disgustin' stuff, but maybe with someone you really loved, well, maybe not so disgustin'.

As I step out of the doorway, I loosen my pants and look down at my tattoo, which is startin' to hurt some, and I see that it's swollen a bit, but Roderigo had said that was to be expected and so I pull my pants back up again and am tying the drawstring just as the boys and some of the *Dolphin* seamen come around the corner so it looks to them like I'm just pullin' up me pants. They hoot and holler and point and make crude jokes and say, "How was it then, Jack?" I blush all red in the face and say that I was just asking for directions and they could each of 'em sod off with their filthy minds. I see Jaimy lookin' at me funny, but what the hell, I think, it helps The Deception.

The boys finally let up on me and get to raggin' on poor Willy who had fainted dead away the first time the

for food and we get stews and fishes and oranges and, even though I loves me old-horse-and-biscuit back on the dear old *Dolphin,* the change is just the thing.

"Another pint wi' ye, Jackeroe!" says Saunders, clappin' me on the back, but I say, "Thank ye kindly, Joe, but seein' as how I can barely get this one down my gullet, I'll say no. Please, Mate, have one on me." My head is reelin' wi' the excitement and the ale and the food and the music and the noise and the exotic smell of this place. It crosses my spinnin' mind that should I be discovered and put off, this would not be a bad place to be dumped, all warm and rich, but no, I can't leave my mates and I can't leave Jaimy and I'd prolly end up like Mrs. Roundtree, bless her, when all was said and done.

It don't matter what I say, another pint of ale is shoved in my fist and I stick my nose in the foam and drink some of it, but I give the rest to Jaimy, and he passes it off to Willy, who seems to be swallowing up everything in sight, a growin' boy is our Willy.

The Dolphins ain't the only ones in this tavern; there's men from the *Endeavor* and the *Surprise,* and some merchantmen, too, and the talk is swirlin' about, and some of the talk is that the *Dolphin* is headin' for the Caribbean to search for more pirates 'cause we're so good at catchin' 'em and makin' squadron commanders rich. Then I hear *Bloody Jack* said in the talk and I know they mean me and I don't like it. I wish they'd stop with that. My ears burn 'cause I know I'm bein' looked at behind my back.

My good sense, which has been hangin' back all day, tells me it's time for the Brotherhood to get back to the ship before we get knocked on the head for the few pennies we have left or get so drunk we can't get back to the dear *Dolphin* and are left here and other lads take our places. Other lads like the ones in this tavern who are jealous of our good fortune and ain't shy in showin' it. I see a couple of boys from the *Surprise* glarin' at Davy and Tink and Jaimy at the bar with all their prize money to spend. I know they're about to make a comment on the boys' cute outfits and the blood will flow.

"Awright, lads," I say. "Drink up. Time to get back before they discover we're gone. Looks like we're gonna have to help poor Willy."

They groan and say no, but Jaimy finishes his and gets up and the others follow. Tink and Davy put a hand under Willy's arms and we head out into the sun. Before I go I slap my last few coins on the bar. "A drink for every mother's son of a ship's boy in the house," I says loud enough for all to hear. "God bless ship's boys!"

We are not followed as we roll back to the ship, singin' and laughin' and exultin' in a great day. We have tasted oranges and ale. We have seen a foreign country. I have found out that I am not dying, not of *that,* anyway, and it all makes me so happy that I can barely contain the poundin' heart that beats in my chest.

I'm with me mates, and Stewed, Blued, and Tattooed, we sail for the Caribbean Sea.

PART III

As the Scholar Has Said,
"The Knowledge That One Is to Be Hanged
in the Morning,
Concentrates the Attention Most Wonderfully."

Chapter 19

We've been in the Caribbean for three months now, and the sea is such a color of blue that I can't believe my eyes are seeing it. It's so clear that when we come around an island in our search for pirates and get in shallower water, the most astonishing rocks and reefs pop out of the depths and look like strange castles, right there up close instead of fifty feet down like they really are. Tilly has rigged up brightly colored lures with feathers and hooks and trailed them on long lines off the fantail. Fishes bite on them and Tilly cranks them in on a reel that he has mounted on a stiff pole that bends with the fishes' desperate struggles, and when the fish get close to the side all brilliant in their colors but all tired out now, men with gaff hooks lean over and hook them in their gills most cruelly and hoist them aboard where they gasp and flop on the deck for a while. Their color slowly dulls as they die. It's a shame, but they are very tasty.

Tilly goes on about this book *The Compleat Angler* and has us all make small lures and lines, and we catch fish, too. A useful skill, I decide, and resolve to keep my lure and line for future use. Like when I have my own ship and need something to eat and can't afford the Horse.

This part of the voyage has proved uneventful, except for some fearsome hurricanes during the hottest months when I thought we were all lost for sure. I could not believe that such mountains of water could be and that we could survive them. We sailed under bare poles with only a scrap of canvas aloft to keep the *Dolphin*'s head into the wind, and all of us were up for days without sleep, but the good ship held, and so did we. Now the weather has turned cooler and the storms have stopped and great slick swells are all that move on the water, except for us.

We prowl on.

We have not caught any major prizes yet. Once again the pirates prove quite wily, slipping in and out of tiny bays and behind little cays and islands. We have seen some burned villages, and the Captain has sent boats full of armed men in to investigate and they came back with stories of the pirate LeFievre and how he ravaged the town and stole everything worth taking, and not just gold and silver. He also takes women and children, for ransom if white, for selling as slaves if black. The rest of the townspeople flee into the hills, and LeFievre burns the town. He has many ships now, and reports from survivors are that he is growing in his pride and struts about in fine silks and talks of setting up his own kingdom on one of the islands. But he could not grow so foolish as to take on a King's ship, could he?

We have chased down some suspicious boats but have

turned up nothing. Once we chased a ship and were running her down when the pirate crew began tossing their captives overboard. We put the boats in the water when the first people were thrown over and kept up the pursuit, but the pirates kept throwing more captives over, one at a time so they got strung out in a line that was too much for the boats, and so we had to stop, so ending the chase, and then the pirates stopped pitching captives. The Captain was fuming, and I know he's trying to think of a way around this caper for the next time it happens. We took the lucky hostages—the ones that didn't drown or weren't still on the pirate ship—back to their town and at least gained the good will of the people. Can't spend that, though.

Whenever a boat is sent out on errands away from the ship, several of us ship's boys are always included in the boat's crew so we can learn to sail and handle small boats. We learn about booms and mainsheets and downhauls and the parts of the sail and how to hold the tiller and tuck the sail in just so, which I think is just fine till one day Tink and I are out in a boat with about ten seamen, which is going into a small deserted cay to look for fresh water. Tink is trimming the sail and I'm on the tiller, keeping the course true for the little dot of an island bobbing up ahead, when I says to the coxswain how grand it is that he's teaching us all this useful knowledge, but he shakes his head and says all ruefully, "Ah, Jacky, I'm afraid that's not what you're here for."

I find this a good deal strange and ask, "What are we here for, then?"

The coxswain, who's in charge of all the small boats on the ship and whose name is Hardy, looks away all shy. "It's a delicate thing, boy," he says, "and not spoke of much." There are grunts of agreement from some of the men. Some of them shake their heads and look off, somber.

"All right," says I, not to be put off, "let's have it. Just why are we here, then, if not to be taught our seamanship?"

After some silence, Hardy sees that I'm startin' to get really steamed at all this, and he says, "Well, Jack, it's this way, and it's nothin' personal, but when a boat goes off out of sight of the mother ship it always carries a couple of boys 'cause..." He hesitates.

"Oh, for Chris'sakes," booms out a seaman named Javerts, "I'll tell the boy. It's 'cause the ship's boys is the first ones eaten if the boat gets lost and can't find its way back."

I look for signs that they're jokin' with Tink and me, but their faces don't betray it.

"You've got to see the wisdom of it, lads," says Hardy. "We wouldn't want to be eatin' a sailor what could pull a decent oar, now, would we?"

Javerts, who's a really disagreeable-lookin' cove with a red gash of a scar that goes clear across one cheek, over his grisly lump of a nose, and onto the other cheek, reaches over and grabs me leg and squeezes it, as if checkin' it for tenderness. His fingers go completely around my thigh. "I wants little Jacky in any boat I'm ever sent out in, for sure. I'll take one of the hams."

I jerk my leg away. "You sods are just havin' us on," I say, but still their faces stay stony and grim. "Ain't you?"

Snag is in the boat and he chimes in with, "It ain't just for our own nourishment and enjoyment, oh no," he says. "Say some nasty sharks happen to circle around the boat, lookin' to make trouble for poor honest seamen, well, we just toss 'em a spare ship's boy and behold—them sharks turns just as nice as any gentlemen and they tips their fins to ye as they leave."

This cuts it, and roars of laughter at my red and gullible face go out across the water.

The sods.

It is good that the weather has turned cooler. I would be stifling otherwise because now I have to wear Charlie's old vest on the *inside,* under my white shirt, to squash down my chest, which is suddenly and traitorously growing and threatening to give me away. It works, but I fear that soon I won't be able to breathe. Maybe I won't grow very big.

Yesterday, Tilly's words were *billowing, burgeoning,* and *blossoming.* I could have swatted him.

"All I really want is a small ship," says I, "that could carry a respectable cargo and be able to be handled with just a few—"

"We *know* what you want, Jacky," says Davy. "Just put a sock in it."

"Piss off, Davy," snarls I, steamed up at being interrupted. "Someday, you vile little scab, someday when the wars are all over and you're stranded on shore, you'll come to the fine offices of Faber Shipping Company Worldwide and say, 'Will ye be givin' me a post now, Jacky?' and I will not."

Davy laughs. "You'll have to, Jack, because of the Oath of the Brotherhood."

"Well then, Davy, I'll give you a post as ship's boy and I'll keep you as ship's boy till you go all bald and stooped in the back, and won't you scrub the head till it shines, by God!"

They all roll around and hoot and snort at the very idea of Faber Shipping. *I'll show you, you sods. Just you wait.*

I go back to fingering my pennywhistle, which I find I can play very softly up here in the top when the wind's blowing and not get in trouble. I've added a few more jigs, "Haste to the Wedding" and "The Hare in the Corn," and another mournful one, "My Bonnie Light Horseman," which is powerful sad and beautiful, but the girl don't get killed and thrown in a lonesome grave in this one, for a change. It's the boy who dies. In war.

The lads are back to predicting what noble sailors they're going to grow up to be and how brave they were in the last fight, but Jaimy don't join in and is quiet, and I know it's because he don't think much of the way he acted in the fight on the pirate ship. And maybe it's something else.

A few nights ago Jaimy and I were on the midwatch and it was calm and peaceful on the ocean, just a gentle breeze, and after we got coffee for the men on watch we got some for ourselves and sat sipping it and watched the constellations wheel about the night sky.

Jaimy starts talking about his family, how there's three sisters at home and one older brother what got sent off to school, but there wasn't enough money for Jaimy, so he got sent off to sea but couldn't go as a midshipman 'cause his dad couldn't buy him a place and he had no influence with the Navy, so ship's boy was the best he could do. It purely mortified his father to send him off, and his mother like to died with grief, but what else was there to do, what with the family wine business having just about perished because of the blockades of the French ports. His father had inherited some money and his mother came from a good family, but everything was gone now. His brother, George, was in school to become a solicitor, but it would be years before he could practice law and make any money.

"So I guess it's up to me," says Jaimy, all glum. "And I haven't made a very good show of it so far."

"Sure you have," says I. "You're sure to be made midshipman soon. You're quick at the studies and Tilly's sure to recommend you, and I know the Captain's noticed your bravery."

"My bravery," he snorts, hanging his head.

"Jaimy, you were the first one over. Everyone saw that. You could not have been braver."

"But when I got over, I just stood there like a fool. I didn't know what to do."

Aye, Jaimy, I thinks. *It's one thing to dream of glory in battle and quite another to actually stick a sword into another person's soft parts. Or a bullet.*

"You were right behind me and you actually did something. You acted like...like an officer. You should be the one picked for midshipman. You and Mr. Lawrence took that ship. You saved my very life."

"I shot a man in the back, that's all I did, and I'll probably have to answer for that someday. There was no bravery in it."

"No, you conducted yourself with honor. You should be proud."

"*Honor?*" I hisses in the dark. "*Honor?* Honor to me is keepin' my head down and my tail covered and hopin' I don't disgrace myself when things get chancy."

He laughs softly in the dark and says, "But you're Bloody Jack, famous in legend and song."

In the gloom, I see him reach out, as if he's going to give me an affectionate head rub, but then he stops and takes back his hand. He turns his head and looks away.

"I don't like being called that, Jaimy."

I would have liked the pet, but I don't say so.

"Why not?"

"Because I'm really not bloody-minded at all. I'm really a peaceful sort of coward."

"Right," he says. "Look. There's Orion up there."

I look up to see The Hunter turning about high in the night sky.

"Yes. There's Rigel in his leg and good old Betelgeuse on his shoulder."

"And Aldebaran up in Taurus."

The breeze slips down from the curve of the massive sail hanging over our heads and flows around us, a warm river of air. Some of Jaimy's hair has come loose from his braid and whips gently across his face. I gaze upon him in the moonlight as he looks off across the water.

Oh, Jaimy, I want to tell you so bad.

Chapter 20

It's just another Sunday, just another inspection. We scrub her down, we shine her up, and we wait for the Captain to come around.

At least we're presentable now, and I make sure the boys are all lined up nice in our kip and their uniforms are clean and crisp. Now that they're all used to wearing them, I think I shall have to make us some neat caps. A cap would be good for me, too, because I could hide my growing hair up in it. My hair ain't long enough for a pigtail yet, but it's getting long enough to make me look more like a girl and that's not good. The caps will be blue, of course, with white stripes around the headband and a blue ribbon hanging down in back and...

"Who made you the bleedin' boss?" growls Tink.

"Someone's got to get you swine all in a line, all ship-shape and Bristol fashion," says I, and then Captain Locke is there, with his usual party.

"The boys are looking tidy," says he. "And they're certainly growing." He's looking at Willy's hairy legs sticking out from the bottom of his trousers.

"Very good," he says, looking about, "however, we're going to have to do something about this." He points to the pile of our bedding behind us, which I did try to fold and neaten up before, but of little use. "I won't have my guns cluttered up so."

He casts his eyes to the overhead, where the hammock hooks are attached. The hammocks are only put up at night. During the day they are rolled up and stored with the seamen's seabags over by the bulkhead. "Let's rig up some hammocks for them."

The Bo'sun murmurs something about not bein' enough room, Sir, not for five, to the First Mate, who passes on the information to the Captain, who heard it well enough the first time but naval custom must be observed.

"Well, then, set up three," he orders firmly. "We lost that many men from the lower deck in the last fight. Put the big one"—and he points to Willy—"in one by himself. The others can sleep two by two in the other hammocks, head to foot. It will do for a while. Make it so."

"It should be Jaimy and me in one hammock, Tink and Davy in the other, 'cause Jaimy and I got watch together and that way we won't be woke for nothing when the watch changes," says I, all firm and full of sweet reason. "Plus, he's biggest, not counting Willy, and I'm smallest, and Tink and Davy are the mediums, so it all works out equal, like."

"Why you want to sleep with Jaimy?" sneers Davy all leering and snide. "I swears you *are* one of those pederasties, Jacky, wi' all yer airs and all yer—"

"I'd rather have a hammock of me own," I lies, "but if I have to share, I'd rather it not be wi' *you* whose feet stink or Tink, who snores like an old sow!"

Willy's sitting with his back leaning on the mast, beaming with joy to be above the argument. "Cheer up, Davy," he says. "Ye and Tink can de-light each other wi' yer farts all the night long."

Such a delicious bit of wit from the usually dim Willy brings such gales of laughter from all of us that the question is decided in my favor.

"I still thinks ye t' be a bleedin' little fairy," says Davy in defeat.

That I be, Davy, that I be. A right little elf.

It being Sunday we have our dancing and playing and singing, and me and my whistle are a real part of it now. It ain't all just one big show, sometimes it's just quiet trading of songs and tunes and words to ballads amongst mates, and that's the way it was today. It's hot and the Brotherhood takes the time for a dowsing in the bowsprit netting and they calls for me saying, "Come on, Jacky," but I says, "No, I'm needed for the playing on the whistle," which ain't exactly true, but the lads are in there all starkers this time and I can't even take off me shirt now, let alone me pants. I get away with the excuse this time, but it won't be long, I know.

I notice the boys are growing a bit of hair under their arms and around their dangly bits. I make a note to myself to make my fake cod a little bigger.

I, too, am furring up in the same sort of places. Soon I'll be a proper little ape, I will.

———

That night we climb into our hammocks. Willy makes contented sounds of single comfort, and Davy and Tink make fart noises and laugh themselves stupid. Jaimy and I, after a few kicks and threats about what goes where, settle down for the night.

I know I'm tempting Fate, but I allows myself a moment of glee, thinking about how my cunning and my trickery and my generally devious nature has got me to this spot.

Grinning in the dark, I thinks, *Ain't this* just *prime?*

Chapter 21

Tilly has all us boys on the fantail for the morning class and he's testing one of his new ideas. He's become quite the engineer of late; first the lures and now the kites. This one, his latest, is the biggest one yet and is made of six stout poles, the ends of which meet and are wired together and the other ends splay out and the whole thing is covered with the thinnest canvas we got on board. There's a cross stick to make sure the poles stay spread out and there's a hook to attach the line to.

"It's all about air pressure," he says, flushed and excited. "The same physical effect that lets our ship sail into the wind. I attended a lecture in London, concerning a fellow name of Bernoulli and his work. Damned interesting. You see, it's the rush of wind over the curved surfaces of the sails and the kite, which set up a high pressure on one side and..."

I'm finding all this very interesting, but what puts a little bit of fear in me is that I spy under the kite a little leather harness that seems to be made to hold a small object. A small object like me, perhaps. Tilly has strapped a sack of flour into this harness, and with he and the boys and a few hands holding on to the rope, they let the kite lift off.

It's lucky it's a calm day with hardly a breeze blowing, or kite and all would be torn out of their hands and away, but, as it is, the kite lifts very prettily and hovers high above the waves.

Tilly laughs in triumph and gets a round of cheers from those on deck. As for me, I slip away in case he gets the idea in his head of putting the smallest seaman on board in that harness. Tilly is a dear old fool, but he puts too much faith in science.

I figure I'll make it up to Tilly for skipping out on his show by making myself useful setting up for the midshipmen class, and I break my rule about never going into the midshipmen without Tilly.

As I enter, a boot shoots out and catches me on me rump and knocks me down. I hit the floor and turn over in horror to see Bliffil standin' over me, a cup in his hand and a broad smile on his face. No one else is in the room; they're all out lookin' at the kite flyin', and I knows I made a big mistake comin' in here alone but it's too late.

"Snot the Sideboy, well, well," he says all jovial. "Come in, snot, you're just in time for a little sport."

His next kick catches me in me side and I feels somethin' let go and the breath is knocked out of me and I can't take me breath back I can't I can't and he kicks me again and again and somethin' crumbles in me other side, and *I can't breathe God help me I can't breathe.*

"Ain't this some sport, runt?"

He hauls back his boot again and he puts it in me belly

and I retches and he kicks me in the face and I gets enough breath back to scream and I screams and then he kicks me on me forehead and there's blood flowin' over me eyes and out of me nose and out of me mouth and I screams and screams and—

"*Mister Bliffil!*" I hears someone shout, far, far off in my misery and pain.

"The boy misspoke me, Sir! He was insolent!" says Bliffil.

"I'm sure the boy has learned whatever lesson you are teaching him," says the Captain, his voice low and even. "And the next time, Mr. Bliffil, you will bring the boy up on charges if he misbehaves and we'll do things in a proper military manner. Is that clear, *Mister* Bliffil?"

"But, Sir—"

"*Is that clear, Mister Bliffil?*"

I ain't screamin' now, just gaspin' out rackin' sobs, my face against the deck, awash in blood and tears. Other boots and feet are about me now.

"Yes, Sir."

"Very well. You are excused, Mr. Bliffil. You, there! Clean up this mess!"

I'm picked up by Jaimy and Willy and hauled off down to our kip and they put me on a blanket and I don't know nothin' what's happenin' around me; I just knows the horror and the pain. They must 'ave sent for Liam, 'cause he's there wipin' me face off and sayin', "*The filthy bastard!*" over and over and feelin' me ribs and lookin' at the cut above me eye and sayin', "Ah no, we'll have t' go t' sick bay to have that stitched, it won't stay together," and he picks me up, and I puts me arm around his neck and me face in his chest and I just keeps on sobbin'.

The Doctor takes his needle and thread and sews up me eyebrow—more pain but it don't matter, there's only so much pain and Jaimy's there, *Oh Jaimy,* and he holds me shoulders steady while the Doctor's stitchin', and then the Doctor opens me mouth and feels around in there and says, "Some teeth are loose, but maybe they'll tighten up again if you don't worry them with your tongue. All right, sit him up. There's no use wrapping floating ribs, they'll either set right or they won't."

They sets me upright and the Doctor puts a spoonful of somethin' in me ruined mouth and Liam carries me back and our hammock has been slung and they puts me in it and I feels me nose and lips a'swellin' and me teeth wigglin' round in me jaw and I knows now that I'm goin' t' be all ugly and hateful lookin' when I grows to be a lady and Jaimy won't want me—no man will want me—and I falls off a cliff and sleeps.

I sleep clear through till the next morning. I wake up and the lads are there and Jaimy has a cup of warm broth, which is good 'cause I sure ain't goin' to be chomping on any horse for a while. My right eye is swollen shut and my lips are out like a duck. I can't close my jaws. I remember what the Doctor said and try not to run my tongue over my teeth, but it's a powerful temptation. My chest hurts like hell, but when I reach up and feel my nose, it don't hurt, so that's something, anyway. I don't think I'll be able to get the broth down, but by takin' really small sips,

I do it. The broth cleans the thick clots of blood out of my mouth.

Jaimy's mouth is set in a grim line and his eyes are full of cold fury. He reaches out and pulls away a lock of my hair that has gotten stuck in the mess around my eye. His look changes to one of warm concern and then back to anger.

"Lor', Jacky, you sure can scream," says Tink. "They musta heard you all the way to London!"

"You was talkin' out of yer head last night, too," chortles Davy. "*No one's gonna* fancy *me. I'm gonna be ugly and no one's gonna* fancy *me!*" he mimics, mincing about the hammock. "You are such a rum cove, Jacky, for thinkin' such things when yer just about beat t' death! *Fancy me? Fancy me?* Jacky, no one's gonna *fancy* us, we're all gonna end up lookin' like Snag!"

"Which is how a salty dog sailor's supposed to look," says Willy with a firm nod.

"And you're halfway there, Jack-o!" crows Tink.

Ah, the sweet comfort of friends.

Liam comes by a little later and tells me that the Doctor has put me on the sick list so I can spend the day in bed. The Doctor gave him a little vial of the juice to make me sleep. I swallow it. It tastes like I remember candy tasting from long ago, before That Dark Day.

"Sleep is the best thing for ye right now, Jacky," says Liam. "Just sleep and you'll get better. Soon you'll be dancin' again." He puts his hand on my shoulder and looks at me in a curious way. "But you've got to be careful,

Jacky. There's bad blood brewin' on this ship and you seem to be in the middle of it."

My one working eyelid is drooping and I'm drifting away into crazy strange and lovely dreams. I dream of Cathay Cats and Bombay Rats and I dream of Kangaroos. I dream of Jaimy and I dream of Charlie.

And I dream of mutiny.

Chapter 22

"You can hit me if you want to, Sir," I says to Mr. Jenkins, "but we've got to talk."

The midshipmen's berth is empty except for Jenkins and me, and I know Bliffil's got the watch so he ain't likely to come in. He'll be out parading around in front of the Captain, all dressed up fine and looking handsome, his eyes gleaming with zeal in the performance of his duty. He puts on a good show. I hope the Captain ain't fooled, as I'd hate to see Bliffil advance in the Navy. Captain Bliffil...Lord, what a thought.

"I...I...I think you've been hit enough, Faber," says he. "What do you want to say?"

"You've got to do something about Mr. Bliffil, Sir. You've got—"

"It's not your place to be telling me this," he says, his face reddening. "I'm sorry you were beaten—"

"This ain't about me, Sir. I'm a ship's boy and ship's boys get beaten. I ain't complainin'. It's about you. You're bein' humiliated in front of your men. They like you, Sir, I know they do, but they got no respect for you 'cause of

Bliffil's rubbin' your nose in it every day. Like that thing yesterday on the fantail, when he..."

"Stop." He gets redder yet and hangs his head. I hate to be so brutal but I go on.

"The officers notice. They talk amongst themselves about who's gonna make good officers and who ain't. I'm up there on the quarterdeck with them and I hear them. The Captain notices, too. He seems high-and-mighty, but he don't miss much."

"What do you think I should d...d...do?" he says miserably.

"You've got to fight him, Sir. Fight him straight out. You can't be any more shamed than you are now. If you don't do somethin,' you'll lose your commission and live in shame for the rest of your life."

I look at him steady. I am being as cruel as I know how. "The Captain's gonna put you off soon, you know that."

"Perhaps that's best. Maybe I'm not cut out for this life," he says. "I could do other things."

"Right," says I. "And you might be right good at other things, but every morning you'll have to look at yourself in the mirror and you'll remember, *every day* you'll re-member, for the rest of your life you'll remember what Bliffil made you eat."

That jerks him up. "What..."

"Your pride, Sir. Your honor. That's what he made you eat. And you'll eat it every day for breakfast, lunch, and dinner from now on if you don't fight him."

I put my hands together like in prayer and put a plead-ing look on my face. "Please, Sir, go at him just once. I know you've got the stuff, I know you stood up straight beside your gun in the fight even when the gun next to you was blown away, 'cause I saw you. Your men saw you. And you went over in the Boarding Party like everyone else. I saw that. The Captain saw that."

I'm runnin' along full bore now and hardly pause for breath, pressin' the truth of what I'm sayin'. "What nobody but me saw was that Bliffil hid behind the cabin when the fight was goin' on and only come out later all roarin' to finish off the helpless pirate when all was done."

Mr. Jenkins seems surprised by this. "But I thought…"

"You thought he was a bold and fierce fighter? Is that what he told you?" I can imagine Bliffil holding forth in the midshipmen's berth on his glorious taking of the pirate ship, waving his bloody sword about under the other middies' noses.

Mr. Jenkins sits and thinks for a while and I let him. Finally he says, "He scares me. He's so big and his fists look like blocks of stone. He puts that hard look on me and I freeze like a mouse before a snake. There. That's the way of it. I'm sorry."

"But, Sir…"

"No, Faber, that's the way of it. If the Captain hadn't forbidden duelling amongst his officers, I'd have called him out when we went ashore on Palma, and he'd either have killed me or I would have killed him and it would have been done with. I am not afraid to die." He pauses. "Sometimes I want to."

There's something I didn't know, that about the duelling, I mean. I press on. "Sir, there's one thing I think you're mistaken about, if you'll forgive me. You've got the mistaken notion that you've got to *win* the fight to accomplish anything, and you're wrong. All you have to do is put up a decent fight and you'll see, he won't bother you anymore."

Mr. Jenkins looks doubtful.

"You see, Sir, Bliffil is a bully, and bullies like to hurt people but they don't like bein' hurt themselves. If he hits you five times and you only hit him once, he's still gonna remember that one hit and he'll pick on someone else, 'cause he's got plenty of victims to choose from."

I believe he's starting to see the force of my argument. His head lifts.

"And you got to fight him crude, just as crude and dirty as he fights," I says, seein' hope. "Don't hold back and try to box with him, he'll only laugh at you and pop you one on your nose, which'll start your eyes waterin' and you'll be done. Just go at him, Sir, just go in with your head down and your arms and fists a'flailin'."

I crawl up on the table so I can look direct in Mr. Jenkins's eyes. "I've known many a tough one in my day, and I knows him for a soft one. Just close in, Sir, and punch at whatever ye can punch at, be it face, body, legs, or crotch. Just hurt him, Sir, and he won't be back for more. *Hurt him.*"

I don't know if my call to arms with Mr. Jenkins will do any good, but at least it's a start. I swear the Brotherhood to secrecy and tell them of my plan, and Tink says, "This gets awfully close to mutiny," and I say, "That's why I swore you to secrecy, you ninny, and it ain't really mutiny, it's more like fomentin' revolution, like." I tell them to be real kind to Mr. Jenkins, buck him up some with nods and winks and poundin' your fist in your palm and grinnin', and talk to the men in his division. Who are they? Smyth, Harley, Gonsalves, and Joad? Right, get them to do the same thing. Let's get our Mr. Jenkins charged up for this. What say? Except for Jaimy, they still look uncertain. Jaimy just looks grim, staring at my battered face.

Then I dredges up somethin' from my broadside readin' days and I sticks me fist up in the air, "Remember, lads, 'Rebellion to Tyrants Is Obedience to God!'"

That nails it.

Chapter 23

The boys are talking about the Nature of Things Between Men and Women *again*. It seems it's all they ever talk about anymore, and what's really maddening is they've got it all wrong. I want to lay it all out for them like Mrs. Roundtree did for me but that would be stupid. Plus I paid a shilling for that knowledge and if they think I'm givin' it out for free, they're wrong.

I guess I snort too loud after a particularly choice piece of falsehood concerning The Parts of the Female and Tink rounds on me like he was reading my mind.

"Awright, Jacky," he says, pointing his finger at me, "you was the one what was in the 'orehouse in Palma. You be the one wi' *ex-per-i-ence*, you little pervert, and so *you* be the one to set us straight. Let's 'ave it. Straight now."

They're all looking at me, expecting the true and straight skinny. Even you, Jaimy, you fool.

"I *told* you I was only asking directions," says I.

"Yeah, right, and me mother's the Queen o' Sheba. C'mon Jacky, you black sinner, you've been there and done it and you've prolly got the pox now, so tell us about it afore you swells up and dies."

I get to my feet and face them. I put my right hand on my hip and my left hand in the air and says, "I, Jack Faber, swear on my tattoo and on my honor as a member of the dread Brotherhood of Ship's Boys of HMS *Dolphin* that I did nothing at that house except ask for directions." I looks them each in the eye.

Directions in how to be a girl, I finishes to myself.

That satisfies them 'cause they know I wouldn't lie under that oath, which they allows was a right fine oath and ought to be the form for giving oaths from now on. So adopted, say you one, say you all, done.

They fall back into their talk and I reach up and touch my eyebrow. It's just about healed and the stitches are out, leaving a little white scar. The hair of my eyebrow is coming in white around the cut. Jaimy says it gives me a rakish look, like I'm a gay and raffish rogue, but I don't know. I do know my teeth have tightened up and my ribs don't hurt no more and all the swelling went away. All in all, I ain't no uglier than I was before, for which I am thankful.

One thing that worries me, though, is that Jaimy's been acting kind of odd. Sometimes he's real warm and friendly to me and sometimes he ain't. Like, sometimes we lie in our hammock at night and talk real low before going to sleep, him about how much he'd like to help his family, and me about carrying tea from China in my little ship, and him laughing and calling me Captain Jack, Fearless Jack, Merchantman of the Orient Trade and me saying that it could happen, don't laugh. But, like, sometimes he don't talk at all. Maybe he's just moody, off and on, like me. That's got to be it.

Now that I'm better, I keep on Mr. Jenkins, pushing and prodding. He still looks doubtful and confused, so one day I look around all furtive and say, "This is going to send my Immortal Soul straight to Hell for the breakin' of me oath, Sir, but I'm goin' to break the Code of the Secret Society of Street Urchins and show you the Secret Choke Hold, known as The Jaws o' Death throughout urchin-dom. Now, Sir, you just close the door and I'll show you, but you must swear never to tell anyone or the Society'll hunt me down and kill me in a most horrible way, and they're all around, Sir, don't think they're not. Awright, I put my left arm across your throat and my left hand..."

'Course, it's just a regular old choke hold, but he don't know that, never having had to fight physical before. These young gents, if you need a sword or a bullet put in some-one, they're just the ticket, but if you're down to the rough and tumble, you're better off with your common man.

I tighten my arms a bit and he lets out a little choke. "Now, Sir, you do it on me. That's it, not too tight now, you don't want to break me neck. Now, to *break* the hold..."

I got all this stuff from Charlie, who had to scrap all his life, what there was of it.

I bring my mind back to the foretop, and now Davy is talking about how since we got tattoos and oaths and such, the next thing is a gold ring in our ears. What hap-pens is some bloke pokes a hole in your earlobe and runs a gold hoop through it and then welds it shut so it can't come out. They all allow that would indeed be a fine thing but why?

"It's tradition, y'see," says Davy. "When you stands your Last Watch and dies or gets killed and yer body washes up on some beach somewheres and some farmer or fisherman walks by, why, he'll say, 'Ah, poor Jack the Sailor, done at last,' and take yer poor bones and give 'em a fine burial and take the gold earring for his just payment. It's tradition, like."

We nod and solemnly consider this bit of naval lore.

"But what if he just cuts the earring out of your ear and leaves your corpse for the crabs?" says the ever doubtful me.

"He wouldn't. 'Cause the curse would be on him then, and he knows it," says Davy. "No, he'd do the job. No mistake."

The force of Davy's reason carries the day and the Brotherhood resolves to get earrings.

What's next, I think, *a bone in my nose?*

The boys have gone to the bowsprit netting again and I plead my wounds as an excuse not to get naked with the rest of them. I go over to the port rail in the waist of the ship out of sight of the lads but not out of hearing, and I can hear them hooting and shouting, and I swear I can hear their voices changing before my very ears. Willy's voice has already changed over, and he sounds like a bull roaring over the squeaks of Davy and Tink, but Jaimy's voice is cracking, sometimes low and sometimes high, and I love to hear it. I know that my voice won't change.

It won't be long now, girl.

My hair, too, is growing out as the Captain ordered and soon it'll be long enough for a pigtail and that ain't helping The Deception none, neither. I can see now by looking sideways my hair hanging by my face and blowing in the breeze. It's a sandy color, not blond, not brown, just like my mum's hair what hung about her face as she leaned over me at night. Same as her hair hung over the edge of that cart on That Dark…No. I've got to let her go, too.

I'm looking out over the calm Caribbean and thinking of the pirates we ain't caught and how it's wearing on the crew who are my dearest friends on the whole, but who are, at the same time, a gang of bloody-minded cutthroats who lust for action and plunder. Who's the pirate and who's the King's man when it comes right down to it? And who am I to blame them? Liam with six kids to support on a rocky scrap of a farm that he don't want to lose even though it's worthless. And Sanderson and Snag and the rest of them? One good prize and they could buy a tavern or a boardinghouse or a chandlery and live snug the rest of their lives. The officers want to buy fine houses and buy their wives a way into a society above what they got now, and why should I say no. Everybody wants something. I ain't no different. I want my own little cargo ship. Just a little one.

I lean over and put my forearms on the rail and my chin on my hands as I gaze out to sea. My ankles are crossed and I idly wave my tail back and forth in rhythm to the roll of the ship.

Sometimes I am *so* stupid I cannot believe it.

He comes up behind me and rams himself up against me back. He puts his arms over mine so's I can't escape and he grinds against me.

"Please, Sir," I plead. "Please…"

"Now, now, Jacky," whispers Sloat, all soft. His mouth is right on my ear. "I'm just seeing 'ow my little Jack the Sailor Boy is doin' after 'is 'orrible beatin'. Was it so bad, Jacky, was it so bad? Tell yer dear old uncle now."

His voice has a singsong to it, and he keeps rubbin' against me and I'm strugglin' to get loose, but it ain't no use, he's got me pinned. I don't want to cry out 'cause that'll be trouble, but I gots to…

I feels the roughness of his beard against me cheek and me skin crawls and I'm sick to me stomach and he says, "Soon, Jacky, soon…for our little talk belowdecks, soon…"

He draws out the words as if he's talkin' to an animal he's tryin' to calm. "*Soon—*"

All of a sudden he lets me go, and I turns around to see Liam lookin' at Sloat wi' pure murder in his eye. He's got one hand on Sloat's shoulder and the other all balled up and cocked to slam into his face.

"Touch any o' the boys again and I'll kill you where you stand," says Liam. Not loud, not showy, just real even and slow.

Sloat knocks Liam's hand off and steps back a pace, but he is not cowed. Other men are gatherin' about.

"Well, if it ain't Father Delaney, the Patron Saint of All the Micks," sneers Sloat. Some of the men laugh. Some don't.

"Mark me, Sloat. Touch any of the boys again and I'll kill you."

"Tell me, Father," says Sloat, "might ye be savin' a bit of this fer yerself?" I slinks back into the shadows.

Liam lunges forward but is held back by his mates.

"Awful friendly wi' our little Jacky sailor boy, ain't-cha, Father McSwine," taunts Sloat with a leer. "Teachin' 'im all manner o' sailor stuff, I'll wager. Showin' 'im stuff, too, I imagine. I imagine all sorts of things. My, my."

Liam looks pure murder, but Sloat looks him right back and he ain't banterin' now and he says, "You son of a bitch, Delaney. You son of a bitch."

Sloat's toadies haul him away, and Liam's friends do the same to him, but the damage is done. The two are separated but the whole ship knows that words have been said and they cannot go unanswered. I just hope they get over it or settle it off the ship, 'cause I couldn't bear to see Liam lashed to the grating and whipped for fighting, but I know they won't, it's just more bad blood.

The ship is awash in bad blood. The ship don't feel lucky no more. Instead of dolphins following the ship, we got sharks, big black brutes what never go away.

Bad blood.

And it all seems wrapped up in *me*.

Chapter 24

Jaimy's been acting right funny lately. Like, if all of us are in the top and some leave so that it's just Jaimy and me up there, he'll swing over the side and leave. And he's taken to hangin' around with Willy and not me. If I come up and say something, he'll just grunt and walk away.

In our hammock at night I've got to be real careful to stay over to my side and touch Jaimy as little as possible. Our hips and legs got to touch, of course, no way around it, it bein' a hammock and all, and our feet are up in each other's face, but that's it 'cause of the way Jaimy's been. I mean we didn't do nothin' but lie there and sleep before, but now he lies there all unnatural stiff and don't say nothin'.

Tonight when I talk about my dream of a little ship and say, "Wouldn't it be grand to have a little seaside cottage to come back to and dry out between the voyages and the adventures and the cottage would have a big fireplace and roses and things," he don't say nothing, doesn't even snort at my silly dreams, just lies there all silent and I know he's awake and it hurts me.

When we're awakened for the midwatch, he don't say nothin' to me. When we're on watch he don't come talk to me like he used to.

When the watch is over, I don't go back to the hammock. I find a blanket and curl up in the old kip between the guns. I don't sleep.

Maybe it's because I'm a proven murderer, thief, liar, and mutineer. But I was all those things before. It's been this way ever since that thing with Sloat. Why should that matter? I didn't do nothing wrong. Why does Jaimy hate me now? What did I do?

I think about how happy I was when we was first put in the same hammock all those weeks ago. Thinking on it now just brings me sadness.

Things ain't no better in the foretop. The boys have been quiet and sullen and castin' side glances at me. The Sloat thing and the Bliffil thing is weighing heavy on the ship and it seems to be weighing heavy on the Brotherhood, too.

Finally Davy gets up and points at me and says what's been on his mind.

"If you weren't forever prancin' about and wigglin' yer ass the way you do, maybe stuff like this wouldn't happen. All this bad blood and bad luck is on account of *you*."

I feel like I've been punched in the gut. This can't be happening. This has got to be just some more Jacky and Davy bickerin'. But no...I look at the others. They look away. They don't say nothing. I look at Jaimy and say, "Jaimy...," and plead with my eyes, but he don't say nothin'. Jaimy shakes his head and looks down at his feet.

I jump up and grab the shroud and take a last look at them standin' there all quiet. Then I go over the edge and slide down to the deck. As I leave the Brotherhood, I hear a mutter.

"The little fairy…"

I go down and get my gear from where it's stored, rolled up beside our…his hammock. I go back up on deck and look about. After a bit of thinking, I head for the mizzenmast, which is the most aft mast on the ship, and climb up into the mizzen top. Later on I'll stow my gear down in my hidey-hole and I'll probably sleep in the rope locker on the port side, well away from…them.

I survey my new home. I have a good view of the ship from here and I can't see the foretop, which is good 'cause I don't want to see the foretop or anything on it. The quarterdeck with the watch and all the officers is right below, so it ain't a very popular spot on the ship, but it's fine with me. I'll lead my solitary life up here and get ready for my departure. I resolve to make a seabag for my things as I will have need of it soon. I might think about making a dress.

He's just a boy. I thought he was something more, but he's not. He's just a boy. Everthing else was just something I'd made up in my mind.

This is a good thing that has happened. Events have been spinning out of my control. It's time to get things in order. Time to get on with my life. I must make plans.

I must go down and get some canvas for my seabag. That's the thing to do now.

Chapter 25

I do my duties and stand my watches.

In my off time I sew and play my whistle in the mizzen top. I eat by myself. At night I sleep in the rope locker. I don't need to be awakened for my watches, as I can tell from the bells when it's time to get up. I don't bother anyone. I set up the classroom and I help with the teaching, but I don't joke and I don't laugh. I stay out of Bliffil's way and I'm done with Jenkins. Davy says, "I'm sorry, Jacky. Come on back to the top," but I shake my head and say "No, it's different now, it ain't the same," and they know it's true. Jaimy don't even look at me.

Mr. Tilden gives us the words for today, but I don't remember what they are and I don't care.

One thing that grieves me, though, is that I've got to stay away from Liam 'cause it ain't good for him to be seen with *the little fairy,* and so I miss the comfort of being with him and I ain't picking up any new tunes, but that's all right 'cause there ain't much singing and dancing going on now, anyway. The ship feels wrong...what with Bliffil and Jenkins, Sloat and Liam, and me in the middle of all of it. But I'll be off soon, anyway, and maybe their luck will come back.

I guess the old superstition about girls on board being bad luck wasn't too far from the truth.

All that is not my concern now. My plans are in order. One day out from Jamaica I will inform Mr. Tilden of my gender and he will tell the First Mate and he will tell the Captain. I will be confined and hopefully not beaten and put off the next day. I hope they will give me a little of my pay so I will have a bit of a start and not have to beg right off.

I am settled in my mind. I am content.

I'm coming from the Doctor's, where Tilly has sent me to get some books, and I see Davy come rolling in the after hatch and I see Bliffil sitting there all bloated up with drink and I see him trip Davy and then get up all smiling, saying, "Another little snot in need of a lesson," and he rears back and kicks him and *Oh no, not again.*

Just then I sees Jaimy comin' across the room with blood in his eye and I drops the books and lunges forward and tackles Jaimy about the knees and holds on for his dear life and hisses at him, "Jaimy, no! If you touch him they'll hang you!" And I won't let go of him even though he's strugglin' and beatin' at me shoulders. Bliffil takes another kick and then...

"That's enough, Bliffil."

We look up from the floor and it's Mr. Jenkins standing there. *Glory be.*

He goes at Bliffil, head down and fists a'flailin'.

I lets go of Jaimy and we both circle around and drag Davy out by his ankles. It ain't the place of ship's boys to hang around and watch officers fight, but we don't miss much of the battle.

When Bliffil gets over his initial shock, he throws Jenkins up against the wall and goes to punch him, but Jenkins moves his head and Bliffil misses and hits the wall and howls with the pain. Jenkins gets behind him and puts on the Jaws o' Death, and Bliffil lunges around the room, his eyes bugging out and his face turnin' red. Bliffil loses his footing and falls against the table, smashing his nose, and the claret flows but he manages to shake Jenkins off and get one good kick in, and Jenkins is doubled over and down and I know it's over when Bliffil gets on top of him, and I say, "Jaimy, go get Mr. Jenkins's men and I'll get Mr. Lawrence," and I runs out and gets up in front of the Second Mate and points to the midshipmen's berth and make mumblin' sounds, and he says, "What the hell are you on about, Faber?" I keeps pointin' and he goes over and sees what's up and he stops the fight. Mr. Jenkins's men go in and pick him up and take him out.

Bliffil gets to his feet and his nose ain't so pretty and noble no more. It's smashed over to the side and looks likely to stay there. When he opens his eyes and looks out, I make sure the first thing he sees is me lookin' at him. Then I leaves.

Mr. Jenkins's men have got him propped up against their gun, mopping at his face, and I can see he ain't hurt too bad. They're patting him on the back and grinnin' and sayin', "Good show, Sir," and he's tryin' to smile.

I go up and say, "You did it, Sir. I'm so proud of you," but when the boys come up to say, "Well done, Sir," and Davy says his thanks for the rescue, I leave and go back to the mizzen top.

I've got the canvas for my seabag and I start by cutting a round piece for the bottom. Then the big piece sits on that and I sew it up around the bottom and up the side. I flip the top edge over about an inch and put a seam along the bottom edge of that so it'll hold the drawstring. I work the string through it and turn the whole thing inside out so the neat seams are on the outside, and it's done. It looks right fine, I says to myself.

Tomorrow I'll stitch my name on the side: J. M. FABER. It's getting too dark to do it now, and the seas are really working up and the after top is drawing quite an arc in the air, back and forth.

Right now I'll occupy myself with planning my future.

I've definitely decided on Kingston, Jamaica, as the best I can do—they speak English there, or sort of, and if I make a few shillings I can book passage for the States, where I'm more likely to find a living. As for that, I don't think my sewing's really good enough to get me a job doing it. I mean, most girls have been doing it all their lives. And very little else.

I maybe could play the pennywhistle and sing on street corners for a few pennies if it's allowed. Maybe dance, too. Prolly end up in jail as I don't know what's allowed and what's not in Kingston. I shall have to get next to some of the Jamaican hands at breakfast in the morning.

There are two of them, I believe. Since it'll be broad daylight I don't think they'll be tainted by talking to *the little fairy* and maybe I'll get some useful information.

Before I go to the singing and dancing, though, I think I'll try knocking on the doors of some of the better people in the town and see if their children are in need of a reading tutor. That might be a bit more respectable. A dress would be a help there. I must get on it. The best families would probably balk at a girl dressed up as a sailor boy—not a good example to their little darlings. Best not to worry, though, just deal with what comes up.

I pull out my whistle and play very softly till it's time to go down to the rope locker to sleep.

Chapter 26

I'm in my new kip in the rope locker, at least for part of the night since I've got the Four-to-Eight in the morning. *I'll get myself off to sleep,* I says to myself, *with more planning for my new and exciting future.*

Maybe I wouldn't have to do the singing and playing in the street, after all. Not that I'd mind doing it in the street, but I don't want to end up in jail, either. Maybe I could make a deal with a tavern owner to set up in a corner of his place, playing for the sailors when they come in on shore leave. I'd give the owner part of what I brought in and maybe he'd give me a place to stay. A little room of my own, and I'd help clean up, too. I ain't proud. I'll turn these hands to labor, I will. Maybe that would be best. The music would surely be more fun than the tutoring.

This rope ain't the softest stuff, I think as I squirm around, trying to find some comfort.

If I'm going to do the music, I'd probably best settle on what tunes I'd do right now and practice up on them. The usual jigs and reels and dancing ones, of course, but what would really make it good would be some funny songs. Get 'em laughing and they'd be more likely to part with their coin. I'm slippin', slippin' down into sleep, and from up out of nowhere comes something to my mind from long ago, from long, long ago. *Now I lay me down to sleep, I pray—*

His hand is over me mouth and it's so big he has me whole jaw and me nose in it and I can't breathe and he's all on me and I can't move and...

"Time for our little talk now, Jacky," Sloat whispers in me ear. I can smell the sweat on him and the rum and I can taste the dirt in his hand and I tries to wriggle and squeal, but he's on me so that I can't, I can't get away.

"Oh, little Jacky, you're going to like this, you'll see. I knows you was sleepin' down here so I'd come and find ye. Wasn't ye, Jacky? You'll be back every day for more and more, I know you will, and you'll love yer uncle Bill more and more every day. Oh yes, you will."

His beard is on me face and neck and then he's kissin' me and with his other hand he's pullin' down me pants and the drawstring breaks and then his hand is on me. *Oh, God.*

He stops moving all of a sudden. His head jerks up and he looks in me eyes.

"Well, well, what have we here? Not a little rooster, but a little hen, my, my...Well, well, even better." He chuckles deep in his throat and puts his head back down on mine. "Got a little henhouse there, Jacky? A cuckoo's nest? Such fun," he says low and thick, pantin' the rum hard in me face.

He pulls me pants down around me ankles and keeps laughin' and whisperin' in me ear, "Oh yes. This is gonna be fine, you'll see, Jacky, you'll see...Bill Sloat, you old rascal you old devil, you could always smell it a mile…a mile…"

I pulls me shiv back out of his gut, and he roars and stands up and looks at the bloodstain growin' on his shirt. I only meant to prick him a bit to get him off of me, that's all I wanted, but I look at me shiv and the blood is on it all the way down to the hilt, and he keeps roaring and sayin', *"Son of a bitch, son of a bitch,"* over and over. He's teetering back and forth from the rum and the stabbin' and the rollin' of the ship, and there's voices yellin', *"It's Sloat." "He's drunk again." "He's stole Tommy's ration again,"* and he keeps reelin' backward and hits the rail just as the ship rolls, and he's over the side and there's a splash and then nothin'.

There's shouts of "Man overboard," and bells ring and the ship comes about and men call out over the water, but nothin' is heard back. I pulls up me drawers and me pants as men are runnin' by me to the rail, and I hobbles over to the hatchway and dives down headfirst and gets out of sight fast. I'm hopin' nobody notices me in the confusion as I slides down a ladder and heads for me hidey-hole, shakin' all over.

The boats are put down in the rollin' sea and they rows around, but nothin'.

Nothin' but the dark and rollin' sea.

Maybe nobody saw. Maybe nobody heard. Maybe they'll think he was just drunk again and fell over the side in his drunkenness. Maybe nothin' will happen. Maybe.

I quivers in the dark for hours, huggin' me knees, and I thinks of Mary Townsend again and again and the rope across me throttle and the Bo'sun droppin' down on me shoulders to crush me throat and snap me neck, the same picture over and over and over till I'm whimperin' out loud, and then I hears the faint bells of the Four-to-Eight and I go up to stand my watch. I look over the side and I think of him down there, his blood leakin' out of him and his arms all out like he's flyin', but he ain't flyin', he's sinkin' down, down, and I'm thinkin' about him rollin' about in the dark depths of the black sea with his eyes open and starin', and *I didn't do it I just wanted to get him off of me,* and *I didn't kill him I didn't kill him I didn't kill him.* He drowned. He fell overboard. He drowned.

But that ain't the end of it, of course. The next morning blood is found on the deck near to where he went over, so all hands know it wasn't no accident. Sloat's friends swear the last thing they heard Sloat say as he went over was *"Son of a bitch,"* which was just what he called Liam Delaney the last time they tangled, and Delaney, the dog, said he'd kill poor Sloat and damned if 'e ain't done it! Right, and Delaney had the watch, too, so 'e 'ad plenty o' time t' do the rotten deed! The murdering Irish bastard!

So it ain't me they're gonna hang.

It's Liam.

Chapter 27

They've got Liam all tied up and it tears my heart to see him treated so, him what only had kind things to say to me and who taught me stuff and never asked for nothin'. He blinks in the sunlight as he's brought out of the brig and into the Captain's cabin, where the trial is bein' held. Liam's face is a mask of anger, but there's hopelessness there, too. He knows.

The trial drones on and on. There's two Marine sentries in dress uniforms all red and white outside the cabin, with their rifles held across their chests so that their bayonets cross in front of the door. The witnesses are called in and then come back out, satisfaction on the faces of Sloat's mates, despair on those of Liam's friends. The Captain and his officers talk on and on.

The men listening in at the cabin window shake their heads sadly.

It looks like it's over.

Liam to be hanged and I'm the cause. I'll have to beat the drum as he's hauled aloft, all twisting and...

No. This cannot be.

I runs down the passageway and ducks under the bayonets and beats on the door.

"What the Hell?" from within and, "Stop there, you!" from the sentries. One grabs me by me neck.

The door opens and Mr. Haywood is standin' there, all outraged as he looks out over me head and finally down at me.

"What do you want, boy?" he thunders.

"Please, Sir, I got somethin' t' say," and that's about the last clear thing I says as I plunges into the room and throws meself down in front of the Captain, who's standin' at the lectern and about to pronounce sentence on poor Liam.

"I was the one what did it, Sir," I wails, me hands up and prayin' and the tears gushin' out o' me eyes. "He was on me and he had his hand across me mouth so I couldn't call for help and he wouldn't get up and he's so heavy and he was kissin' me and I couldn't breathe and he pulled down me pants and put 'is hand on me and I was out o' me mind wi' the terror so I pulled out me shiv and I only wanted to poke 'im a little so's he'd get up and leave me alone but instead he jumps up and he's bleedin' and yellin' and then 'e goes over the side and I didn't mean it, Sir, I didn't but 'e was so heavy and awful and I didn't know what else to do, I didn't know what to do…see, look ye here…"

I pulls me shiv out o' me vest and tosses it on the deck. Sloat's blood is still on it and it sickens me to see it.

"See, Sir, it warn't Liam, it was me and I'm sorry, Sir, I'm sorry."

And now the snot's runnin' out o' me nose and mixin'

wi' the tears and runnin' in me mouth, and I can taste the tears and the snot in me mouth but I don't care. I'm just howlin' wi' fear and gaspin' wi' sobs and snortin' tears and snot all over the Captain's rug and I keeps on sayin', *"Please, Sir, I couldn't stand the hangin' wi' the Bo'sun jumpin' on me shoulders and me neck all wrung. Couldn't ye just knock me on the head and put me over the side if ye have to…"*

"Take him out of here!" roars the Captain, but I don't hear him 'cause I'm out o' me mind, and when hands are laid on me I thinks they're gonna take me right out and do me right then and I lets out a scream that's got all the horror and terror that's ever been in me, and I screams and screams.…

But all they do is take me out and throw me in the brig till I calm down and they have a chance to talk over what I just told them. Liam's in there, too, but at least he's untied now and sittin' on the bunk.

"That was a brave, brave thing to do, comin' in there like that," he says. "I owe you my life, Jacky."

"I don't feel so very brave," says I, and I goes over and lies down and puts me head in his lap and falls into a dead sleep.

The Marines come and get me in the late afternoon. They tie my hands in front of me. "Sorry, boy, rules are rules," and they take me in the Captain's cabin, where all the officers are looking dreadful and stern, and they take me up and make me face the Captain at the lectern. He looks haggard and there are dark bags under his eyes.

"Faber, I swear, if you start that screeching again I'll take you out and hang you myself. Do you understand?"

"Yes, Sir."

"Good. Place your hands on the Bible. Do you swear to tell the truth, before Almighty God?"

I swears that I do.

"Now, where did all this take place?"

"In the starboard-side rope locker, Sir."

"And what were you doing in this rope locker?"

"Sleeping, Sir."

"And why were you sleeping in the rope locker instead of in your hammock?"

Deacon Dunne is sitting at a small table writing all this down.

"Because my mates don't like me anymore."

"And why don't your mates like you anymore?"

I hesitates a bit before answering. "They think I'm queer, Sir."

"And are you?"

"No, Sir."

"What do you mean by 'queer'?"

"They think I stirred up the trouble between Liam and Sloat when I didn't do nothin' to stir up nobody."

"You didn't lead Sloat on in any way?"

"No, Sir. He scared me. I tried to stay out of his way."

"All right. Now tell us what happened in the rope locker."

I tell them, this time without the howling and crying and groveling. When I am done, there is only the sound of Deacon Dunne's quill scratching.

"Very well, Faber, you may stand down. Sergeant, take him away."

I turn away from the lectern and the Marine leads me back to my cell. They untie my hands. This time I am alone in the brig. They have let Liam go. I am the only one on trial now.

I look up to the light from the small grating in the ceiling high overhead. The grating lets out into the hold above and allows in a little light and air. I've seen a lot of things in my life, but this is the first time I've seen bars between me and the world.

"We're sorry, Jacky. We didn't know. We thought…"

It's night now and the boys have snuck up to the grating.

"That's all right, lads," I say, looking up. I think I can make out four heads in the gloom. "What do you hear?"

"They was in there for hours talkin' about it. They brought back some of Sloat's mates and Liam, too." I recognize Davy's voice in the darkness.

"Right. And they went down to check the rope locker and sure enough there was your blanket still there and there was blood, so that helps your story," says Tink. "And you got some of the officers on your side. I know Mr. Lawrence is."

"Mr. Haywood ain't your friend, though, that's for sure…"

This sends a shiver through me. I know the First Mate hates disruption and disorder above all things, and I ain't exactly been helpful in that regard.

"Jacky." This from Jaimy. "You wouldn't have been sleeping down there if I hadn't been..."

Silence.

"No. It's all right," I say finally. "You couldn't know."

Silence, again.

"I want you to go away now," I whisper. "My Will is here in my vest, and my stuff is in the third level of the middle hold, back behind the casks.

"And lads...," I says, tryin' to hold steady, "if they do me...I don't...I don't want you to watch. Find an excuse. Go down below. Or at least close your eyes. I...I don't think I'll be very brave."

"All right," they say, all quiet and low.

"And Jaimy..."

"Yes."

"No— Nothing..."

Chapter 28

No, they don't hang me or do anything to me at all except let me rot in the jail cell all night long, rockin' back and forth on the bunk, knowin' the morn would bring either the sweet air of freedom in me chest or Jack Hemp hard across me windpipe. I know it's my free and easy ways that got me in this fix, and I resolves to be better if I survives.

At dawn the Marines come back for me and tie my hands, this time behind my back, and I think it's 'cause that way I won't be able to claw at the rope around my neck when I'm hauled up, which wouldn't look military, and I'm glad I used the chamber pot just before they got there 'cause I don't want to be disgraced that way. We march up the passageway and I hear a low whistle, and there's Bliffil in a side corridor, swingin' a little noose between his thumb and forefinger and lookin' at me over it and smilin', and my knees turn to water and my eyes turn back in my head, but one of the Marines slaps me around a bit and I manage to stand up before the Captain, who looks at me sternly and says, "We find that you, Jack Faber, acted in self-defense and therefore are to go free, but it is the hope of this court-martial that your night in confinement will be a lesson to you to be more quiet and reserved in your demeanor, especially quiet for the love of God. Dismissed."

The next Sunday, Deacon Dunne gives a fire-and-brimstone sermon on sodomy that leaves very little doubt as to where he thinks Sloat is roasting right now, and everyone looks piteous at me and I wish they wouldn't. I have to look down all shy and I hear a few mutters of *Bloody Jack* and I guess I ain't never gonna get rid of that, especially if I keep on killing people.

I'm welcomed back into the foretop, and the boys are genuinely glad that I'm not swinging off the yardarm, which is exactly where my mortal remains *would* be hanging if things had gone the other way. It's all right but it still ain't like old times, at least not for me. After a while, when they're all talking and skylarking and don't notice, I go back to my spot in the mizzen top.

I still plan to get put off in Jamaica and I have to get ready. The word is about that we are indeed going to Kingston and we'll arrive in about a week and a half, if the wind holds fair and we don't run into LeFievre.

My dress is basically blocked out now. I didn't have anything to go by in the way of style, so I thought back to Mrs. Roundtree and figured I'd make one like hers, all tight in the waist and looser up top. That's something to look forward to, release from the confines of this vest. The dress is long in the skirt because only little girls wear short skirts and I ain't going to be a little girl for too much longer. Besides I got to cover up the fact that I don't have any stockings and I certainly can't make st— *Shoes!* What the hell am I going to do for *shoes*?

I ain't never had a pair of shoes, not since That Dark Day, but I'm sure the finer families of Kingston will expect them in a tutor.

Next morning I sit next to Joshua Spenser at breakfast, as he is from Jamaica, and I ask him about the fine families of Kingston, the laws on singing in the street, and the wearing of shoes, required or no? I figure it being broad daylight and out in the open, he won't be tainted by my notorious company and he don't seem to mind.

"Well, boy," he says in that musical way the Caribbean sailors have, "I not be knowing of the fine families in Kingston, just some of the fine ladies there."

He grins in anticipation of the fine ladies.

"But I do know all the rich people live up on the high street above the town. They be right easy to spot when they come to town, bein' all white people and all finely dressed. As for shoes, one can get by with the sandals, which they sell in the market square. Very cheap."

That's a relief. If I get put off with any money, that's the first thing I'll buy.

"As for the laws about singing in the street, why, are you t'inkin' of desertin', boy?"

"No, Joshua, I'm only thinking of maybe picking up a few pennies in doing it when we're on liberty."

His face fairly glows with the prospect of shore leave in his hometown. "Wait you see, boy. On market day all the women they come to town with baskets full of foods and spread it out on blankets and in stalls, and there's the best rum and music, such music! And if it's Carnival time, which it is now, the party never stops, boy, I tell you true!"

I finish up my lovely gruel and wait patiently for him to get back on the subject at hand.

"Now as to the Law, boy," he says chewing and thinking, "there is Law, and too much of it to my mind, and the name of the Law is Sheriff John Stone, and he is no man to mess with. If he wants to let you sing and play your whistle in his street, he'll let you. If not, it's the Trenchtown jail for you, boy, and mark me, it's a place you'll not soon forget. Best check with the man first, boy."

I resolve to do it.

We've pulled up next to other ships we've come across, to get information on the pirates' whereabouts. They don't always want to stop to talk, but when a King's ship says stop, you stop. A shot over their bows usually convinces them. Britannia does rule the waves.

If the other captain has been less than friendly, the captains shout at each other through speaking trumpets across the water. If the other captain is civil, Captain Locke sends a boat over for him and has him to his cabin for a few snorts, which helps the conversation right along. One or another of us boys is always listening at the window, and it seems that LeFievre grows even more arrogant and has added more ships to his fleet. He burns all before him, be it village, town, or ship.

These nights I sleep in the old kip between the guns, with the boys in their hammocks swinging overhead. I don't want to be off alone again, as Sloat's old mates might not be of a forgiving nature. I beg off sleeping with Jaimy in our old hammock by saying that I don't like hammocks 'cause you got to sleep on your back in one and I like to curl up on my side.

Jaimy don't protest.

Chapter 29

The mood of the ship has lightened, what with Sloat gone and Bliffil restrained. Bliffil's recovered enough from his fight with Mr. Jenkins to start in to bullying the youngers again, but he don't mess with Jenkins no more. Mr. Jenkins tries to look out for the squeakers, but Bliffil is a sneaky one and he gets in his shots, though not as much as before 'cause now he knows someone may call him on it. I stay well out of his way, as his nose ain't quite so pretty no more and he knows who to blame.

The prospect of a port visit, too, especially one like Kingston is enough to lighten any sailor's load.

I'm stitching a line of white thread across the bodice of my dress to take the place of the lace, which the ship don't stock. The sun is high and bright in the afternoon watch, four bells I hear from down below, when I'm surprised to see Jaimy's head and shoulders coming up over the edge of the mizzen top. He don't say nothin' right off, just sits down lookin' miserable. I don't say nothin', neither.

"Why don't you come up in the foretop with the rest of us anymore?" he says finally.

I shake my head. "No, Jaimy. I just make all of you uncomfortable."

More silence.

"I'll bet you regret getting the Brotherhood tattoo now, don't you?" he says all sad and downcast.

We saw just how far that Brotherhood went, didn't we, I think, but I say, "No, I don't regret it. When I got it we was all mates and I'll always remember that time fondly."

Jaimy seems to be trying to say something to me but he just can't get it out.

"What do you want to say to me, Jaimy?" I put up my needle and look him in the eye. He won't meet my gaze.

"When I was mean to you...I thought I...I was becoming one of those sodomites," he says, the words not coming easy. "Not with anyone else. Just with you."

Well.

"You'll just have to get over that, won't you," says I, all brisk and cruel. "As it ain't natural."

I return to my sewing.

He don't say nothin' at all, not for a long while.

"I know it's not natural and I know I'll have to leave the Service," he finally manages to say, hardly above a whisper. "Good-bye, Jacky. None of it was your fault." He begins to rise.

"Wait," I say, getting to my feet. "Before you go, I want you to hold this up so I can measure it."

"Wh— What is it?" he asks, all confused with the turn in the conversation.

"A dress," I say.

"A *dress*? For whom?"

"For me. Now stand up."

As he gets up, I pull off my white overshirt and pop open the top four buttons of my vest. I run my hand over my hair, fluffing it up a bit in the light breeze. I take a deep breath. "Ah yes. That certainly feels better. Now, Jaimy, hold it up against me...Take the dress, Jaimy, come on. Don't be shy, now. Tuck it up against my ribs... Right, push it up there, while I mark it. Hold it now. There. Thanks."

He stands stunned.

I sit back down and resume sewing, but I don't put my shirt back on and I don't button up my vest. I look up at him. "What's the matter, Jaimy? Ain't-cha never seen a girl?"

It's a good ten minutes he stands there staring. Then he sits down for another ten minutes just lookin' at me. At last, he finds he can speak. He stands up.

"What are we going to do, Jacky?" he asks, all stupid.

I get to my feet. I face him, square on.

"Well, Jaimy," I says, "you can kiss me, if you love me."

PART IV

Shorn of Hope and by Hope Betrayed,
Yet by Hope Uplifted and by Hope Is Saved.

Chapter 30

Oh, and it's a different James Emerson Fletcher who walks the deck of His Majesty's Ship the *Dolphin* these past days. His step is quick and light and his head is high and his gaze is clear and fixed on far horizons, but he is not of this Earth. His mind is adrift and awash in the wonder of it all.

Me, too.

We have to be very careful because now I *don't* want to be put off the ship, not now, and though I know that I'm soon to be caught, I just want as much time as I can get right here right now with Jaimy, and that's all I'm thinkin' about. I ain't thinkin' any farther ahead than the next time we can be alone together in the mizzen top or on watch at night. Yes, I know we've got to be wary, just a little clutch and a kiss-me-quick here and there, but oh, Lord....

In my calm moments I realize that I am going to have to be the wise one of the pair of us. Jaimy, who is usually so upright and self-possessed and clearheaded, gets so carried away that he don't know what he's doin'. My own ardor is not to be discounted, but I know I've got to be strong 'cause I know what happens at the end. Mrs. Roundtree told me and I can't let it happen. Not yet, I can't.

I move back into the hammock. We've still got to sleep end to end to keep up appearances, for after all, Davy and Tink are right there, so it's the same as it was before. But now it's different, oh, yes, it's very different.

Tilly is teaching us some anatomy today. He has a large watercolor painting of the guts of a person—a male person. Jaimy is blushing for me, but I put on a look of keen scientific interest and run my toe up Jaimy's pant leg.

Tilly tells us what each of the organs are for and it hits me suddenly that he probably got the chart from one of those anatomists back in London. I try not to think any more about that as this may be someone I know. Or knew.

Still, it's good to know where the important guts are so as to be able to protect them when one is, say, down on the deck and being kicked. Next time it happens to me I'll make sure to squirm over and get my back to the wall to protect my kidneys. If I do that and curl up and cover my head with my hands and tuck my elbows into my belly, well, there's not much out there for them to kick.

"What are those two little things for, Mr. Tilden," I asks, pointing, and Jaimy gives me a kick and a look.

"Never you mind, Jack," says Tilly, looking at me as if I were beyond hope of redemption. "And you can stop with the silly smirking and grinning, you little fool. Remember, Jack, 'Whom the gods would destroy, they first make happy.' Class dismissed."

And it's true. I am as happy as I have ever been, and I can only hope the gods cut me some slack. At least for a bit.

Willy is taken up as Ordinary Seaman. He's to be a Waister to start off, which means he'll work in the center part of the ship, on deck, and it's the lowest kind of seaman there is, but still it's seaman and not ship's boy and he gets full pay and a full share of prize money and a full ration of horse and biscuit and rum now, too. We're all happy for him and clap him on the back, and he swears he won't forget us in his new grand state and won't kick us even though it's now his right.

I take the seabag I was making for myself before everything changed and stitch WM. SIMPSON, SEAMAN on the side, and we give it to him as a farewell present and he starts blubbering, good old Willy.

Jaimy and I force ourselves to sometimes go up on the foretop to be with Davy and Tink, all that's left now with Willy gone off to new duties and new mates. We talk and hang about like in old times, but all Jaimy and I want to do is be alone together, our arms and legs around each other and our lips mashed together and…well…We don't *do* that when the others are around, but that's all we're thinking about, so we ain't very good company.

I do come to my senses sometimes and insist that we act a little bit normal, so I send Jaimy away to hang about with the other sailors for appearances' sake, although it pains me to do so. Then I go up into the foretop with Davy and Tink, and I work on my cap.

My cap has a blue top that is gathered into a white headband on to which I have stitched HMS *DOLPHIN*. The blue top part is loose and floppy and roomy enough to stuff my hair up into. Davy swears that he will put a marlinespike in my belly and twist it if I wear *that stupid thing* in front of the Captain so that the Captain orders me to make them for all the boys, so that Davy his ownself has to wear the damned thing in front of the entire crew and so die of shame. Tink backs that up with a promise to gut me with a rusty knife if this comes to pass. I invite them to go do something unnatural to themselves and we fling curses back and forth, just like in the old days.

I fear discovery more than I fear either Tink or Davy, so now that I've completed my cap, I wear it constantly.

I have taken up my lessons in music with Liam again, now that the curse is off me, and he is starting me on the concertina, which is good 'cause even my love-addled mind knows that the time ain't long when I'll have to make my way alone. Jaimy says that no, that won't happen. He says that we'll get off the ship together and that we'll get married and that he'll take care of me, but I don't know. They could kick me off and keep him on, which is much more likely, the Service having put a lot of time and training in Jaimy and in me, too, but what's put in me will be lost to them and they'll probably be mad and in no mood to grant the wishes of two ship's boys. One ship's boy, rather, and one worthless ship's girl.

I did like hearing Jaimy say he'd marry me, though.

———

Liam's noticed a change in me. He looks at me sideways and smiles like he knows something, and I blush and look down and say "What?" and he says, "Oh, nothing, Jacky. Just you be careful is all."

I go to the Sunday music making and dancing, but I don't dance anymore and Liam doesn't push me. I'd love to dance and sing and play and just show off in general, 'cause it's in my nature, but the poor and faltering Deception must be preserved as long as possible and showing myself off ain't the way to do it. I sit back under my cap at the edge of things and help out with my whistle and sometimes the concertina. The other sailors don't comment on my new shyness. They figure I've been through a lot. Little do they know.

Jaimy takes my sailor cap off my head when we get together, he takes it off with feeling, tossing it aside and running his hand through my hair and turning my face up to his and...

He has tried to talk me out of some of my other clothes, too, but I don't let him win, 'cause I know what's gonna happen if I do.

Ain't I bein' a good girl, then?

Chapter 31

We are in Kingston. We had about a two-day warning and here we are. We came in with flags flying and cannons booming and everyone turned out all smart, and there was the usual parade of nobs and officials and such, and then the Governor came aboard. Us sideboys were decked out and lined up and I wore my new cap and the Captain put in an order for three more for the other boys. "Make it so, Mr. Haywood," and the First Mate looks at me with so very little love in his heart and I look back at the man who would have had me hanged with even less, and Davy beside me risks a beating by gouging my side with his thumbnail, and then there's more whistles and pipes and then everybody leaves. It's easier getting ashore this time 'cause we're right next to the dock with a gangway going down. Ten minutes later we're off on the town.

There's great crowds in the streets, it being market day and Carnival just like Joshua said, and Jaimy and I manage to get separated from Tink and Davy, which wasn't too hard to do 'cause I think the two little baboons have got something nasty planned.

So Jaimy and I walk around the market and it's all bright and colorful, even more so than Palma, with the people dressed in their holiday best. We watch a trained monkey dance to a man playing a concertina, and there are men (and women!) walking about playing guitars and singing, so I guess that's allowed. Good to know. The dancing is wild and loud—much more spirited than us somber Brits, but I could get along. I could learn these tunes.

We look at all the stalls selling the most wonderful things like carved monkey heads and bright necklaces and bracelets and...there are the sandals. I try on a lot of them with the owner of the shop pointing out the virtues of each, and finally I settle on a pair. A cheap pair, but my first footwear and so therefore precious. I put them on and we move off through the fair. We're having a grand time, but we can't even hold hands. It ain't *that* free a city.

We're about to duck into a tavern, when I spy a stall all piled up with used clothing.

"Wait a minute, Jaimy," I say, and I go over and rummage though the dresses and find one that looks like it would fit and the price is right. I haul out the few pennies to pay the woman and she looks at me funny and I say that it's for my sister, and she laughs and says, "Whatever, child," and I grab Jaimy by the arm and say, "Let's go."

"Go where?" asks the dear stupid boy.

"We're going to walk for a bit, and when the town thins out I'm going to change into this dress, and for once, just once, we are going to walk out in the world as a boy and a girl."

———

The town does thin out quickly after we leave the main square. The houses get farther apart and vacant lots appear, and then small fields. At last I see some bushes that will serve.

"Wait here, Jaimy, and turn around," I say and give him a level look. "On your honor. Right *here*." He waits.

I go behind the curtain of small trees and, seeing that it's safe, pull my jumper off over my head and then unbutton the vest (*ahhh...*) and then hurry off the vest, down the pants, off the sandals, and on with the dress. The dress comes down only to my knees and my underdrawers show below the hem. My fake cod pokes out the front of the dress. Plainly, this will never do, so I shed the drawers, too. I know it's risky, but there's no other way. I roll up my clothes in a neat bundle and put the sandals back on and look at the dress. It's a little shabby and worn and the colors are faded, and it's been washed so many times it's flimsy, but it's wondrous soft and it's a good fit. The neckline comes low across my chest and it's got puffy little short sleeves. I could have done worse. A lot worse.

I fluff up my hair and run my tongue over my lips and I step out to show Jaimy.

"So, James Fletcher," says I, and I stands there and cocks my hip. "What do you think of your saucy sailor girl now?"

He turns and looks at me. His eyes widen and his mouth opens slightly.

"Beautiful," he whispers. "You are so beautiful."

I look down at the ground. I'm suddenly flustered by the warmth of his gaze. "Ah, g'wan," I say lamely. "I bet you say that to all the girls."

"No, Jacky. You are the most beautiful thing I have ever seen or ever will see. I know I will never be happier than I am at this moment." He comes to me and takes my hand.

"Well. We'll see about that, won't we?" I say, having much more happier moments for him planned out in my head. "As for now, you may take your lady to lunch."

I twine my arm through his and we wend our way back into the town.

We find a little café on the outskirts of the busy center and we go in and find a table in the gloom, and Jaimy pulls out my chair for me, which shows he did have some manners as a youth, and I sit down with my dress pulled up proper under me, which shows I'm learning, too, 'cause I ain't never had a dress on before unless you count my shifts.

A large woman comes over and beams at us and asks us what we'd like to have, and Jaimy says for her to bring us some food and ale. I say that I'd rather have a little wine, thank you, and I say that 'cause I've noticed that the beer and ale run right through me, which makes it difficult, given my usual situation.

"The lads will never come this far out," says I, looking about. It's deliciously cool in here. And quiet. And dim.

Jaimy puts his hand on mine. "I don't care if they do. I meant what I said before. About leaving the Service and getting married."

"Jaimy, you've got to be sensible. They're never going to let you just leave the ship."

"I'll desert."

"No, you won't. The Navy's your life, as you've often said. You're sure to be made midshipman soon. You don't want to mess that up. If you deserted, you'd never step on a British ship again. I don't think you could live with that."

"No." He looks at me steady. "You're my life, now."

Although I appreciate the thought, I see that some female charm is necessary. "Jaimy," I breathe softly and lean over and put my arm around his waist and look real close in his eyes, "I will be *ever* so proud of my Mr. Midshipman James Emerson Fletcher, I will."

Just then the woman brings us our food and drinks. "Now, now, children, plenty o' time for that. Eat up now." Everyone in the place seems to be grinning and winking at us.

My simpering little speech seems to have had the desired effect on Jaimy, 'cause he doesn't say anything more about deserting. We turn to lunch.

I shovel in a mouthful of the food, which seems to be a spicy chicken thing with vegetables all fried and all greasy and good, and I start laughing and almost choke.

"What's so funny?" he asks.

"I was just imagining," says I, wiping off my mouth with the back of my arm, "Mother Fletcher back in London getting word that her son James had forsaken His Majesty's Service and run off with some little trollop in Kingston, Jamaica!"

I look at him over the rim of my wineglass and giggle.

He smiles at the thought. "Perhaps you're right," he admits, dabbing at his mouth with the piece of cloth that was in front of him on the table. I look and there's one in front of me, too. *So that's what it's for,* I think, all shamed. I pick mine up and dab my mouth, too, daintylike. I know he's watching me, so I take the cloth and wipe the back of my arm, too. He laughs.

"I know I've got a lot to learn," I say, "like, what is this?" I hold up the third eating thing at my place.

"It's called a fork," says Jaimy. "You use it to spear things and scoop things, too. Like this. Careful you don't poke your tongue with it, now."

I let my mind wander back to our little walk down here and how wonderful it felt to walk natural like a girl with my hips swaying a bit and not having to walk all clenched up like I do the rest of the time to look like a boy. It was grand just to walk along swinging our clasped hands between us and, just for a moment, forget about the ship and all that and think only of the moment and each other. That and stopping every few steps for a bit of a nuzzle and pet.

Jaimy asks if I want another glass of wine or anything else to eat, and I say, "No, let's go back outside in the world, you and me under the sun," and so we get up and pay and thank the woman for her hospitality and step back out into the bright sunlight and head back up the street.

We come to a low wall in the curve of the road, and the view of the city opens up. The streets are like steps up the hillside, and one street level is above the rooftops of the street below. We pause there and turn toward each other and come together and...

"Hey, Jaimy!"

We both jerk our heads around, and there, three streets below, are Davy and Tink, and Davy is shouting, "It's Jaimy, and he's got a girl!"

I think fast.

I grab Jaimy by the shirtfront and hiss, "Do what I say. Step up on the wall. Point to them and smile real broad and pretend you're telling me they're your mates!"

He does it. He gets up on the wall. He gives me his hand and I get up on the wall. He points. He smiles. He mouths to me, "Those are my mates."

I take it from there.

I turn to them and smile and wave, with my dress blowing about me in the breeze, and I call out, "Allo, freens of Jay-meee! 'E ees most wonderful boy, yes, I theenk I lof heem!"

The boys stand down there thunderstruck.

"I em mos' sor-ree I cannot stay to meet you var-ree preety boys but I mus' go. My papa weel keel me eef 'e see me here with Jay-meee!"

I turn to Jaimy and say, "I'm about to make you a legend, my dear." And I take his face in my hands and kiss him long and slow up there on that little wall with my lovely, lovely dress blowing about me.

Jumping down from the wall I say, "Now, you walk down toward them and I'll go back and change and catch up with you. All right? There's plenty of time."

I give him a peck on the cheek and head on up the road. I know he's watching me, so the evil in me makes me sway my bottom a little bit more than natural as I walk along. A breeze whips up and lifts my skirt some and

I feel a coolness on my backside and I put my hand behind me to smooth down my dress.

I point on down the road and say, "Down, Jay-meee."

"You dog. You hound. You lucky bastard. It's not fair. It's not fair. It's not bleedin' *fair!*"

Davy is having a hard time dealing with Jaimy's seeming success with the local women.

"Who is she, what…"

"She's just a local girl, that's all. A simple girl, really," says Jaimy, all offhanded and cool, "but a gem in the rough, you might say."

"But what did you…"

"Now, now, Davy. You know a gentleman never talks about things like that," says Jaimy, shaking his head and looking off all dreamy.

Davy utters a long and low whimper of pure envy from deep down in his soul.

I had changed and caught up with Jaimy well before we met up with Davy and Tink. The changing went all right except that I was surprised by a donkey right in the middle of it and I near died of fright. I need a rest from fright, I'm thinkin'.

Anyway, I'm back in my sailor gear, all harnessed back in and not liking it much.

"And where was you durin' all this?" demands Davy of me.

"I had to sit and wait in a bloody tavern while he was off wi' the tart," says I, looking out all angrylike from under my cap.

"And she was a *real* girl, too," wails Tink, "not one you have to pay for. A *real* girl."

"She is certainly real," allows Jaimy. "Every lovely inch of her."

Davy's fairly squealing in frustration.

"And how did your little plan go, *Davy*?" I says, all snide and insinuating, to change the subject. "Are you now a *man*?"

"Stuff it, Jacky," he says resentfully, and kicks the dirt beneath his feet. "They wouldn't let us in. They said we was too young."

"Aye, they laughed at us, they did, the sods," says Tink mournfully.

"Anyway, all's not lost," says Davy, brightening. "We've found a place for the earrings."

Chapter 32

We are back on the prowl and exercising the big guns. We are so good at this now that even I, Jacky Faber, Ship's Coward, am looking forward to an encounter with the pirate LeFievre. We drill, we practice, we blow barrels and rafts and floats to kingdom come, but still we catch no pirates. From some of the ships just come from England we hear rumblings of war with France and Spain, and if that happens we'll be called off station and sent back to England to join in the fray. We'd certainly like to see some more prize money before that happens.

I, of course, did not have myself put off in Kingston as planned. I'll stay with Jaimy to the end, and whatever happens, happens.

On that day, Davy led us down to the goldsmith's shop he had found in the middle of the market square. We went in and picked out the gold hoops that were not closed on one end and paid for them and waited to have them clamped in our poor ears. The shop was dark and there was a small forge glowing in the corner. While Davy and Tink were having their hoops put in, and not being very brave or quiet about it, Jaimy nudges me back to the forge and we stand in the glow of it. I can't figure out what he's up to and I look at him all quizzical, but then he takes my hand in his and takes his hoop and puts it on my finger and lifts up my hand and kisses it. I look up at him in the fireglow and I can feel the tears startin' but I can't let them come, and I take my ring and put it on his finger and lift it to my lips and then we turn and go back. The goldsmith shoves a needle through our earlobes and we take the rings off from our fingers and he shoves them through, then takes a hot iron and welds the ring shut, and I swear I didn't feel a thing.

I also swear to myself an oath right then that I will never, *ever*, take off that ring.

Compared to my filmy little dress from Kingston, *this* dress is a ship in full sail, and it is nearing completion. 'Course I ain't never yet tried it on 'cause wouldn't that be something to try to explain away if I got caught?

My Kingston dress and the girl what was in it has taken on the force of a legend in the minds of all the boys, including Jaimy, who says he wants me to wear it on our wedding night, just the way I wore it on that day. Naughty boy. That little bit of damning evidence is hidden deep in my lowest hidey-hole, but the memory of that day is locked down deep in my heart. Whatever else happens, I'll always have that.

This new dress, though not having the history of the other, is going to be beautiful with its white piping on the blue and the pleats on the skirt and the tight waist and fitted top. I've made another seabag and put my name on the side of this one so I can't give it away, and I would have made one for Jaimy but that would make the other boys look at me funny again and we can't have that. I stuff the dress inside the bag and only pull out a little of it at a time to work on so I could cover it up if surprised. But hardly anyone ever comes up on the mizzen top 'cept me and Jaimy.

I'm thinking that dresses are funny things, though, now that I've actually worn one. Why would a country like ours, which so prizes the so-called purity of its women so much, have them wear something like a *dress*? I mean, trousers and drawers give a certain amount of protection, it's got to be admitted. Like if someone has evil on his mind and he's got to work through belts and pant legs and such, it's going to take him a bit of time and effort, during which such time rescue might be on its way or his ardor might flag because of all the bother. While with a dress, why, you just lift it up and there you are, objective in sight. And it ain't just England, it's all of them. I know I'd have been in a much bigger fix when Sloat came at me if I'd been wearing a dress instead of my good sturdy sailor gear. It's a nagging thing and it probably ain't true, but I'd hate to think that a dress's lack of protection is the whole point of it. Don't seem right, somehow.

It's just the four of us in Tilly's class now, what with Willy gone off. I did finally get him to the point where he can scrawl his name, and I believe that is going to be it for Willy's book learning.

Old Tilly has been doing Shakespeare with us lately and the boys like it for all the blood and murders and such and I like it for the romance and the trickery and twists and things, but I don't think Juliet was very bright thinking *that* plan would work. It was much too complicated and depended on too many other people. Take it from a practiced trickster, they should have just run away and been done with it. 'Course that is *not* what I said to Jaimy in Kingston, so I guess I'm talking out of two sides of my mouth.

"Jaimy found hisself a Juliet of his own in Kingston," says Davy, still not over it.

"Is that so, James?" says Mr. Tilden, looking at Jaimy closely.

"I just talked to a village girl for a while, that's all," says Jaimy, all hot under the collar and looking daggers at Davy.

"Right," says Davy, all nudge-nudge, wink-wink with Tink.

"I hope you haven't done something stupid," says Tilly, "something besides getting yourselves up like a parcel of rogues." We all touch our earrings at that, and I give Jaimy a secret smouldering look.

"She promised to name the baby after him, ain't that right, Jay-mee?" says I, grinning at Jaimy's discomfort. *Take that girl out and shoot her.*

I am taken out, actually, and I am weighed. Tilly's still caught up in his foolish kite experiment and we hear again of the accursed Bernoulli. Today a board is set across a spar and I'm put on one end. Two-and-a-half bags of flour are put on the other end and I'm lifted up. Under Tilly's direction a seaman takes flour out of the half bag until I am level. I find the whole thing a bit demeaning and I wear my best angry glower.

Satisfied, Tilly puts the two-and-a-half bags in another bag and ties it up and puts it in the kite harness. Jaimy is looking at me with a certain satisfaction now.

I'm looking real stormy, with the direction things seem to be taking, and manage to get across my discomfort, and Tilly says, "You silly boy, why, this flying machine is as safe as a cradle, and if I weren't a gentleman of some substance, I'd go up in it myself, I would. You're a very lucky boy to be chosen as the first to go aloft."

Seein' that I still ain't convinced, he goes on.

"Did you know that French scientists sent a man up several hundred feet in a kite last year at the Continental Exposition? And that kite was inferior to this one. Did you know that some people in high places in the government think that's how Bonaparte's going to get his army across the Channel to fight us? Yes, it's true. Kites it is. Kites and balloons. I think they're right, too. It's a brave new scientific world."

Tilly potters about some more and looks at the clouds scudding by and says, "But, I'm sorry to say, you shan't get to go up today. Just a test flight, I'm afraid. We must proceed in an orderly manner."

With all of us and about a dozen men holding on, the kite is lifted aloft. The damned thing works.

Later, in the mizzen top, Jaimy is really steamed with me.

"How could you say that to Mr. Tilden?" he demands.

"Come on, Jaimy, I was only joking," says I. "Tilly knows it. It's all right."

I bat my eyelashes and look up at him all contrite. "Please forgive me, Jay-mee."

"I...I just wish you wouldn't be so...so...crude sometimes."

What?

"Crude! If we're sittin' here talkin' *crude,* I might just ask you whose *crude* hands—"

"No, no...I don't mean that." He searches for the words. "It's just the way you talk sometimes. It's...cheap."

Oh.

I decide to make light of this. "Aw, g'wan, Jai-mee. Oi'm jes' teasin' wi' ye. Coom an' gi' yer salty sailor lass a bit o' a kiss."

"*Please* don't talk that way," he says, frowning. He takes off his shirt. He has been working below with some men trying to fix a winch and he fairly glistens with sweat.

"Why not?"

"Because it isn't dignified, is why. If we're to be married, well..."

I sit up straight and fold my hands in my lap and say, "All right, Jaimy. You tell me what to be and I'll be it."

"Well, be more ladylike, more befitting an officer's wife..."

Oh, ho, ship's boy. Ain't we getting a bit ahead of ourselves here?

"Very well, how's this?" I put my mouth in a prim little line. "Oh, Captain Fletcher, it is *so* good to see you. Did you enjoy your night at the club? The children are *ever* so anxious to see their papa. Will you receive them now? No? Well, then, perhaps after you've had a bit of dinner. I'll have the cook prepare. A glass of sherry with you then, dear husband?"

Jaimy laughs and flings his shirt at me.

"Perhaps I am a bit of a stuffed shirt."

"I love you, anyway. Now come here, Captain, and give your ladyship a kiss before she does something *really* crude."

He really is the most magnificent boy.

Chapter 33

Hamlet was a good one. I thought the deceptions in that one were pretty well thought up. Shakespeare and I could have come up with a couple of corkers together, I'll wager. Poor Ophelia, though. It's always the girl what gets it, be it song or story. Or play. 'Course they all gets it in the end and it serves that Hamlet right, he who could have had the love of a good girl and been prince and all, but, no....

"The words for today are *monologue, dialogue,* and *soliloquy,*" intones Mr. Tilden.

I've also got three words for today, but I don't say them out loud. They are *betrothed, bespoke,* and *forsworn.* I like those words. Also, I like the sound of *Mrs. James Fletcher* and *Mrs. Jacky Fletcher* and *Lieutenant and Mrs. James Fletcher.* Better yet, *Captain James Emerson Fletcher and his lovely wife, Mrs. Mary Jacky Fletcher, were received by His Majesty the...*

I, Mary Jacky Faber, resolve that I must be the good one in this relationship because I'm the one with sense.

My brain is in my head and not in other places, which is not always the case with my very good friend, Mr. Fletcher. He has been suggesting of late that the jolly boat would be a fine place for us to sneak into and pull the canvas cover over it and no one would know we were in there, and wouldn't that be prime? Just to be together, of course. Nothing more. I think that would *not* be prime to climb into the aptly named jolly boat, because our mutual passion might get the better of us, and I know from my conversation with Mrs. Roundtree what the end of *that* would be, and that is just not possible at this time. No, no, I must not tempt Mr. Fletcher beyond all endurance, poor lad, as that would bring ruin upon us both.

Besides, the other lads will surely begin to wonder about our absence.

Yes, it is I who must make sure that our laces stay firmly laced and our buttons stay tightly buttoned and our pants stay up and on. So belay that, sailor, heave to and trice up.

I shall make a point to see James this evening and discuss it with him.

"Oh Jaimy, please Jaimy, I just loses me head and me good sense when we're alone and all pressed up together like this and oh, Jaimy, I don't want to deny ye nothin', Jaimy, but I can't be wi' child now, I'd be put off and have to be put with a bowl to beg and I don't want to go back to beggin', Jaimy, I don't 'cause I hates the beggin' and wi' a baby on me hip, oh God, I don't want I don't want I don't waaaaa..."

"Jacky, please stop crying. I'd never do anything to hurt you, Jacky, please stop crying, someone's going to hear you. Here, wipe your face in my shirt. Please stop, Jacky, I'd die before I'd see you hurt…"

"And I'd never see ye no more, Jaimy, and I couldn't stand that, I couldn't stand that, I could stand anythin' else but not that, to see ye nay more, Jaimy, 'twould kill me it would and why are ye shakin' me, Jaimy, why are ye…"

"For the love of God, Jacky, we're going to be caught right now if you don't quiet down."

"I'm your lass, Jaimy, I am forever and ever, but we can't we can't, oh, Jaimy…hic…not now…hic oh oh oh…hic… hic…"

"Now you've given yourself the hiccups, Jacky, see what you've done. Here, blow your nose. Someone's coming. We won't go in the jolly boat."

I am not at all pleased with my handling of the situation yesterday. I do not know exactly how a lady conducts herself in matters such as these, but I have a strong suspicion that I could have handled it in a more dignified fashion. But it did seem to work, for all that. We do not go in the jolly boat and I remain chaste. Somewhat.

We have been sailing slowly around in mist and fog for over a week, and since we can't see the stars at night, nor even the sun nor the horizon clearly in the day, we don't know exactly where we are. Nerves are on edge. We hear strange noises in the gloom, like other ships are about, but they don't answer our hail. Some of the men have been whispering about ghost ships. But it ain't ghosts.

Two bells into the morning watch the fog lifts and swirls away and there is LeFievre's pirate fleet. They don't run. They turn to fight.

We Beat to Quarters and straightaway down on them we fall.

Chapter 34

We are paying dearly for this victory, as victory it shall surely be. Even with a fleet of well-armed boats, LeFievre is foolish to take on a King's ship. His smaller ships, coasters mainly, swarm about us, peppering us with bullets and cannonballs. No thought of prizes here as we are at this time fighting for our very lives. The Master has been hit with chain shot and has been taken below. Most of him. His leg is still lying over there by the wheel and blood once again flows across the deck of the *Dolphin*. All the decks. I feels the impact of the shells, and I smells the smoke, and I hears the screams from below, and I tries not to think of what could be happenin' down there or what could already have happened. *Dear God, please...*

LeFievre's smaller ships are soon shattered or sunk, and men and wreckage are all around in the water, but we plows through 'em, headin' for LeFievre's big ships, which lie in a line about a half mile off, all pointin' towards us. His ship, the biggest one, is in the middle of the line, and we can see LeFievre himself, struttin' on the deck, all decked out in fine silks.

"Pride goeth before a fall, LeFievre," says the Captain

grimly. "Mr. Haywood, bring her about to take us to the top of their line. The wind will be abaft our beam such that we'll be able to come about again and roll right down their line, raking them with our full broadside, while they can only bring their bow chasers to bear. Do it now, Sir."

"Aye, Sir. *Ready about!*" he roars, havin' taken over the Master's duties from poor Mr. Greenshaw. "*Hard a'lee!*" The *Dolphin* turns.

"I assume they do not hold classes in naval tactics at pirate school," says the Captain.

"If they do," says Mr. Haywood with satisfaction, "Monsieur LeFievre obviously was lax in his studies."

I am a little bit cheered and calmed by their confidence. I try to get my tremblin' under control.

"Hold fire till my order," says the Captain. "Faber, ready with your drum."

Fifteen minutes later, we are in position and we starts our run.

"On my order, fire as they bear!" shouts the Captain. I raises my sticks. The pirates have already realized their mistake and are trying to get about, but it's too late. Their forward guns are shooting at us, but they are causing little damage so far. Then I hears a tiny *ting* and feel a strange *whoosh* of wind past my ear and see the ball disappear in the distance. It had nicked my earring.

"Close one, Faber," says the Captain.

I am unable to reply.

"*Fire!*"

I slams down the sticks and our guns begin to answer theirs, and all take their bloody toll. The pirates, except for LeFievre's flagship, are all converted merchantmen and are poorly armed. Some of them, however, have how-itzers mounted, and they shoot a ball so high up in the air that when it comes down, it can go through all your decks and out your bottom. The awful part is that we can see the ball go up and come down and maybe see our own destruction coming.

The jolly boat disappears in a shower of splinters. Someone on the pirate is a lucky shot. That's the last of the boats. The after ones were destroyed early on by shot and the forward ones caught fire from a hot ball. The fire was quickly put out, but the boats were lost. They blaze up right quick 'cause of all the pitch and tar in 'em. *We'd better not have to abandon ship,* I thinks.

Through all the noise and confusion I have a clear thought of regret. Maybe we're going to die. Both Jaimy and I. Maybe I was stupid to deny us anything. What's it goin' to matter now? Maybe...

Another explosion brings me back to the terror of the moment. One of the pirate ships has exploded and two of them are on fire. One is wallowing and sinking. Men are jumping off. Only LeFievre's flagship is left and it is full of fight. He has managed to bring his ship around and is pouring broadside after broadside into us. LeFievre must be furious with the loss of his fleet, and he means to make us pay.

"In for the kill, Mr. Haywood. We'll take her if we can, sink her if we must."

"Aye, Sir."

Orders are given and we closes with the pirate. His guns are blazin' away and so are ours. We are rocked with a hit on the starboard bow and we knock down his mizzenmast. Then, with a cheer, we see his main teeter all askew and then go down. It should be over. *Please let it be over. Please let me go to see if . . .*

"What's he doing there?" The Captain is peering through his glass at the confusion on the other ship.

"It appears he's off-loading treasure into that boat," says the First Mate, fairly licking his lips.

"I can see that," says the Captain with some irritation. "I mean on the other side of his ship. I see a sail sticking up."

Mr. Haywood shifts his glass. "They seem to be loading it with something, too. Maybe it's more treasure."

Although I don't have a telescope, I can see what they're talking about. It's a small boat, with a single sail. One of their lifeboats. *Maybe they are trying to save their lives,* I thinks. I know I'd be thinkin' that if I was them. Then that boat moves away from the side of the ship and all the pirates run to the remaining lifeboats and get in. *How can they possibly hope to get away,* I wonders.

I finds out.

The small boat heads straight for our bow. The rudder and the sail are tied down. There is no one in the boat, just piles of black kegs and white bags. And sparkles of fire from the fuses.

"*Fireship!*" screams the Captain. "*Hard left rudder! Clear the fo'c'sle!*"

Men pour from the bow of the ship, gunners from the guns, Marines from the masts, men from the anchor locker and the orlop, there's Mr. Lawrence and Davy and . . .

"*Get down!*" yells the Captain and hits the deck. I stands there all stupid, and he reaches out and yanks me feet out from under me. Me drum rolls away as I goes down and I see it bounce over the side, but before it does there's this sheet of white light and I see the skin of the drum go all orange and then turn black and gone. Then the blast hits.

I screams out, but I can't hear my own voice and I thinks I screams out Jaimy's name but I don't know 'cause all is lost in the roar of the firestorm.

Chapter 35

It's been three days now and we're still sinking.

LeFievre's fireship blasted a massive hole in the starboard bow. The bowsprit and its netting are gone. The figurehead, the woman with the dolphins, is smouldering splinters. The seas pour into the blackened hole every time we rock in the swells, as the hole is right at the waterline. The carpenter is unable to fix it; it's just too big and too far across. We have tried stretching canvas across the gap, but that is soon ripped off by the force of the sea. The Bo'sun took a bunch of us down in the hold, and we shifted cargo to put a list on the ship so that it leans over enough so that the hole is just out of the water, but the seas still slop in. If we have a storm, we are lost. If we don't get to land, we are lost. If the water level in the hold gets above a certain mark, we are lost.

We are on the pumps every second. Every pump on the ship, big and small, is taken to the forward hold and put in service. It is killing work, and we go in shifts of half hour on, half hour off. We collapse next to our pump, and we sleep next to it. We ship's boys have been given the small deck pump, the one used to hose us off that day long ago. There's only Jaimy, Davy, and me now, as Tink caught a musket ball in his leg and is in sick bay. The bullet didn't hit the bone, so he might not lose the leg if infection don't set in, and we prays that it don't.

We lost eighteen men dead, thirty wounded, in that battle. Henderson was one, he who was a constant friend to me and always looked out for my poor self when I was green. Lafferty, another good one. Both of 'em blown off the fo'c'sle and never seen by earthly eyes again. And Grant, he who could play the fiddle and the concertina, and I can't make myself believe those fingers will move no more. Mr. Barkley, midshipman, one of the younger squeakers, and Joshua Spense, the Kingston man. I'm glad he had that last liberty in his own town. He should have deserted when he had the chance. Not very military of me to think that, but I don't care. I'm too tired.

Mr. Greenshaw, the Master, is still alive, but only just barely. His leg went over the side with the dead seamen right away after the blast. No time for ceremony now. No time for grief. We'll say the words later, if we can.

LeFievre and what's left of his crew got away.

The pump handle is a T-shaped bar and you put your hands on the cross piece of the T and you lift it up and you push it down. On the upstroke you hear the valve breathe in with a soggy sigh, and on the downstroke you hear the bit of water pushed up through the pipe and out over the side. I've figured that when I do it I get maybe a half gallon a minute out. Prolly less. Up and down, up and down till all sense of time and place fades away, and you do it till your time is up or you collapse and are dragged away.

When we first started we joked and cheered each other on, but after a while we couldn't, just couldn't. We only pushed on the bar and went up and down and up and down, and days and nights went by. Jaimy tried to work harder to take up some of my time and I tried not to let him but I couldn't keep up and I went for food for all of us, and we ate it and pumped and pumped and slept and pumped and in the morning, we saw that we had lost ground. There was two more feet of water in the hold and that just about tore the hearts out of us. I go back up on deck to get some biscuits and tea to take back, but Mr. Haywood stops me. He is stripped to the waist 'cause he has been on the pumps, too, and all the officers and midshipmen and the Captain, too, and I stand there weaving back and forth in front of him with the mugs and the biscuits in me hands and me eyes about to roll back in me head, and I ain't thinkin' too good and . . .

"Faber. What pump are you on?"

"Number-three-deck pump, Sir. Just down there."

"Right. Take that down to your mates and then go to your hammock and go to sleep. I'll send someone to take your place, and then I'll send someone to wake you in two hours."

This must be a dream. I must still be down next to the pump.

"But, Sir, me mates—"

"Do it, Faber. No back talk."

I do it.

I go back and tell the lads, and they nod and take the food. A sailor shows up to take my place. I stumble out and over to our old kip. None of the hammocks are hung 'cause no one's slept since the battle. I fall down toward a pile of powder rags and swabs. I am asleep before I hit them.

I sleep a sleep that's too deep for dreamin', but I'm hauled out of it way too soon, and it's Muck I feel shaking my shoulder and lifting me up and putting me in his cart, and I moans, *No, Muck, I ain't drownded yet*, but it's not Muck. It's a seaman who's saying, "Wake up, Jacky. Mr. Haywood wants you topside. Now."

Mr. Haywood sees me come on deck and takes me by the arm and points up the mainmast.

"See the lookout up there, boy?"

The lookout is standing, glass to eye, on the little platform at the doubling of the maintopmast with the topgallant, about a hundred feet up.

"Yes, Sir," says I, tryin' not to yawn in his face.

"Now see the place *above* him, on the main royal, where the backstays and the shroud lines come together?"

"Yes, Sir."

"Good. I want you to go up and relieve the lookout and take his glass and climb up to that spot and search the horizon. Especially the horizon to the south. When you climb up there, you should be a good twenty-five feet higher and that will give you a better view. Do you understand, boy?"

"Aye, Sir."

"Good. Then do it. Now."

I head for the ratlines and on the way pick up a short length of light line. I hook my toes on the netting and up I climb.

When I get up to Harper, the lookout, I take his glass and turn from him and loosen my vest and jam the glass down in and ask him to give me a boost before he goes. He flings me up so's I can grab a backstay and swing out and climb up it to where it joins the main royal mast. When I get there, I wrap my legs around the mast and sort of sit on the lines. They are under powerful pressure from holding up the mast and all, and it's like sitting on thin, sloping iron bars but I'll have to bear it. I tie the line I brung with me around myself and around the mast and then take out the glass and tie the end of the line around that so's I don't drop it. I put the telescope to my eye and look south.

Nothing.

I brace the glass against the mast and slowly scan the whole horizon. In the glass the horizon wiggles in the heat of the morning but shows nothing else. We're heading dead west 'cause we know the South American continent lies off there someplace, we just don't know where, and there ain't nothin' but ocean in the other direction. I concentrate on the southern part again.

I search the southern sea off the port side of the ship for a full half hour as ordered. Nothing. I figure I'll give it a rest and give all the compass points a quick look. North, northeast, east, southeast, south, southwest, west, northwest, north. Nothing.

Alas, the dear *Dolphin*, my only home ever, my port in the storm, the refuge what saved a poor girl from . . .

What's that?

North-northwest bearing, two points ahead of the

starboard beam: a smudge. Prolly nothing. It's like the horizon was a pencil line and it was just rubbed a little right there. Don't lose it. Prolly just clouds.

Both my legs are falling asleep from sitting on the wires. I try to scootch up a bit, but I can't without taking my eyes off the smudge, which ain't changin' none, since we ain't goin' towards it.

I need to get up higher.

I take the glass from my eye and look up. There's still another ten, maybe twelve feet of bare mast to the top, and then there's a flat place on top of the mast, a small plate to keep the rainwater out of the wood grain to keep it from rotting. I know that 'cause all of us ship's boys have touched the top of the highest mast 'cause we dared each other to do it, and so we had to do it. I retie the line around my waist so that it forms a loop around me and the mast. I put the glass back in my vest and start up.

I lean back against the rope and slowly shinny up, pulling the rope with me as I go, inch by inch. I get to the top and look down at the deck, one hundred and fifty feet below. I could not be higher—every bit of the *Dolphin* is below me now. Well, sort of, 'cause there is actually only water beneath me on account of the list on the ship. If I take a tumble, I'll make quite a splash, but at least I won't smash against the deck and make a mess. Still be dead, though. I pull out the glass and lay it on the top plate and train it on the spot.

There!

I don't think it's a cloud! It seems to have ends, like cliffs. But I can't be sure. It could be a fog bank. But on a clear day like this?

"Mr. Haywood. On deck there," I say not loud 'cause I don't want to get the crew's hopes up. No one hears me.

I see Willy crossing the deck far below.

I call out, "Willy!" and he looks up.

"Get Mr. Haywood. Quiet, like."

The First Mate is up the mast in a flash with his own glass.

"There, Sir," I say with my eye still on the glass. "To the northwest, two points ahead of the beam. About zero seven zero, relative. Maybe it's clouds, Sir, I don't know..."

"I don't see anything," he says, disgusted. Then he looks at me a good thirty, forty feet above him.

"Johnson. Get up here," he calls down. The small and wiry Johnson bounds up to the platform. "Get up as close as you can to Faber. Take my glass."

In a moment, I feel his head butt up against my leg. "Where away, Jacky?"

I keep the glass to my eye and point. He squints in his glass.

"Sir!" says Johnson. "There's something! It's land!"

Mr. Haywood calls down orders and the *Dolphin* slowly turns toward her salvation.

"Good work, Faber. Don't fall on your way down. Report back to your pump."

It takes us the full day to get there, wallowing as we are. When we get close, I'm called up again and sent into the foretop, the dear old foretop, to spot the shallows in the clear bright water. I think they have me do it 'cause I'm pretty useless on the pump.

Already I can see heads of coral poking up from way

below as we head in to the island. They've found a likely little cove that's protected by an arm of sand and coral that reaches out and encircles it. The Captain keeps us off till almost high tide and then we go in under very little sail. It's dangerous for the ship as we could run aground too soon and sink in sight of land, but we have no other choice. At least we know we're not going to drown, and that is a wonderful thing.

I call out when I see something and the ground is coming up fast, but the stands of sharp coral that could rip the bottom right off the ship thin out and then it's all white sand. We slip up on the sand, and I swear the *Dolphin* sighs as she leans over and comes to rest, safe.

There is no cheering. All just rig hammocks and fall into them. The exhaustion is total—officer, seaman, and boy. There are no watches set, no food prepared, nothing but sweet sleep. I meet Jaimy staggering back to our hammock. I take his arm and put it around my shoulders and help him the rest of the way.

"Jacky," he whispers, "tonight I want...I want us to sleep at the same end of the hammock. Just sleep..."

Our hammocks are the kind that fold up around a person so you can't see in. *What's the harm,* I thinks. Besides, no one cares about nothing except blessed sleep.

"Just sleep...," he goes on dreamily. "I just want to sleep...and wake up in the morning with your head on my shoulder and your breath on my face."

We crawl in and enfold into each other and the rough canvas of our dear, dear hammock feels like the finest of velvet.

Chapter 36

The first thing I feel in the morning is someone lifting the flap of the hammock off of our faces, and I open an eyelid and it's Davy's shocked face I'm seeing looking down.

I let out a low moan and lift my hand and tap Jaimy on the chest. His eyes flutter open and sense returns to them and he looks at me and smiles. I point up and he follows my point and sees Davy. He starts. Then he relaxes and strokes my hair with the hand that's connected to the arm and shoulder that my head is lying on and says, "Davy, put your hand on your tattoo and swear that you will never tell a soul about this. At least not yet."

Davy is still struck dumb.

"Is there anyone else in here?" Jaimy asks Davy.

I see Davy look quickly around the hold. He recovers the power of speech. "No, they're all on the beach, but—"

"Then *swear*, Davy, or the Brotherhood was nothing but a bunch of little boys playing games."

Davy stands there scowling a bit and then comes back to his ordinary self. "All right, you sods," he hisses, "I swears I won't tell no one I caught the both of you in disgustin' mortal sin for which you'll roast in Hell forever."

"All right, then." Jaimy takes a deep breath. "Jacky is the girl that you saw me with in Kingston. And, she is actually...well, a girl. Really, she is."

Davy looks at me all in confusion. He silently mouths the word *girl*, all unbelieving. I take my hand from Jaimy's chest and give Davy a little finger wave.

"'Allo, Day-vee, you var-ee preety boy, I theenk. Eet ees nice to see you again, Day-vee..."

He's about to choke. "All this time! All this time you two have been..."

Davy looks like what I imagine a startled fish looks like under water, all gulpy and pop-eyed. I don't care. I've had the most beautiful sleep of my life and I'm feeling deliciously drowsy. And wicked. I burrow my face in Jaimy's neck.

"I've only known for about two weeks. And we haven't *been* anything," says Jaimy. "So remember, you are forsworn, Davy. Don't even tell Tink. He's in no shape for keeping secrets."

I squirm around and let my leg slip over Jaimy and take a deep, deep breath, then let it out oh-so-slowly as a deep sigh of contentment, and I nuzzle Jaimy's ear with my nose and say all sleepily, "David, do you mind? I'm not quite dressed."

Davy lets fly an oath and storms out of the hold. We hear his fist hit the wall as he leaves.

"You really *are* evil, you know," says Jaimy.

"I know," I murmurs. "I shall have to pay."

———

The beach encampment has already been laid out by the time Jaimy and I emerge blinking into the sun. There's a steep list on the ship now that it's fully heeled over on the sandy bottom, and it ain't too comfortable for doin' much of anything 'cept swingin' in a hammock. There's tents been put up to shelter the sick bay, which has been moved out of the ship, and the kitchen has been set up and there's cauldrons steaming and gruel cooking and smelling right good. There's tables, even. I realize, a little guiltily, that some people were working while we slumbered on. Do I really feel guilty, though? Nah. I feel wonderful.

We go over to see Tink and he's all gray and tired looking, but he's cheerful and his wound looks better, if rather grisly. We go to get something to eat and we meet Davy on the way and he joins us but can't stop staring at me till we threaten to hurt him, so he stops, but every now and then he blurts out something like, "In the netting! That's why you wouldn't go splashin' in the swells no more!"

"That's right," says I, shovelling in a spoonful of the heavenly swill. "But you were all *ever* so interesting." That gets me an elbow from Jaimy.

This mush gets better every day. I think there's some peas in this batch.

"And the oath of the Brotherhood," says Davy, pointing at me, "wasn't there something in there about *sharin*'?"

"It doesn't work that way, Davy," says Jaimy, with a warning in his tone.

I let them fight on. It's nice to have someone else bickering with Davy for a change. Being a girl now, at least between the three of us, sets me above the battle. The serene goddess Jacky beams her happiness all around. The sun is warm, and it's so strange to be on land again and so good not to be dead and rolling about on the bottom of the sea.

Liam comes by and sits down with his bowl and that stops Davy's ravings. We find out from Liam that the island has no people on it. It is about seven miles long, half a mile wide, and, while it does have some fresh water and some scrubby trees, there is absolutely no wood worthy of the name. There are many palm trees, but their wood is all mushy and won't do.

It's been decided that planks from the *Dolphin*'s deck will be pulled off to build a small boat that will carry a party of men to go off to get help and supplies. Sailors have been sent up with glasses to the tops of the tallest coconut trees to see if they can spot any land, but no luck, so the boat will just have to strike off blindly to the west, where we know the continent lies, somewhere. It could be twenty miles away, just over the horizon, or it could be a hundred miles off. Maybe two. Work has already begun on the boat. We can hear the hammers and saws.

"And there's sure to be a ship's boy or two in that very boat," says Liam, merrily. We all know the story. Ha-ha. Very funny.

"I volunteer Jaimy," says Davy with a twinkly look at me. "He's the one what wants to be a midshipman and needs to be off studying small boat handlin'. Jacky and me'll take care of things around here."

I spread evil looks all around.

We hear from Liam that most of the men are setting up kips onshore for the long wait for repair or rescue. The carpenter and his crew will be at least two weeks building the boat. Jaimy and I exchange quick glances.

"We'll be havin' the wake for Lafferty and Grant tonight," says Liam, looking at me. I nod and say that I'll be there. Five more of the wounded have died since the battle. At least they're to be buried on land, which is good because sailors really don't like to be buried at sea.

We leave the mess tent and walk up the beach, the sand warm and soft beneath our feet. We mean to look up Tilly and report for duty, and after that, maybe set up our own kip in a nice cozy little spot. Dark it will be, with soft boughs for a bed. And far away from the others. I notice that Davy hangs back.

"Davy, get up here and walk beside us," I warns hotly. "I know what you're doing back there." I should smack him.

Tilly is in a state of high scientific excitement. He takes us about, pointing out edible plants and fruits and nuts and clams and such, and I'm thinking I'll be sticking to my usual salt pork and weevily biscuit, thank you. I'm looking off into the bush, thinking secluded bowers, soft boughs and all, while he rattles on.

I put up with the lecture, but really I'm hoping he'll get done soon so Jaimy and I can go off exploring and such, but it is not to be. Oh no, it is not ever to be. Tilly's scientific blather was all just a ruse to get me to go uncomplaining to my sorry fate. As we go around a stand of small trees Tilly's hand clamps around my arm so I can't run away and there it is: The horror. Staked to the ground, shakin' in the wind like a live thing strainin' against its leash. The end of all my joy.

The Kite.

Aw, Tilly, you couldn't give me one day, could you, just

one day of happiness before you have to take me up and kill me in your stupid machine? I know I was wicked and I know that every time I get happy and sassy I end up getting thumped, but this is beyond all reason and I'll be a good girl from now on, I promise.

But I know it's useless to hope. Instead of having a romp with Jaimy in the bushes, I'm to be executed for my crimes. This ain't exactly like a hangin', but it's damned close.

There's a huge pile of nasty coiled rope next to the hated kite, each loop looking like a noose. Men are beginning to gather to handle the line, and callin' up the beach for more help. Three of them lift up the kite to hold it in position while the line is played out. I look wildly about. I am trapped, there is no escape, none. I am doomed.

A crowd is gathering to watch the spectacle.

Jaimy begins to protest for me.

"Nonsense, James," says Tilly. "My flying machine is perfectly safe and thoroughly tested. We have the proper breeze and direction. We can send Faber up with a glass and he'll be able to spot any land that's out there. He'll be much higher than the trees, higher even than the masts on our poor ship. After he's had a look, we'll haul him back down and he'll brag on his flight for the rest of his life."

I've got a sick feelin' in the pit o' me belly and think I'm goin' to lose me breakfast.

"Beggin' your pardon, Mr. Tilden," I croaks out, "but what happened to that man what went up in the kite at that Exposition last year?"

Tilly shakes his head and *tut-tuts.* "He was a con-

232

demned criminal, anyway, so it didn't matter. Besides, my kite is superior."

"Jaimy, you may have me shiv and Davy me seabag and Tink can have me clothes and me Last Will is in me vest if you recover me body. And here, Liam, take back your whistle..."

My whistle is on a thong around me neck and I goes to lift it off to give it to Liam, who's lookin' at me with fatherly concern, but I know he can't do nothin', and he knows it, too. Tilly stops me from dolin' out me worldly goods and pushes me into the harness.

"Put that stuff away and stop with all this twaddle. It's perfectly safe. Look, the end of the rope is tied to that tree. You're going out over the water so you'll have a soft landing if anything happens. But what could happen? In you go, now."

They're strappin' me in tight, one strap across me chest and another across me hips and a strap around each thigh and up over me crotch to connect up with the hip one, when the crowd parts and the Captain and First Mate walk up. Captain Locke says all hearty, "Well, Faber, all your good work hanging about the rigging on the ship has certainly paid off as you are certainly not afraid of heights. We saw that amply displayed yesterday, didn't we, Mr. Haywood."

"That we did, Sir. Faber has shown himself to be most brave in all our encounters with the enemy and with nature."

Even in the fog of my despair, I am amazed at this. Mr. Haywood sayin' that about *me*?

"This will hold you in good stead now, I reckon," says the Captain, looking at the fiendish kite with approval.

A spyglass has been fitted with a strap and it's hung around my neck. Hands are placed on the rope.

"And, Faber," continues the Captain, all beaming in his countenance, "when next you touch the ground, it shall be as *Midshipman* Jack Faber."

My feet leave the ground.

The group onshore gets smaller and smaller as I am lifted up. The ship itself becomes toylike down there in the blue-green lagoon with all the palm trees around. All I see of Jaimy is his uplifted face gettin' smaller and smaller, and I make that image stay in my mind 'cause that might be the last time I ever see it.

I know I was bad and careless and cheeky with Davy, but the swiftness of the punishment leaves me astounded. One minute I'm planning a bit of a frolic with Jaimy and the next I'm aloft with only the regret of my free and wanton ways for company.

They seem to have gotten to the end of the rope. I peer down and see that the ants below seem to be relaxing, not even holding on. I guess they trust the tree to which the rope is tied. I hope they are right.

Well, since I'm up here and not yet dead, I should do my duty. I lift up the glass and scan the horizon. I can only see three quarters of it 'cause I can't see behind me and there ain't nothin' on the horizon in the part I can see.

I wiggle around and try to see out to the west but the straps cut most cruelly and I can't…quite…get around.

I do manage a bit more but not enough. I bring up the

glass and...maybe there's something there? I yell out, "Hey!" but all of a sudden the kite lurches up in a strong gust of wind. It scares me but I figure it'll give me a few more feet of height so I look again but, no, nothing.

Another gust and this time it gives a real jerk and I gasp and train the glass down on the beach. All the men are back on the line again and there seems to be a certain unsettlin' panic to their movements. I lift the glass a little higher and see that the rope is pulling the tree out by its roots and the roots come out all white and ghostly and the sand falls quickly off them. Another great gust. *That's it, then,* I say to myself, as I watch the tree pull free and the men are dragged toward the shore, falling off, one by one.

Then the tree itself is lifted in the air. It doesn't even touch the water. I'd like to think that Jaimy is the last one to let go.

That's it for me, then. There will be no boat to come get me when at last I settle into the sea.

That's it for me.

Chapter 37

So farewell light
And sunshine bright
And all beneath the sky...

Strange that I should think of that lyric from a song about a man who's going to be hanged, which is what I always feared the most and was sure was going to happen to me, and now I'm to be drowned instead. I remember back to when I first skipped on board, thinking as how a girl what's meant for hangin' ain't likely to be drowned. Well, here I am. It looks like a deep swallow of the salt rather than the jerk of the hemp for me. Cold comfort. Same throat what gets it, seawater or rope.

I think I must have passed out for a while when the kite was climbing ever higher and higher in the sky. I look down now between my dangling toes and see the rope hanging almost straight down with that traitorous tree at the end of it, still high above the water. The island is far away now, just a smudge like when I first spotted it from the mainmast. Only yesterday, was it? The wind is lessening now, as it almost always does in the late afternoon, and the kite is starting to settle. Now the island ain't even a smudge. Now it's gone.

The kite's swooping back and forth as it settles and the rope snakes back and forth, back and forth like a long tail, and I know it's 'cause the wind can't get running smooth across the top of the kite 'cause the kite ain't held steady like a sail is held steady and soon all will drop into the ocean and that will be it for both the kite and me.

I don't rant or cry or anything like that. I don't even pray, hardly. I've prayed for deliverance before and I get delivered and then someone else dies and that someone could be Jaimy this time and I don't want that, but I do hope that he sheds a few tears for me. No, no I don't want that, either. I want him to become a fine officer and marry a fine lady, which I am not and never will be now, but I do hope he remembers me fondly, I do.

The water draws closer. Soon the tree will touch and at least the water will be warm. I look at its blue hugeness and I say, *I will ask one thing please, God, please no sharks, no sharks.* I just want to be let down softly and then go to sleep 'neath the curl of a smooth little wave, gentlelike. A nice little warm wave. That's all.

I imagine Liam and the rest will be waking me tonight, too. The thought gives me some comfort. I hope he asks Jaimy to come to the wake, too, even though it's Catholic stuff and Deacon Dunne would say no, but all the cryin' and hollerin' and keenin' and such is good for a grieving soul. I've never held back my tears, that's for sure.

Closer yet. I've got to get myself ready in my mind and so I think about how far I got from London and how

Muck never got me and how I'll not be put up in jars and I've seen a lot of stuff and how I gave it a good run and got farther than Charlie, who I might be seeing real soon, and how I got to love a fine boy and I think he might love me and I am goin' to cry now but I think that's all right, I never was very brave....

I see the tree hit the water and I'm thinking I'll cut myself out of the harness when me and the kite comes all the way down 'cause I wants to float free and go down when I'm ready. I figure that the best thing to do when I finally slips under is to hold me breath till I get down a ways and then suck in a chestful of water all sharp and fast so's to get it over with quick with not much choking. I hope not much choking. I don't even know if I can swim 'cause I ain't never tried.

At least it's a plan and I feel a little better for it.

The kite steadies down. It don't swoop no more and I'm wonderin' why, and I look down and see that the tree is half under the water and leavin' a wake. I don't pay it no mind and get back to puttin' my final thoughts in order. I look down again in another minute and the tree is still half under water. No change...but wait a minute...I should have dropped down closer and I didn't, I...

Leavin' a wake! I shakes the cobwebs out of me mind and ciphers it out. The tree is draggin' like a sea anchor, just as if a bunch of men was hanging on to the rope so Bernoulli can get back on the job, and the kite stays up and steady! I ain't goin' down no more.

I dare not hope, but I can't help it. No, no, this can't be true, I must be dreamin' or be out of me mind, but it seems too real. It *is* real! I have me own ship and I'm under way with way on! As long as the wind holds, I could fly all the way to Mexico!

I twist around in the harness, tryin' to see behind me, but I still can't, but ain't the water gettin' lighter and brighter and shinin' all like an emerald and, *oh thank you, God,* it means the bottom's comin' up and it's gettin' shallower and shallower and then, as sudden as a slap in the face, there's a white beach beneath me. I don't know if it's Mexico or Timbuktu or what, but it surely looks like home to me! I christen my wonderful ship the *Hope* and in a few moments the tree pulls up on the beach and catches in a grove of palms. The wind lessens and dies.

His Majesty's ship, the *Hope,* settles slowly and gently into the treetops.

Midshipman J. M. Faber commanding.

PART V

Oh, Western Wind, When Wilt Thou Blow,
That the Small Rain Down Can Rain.
Oh, That My Love Were in My Arms,
And I in My Bed, Again.

Chapter 38

After I land in the top of the trees, I pull out my shiv and cut myself out of the harness and swing over to a good limb and climb down. The trees are much bigger here, the Captain and the carpenter will be delighted to know. I find my way out to the beach and to that tree, which was both a traitor and savior to me. Strange to see it with its roots all washed off and white and sticking up in the air. I cut the rope off of it and haul the end back into the brush, so as to keep my presence here a secret from any passing cannibals. I'd hate to think that I'd survived all that I had just to end up on a spit.

I go back to the *Hope* and manage to pull it down from the tree without too much damage. I cut it off from the rope and drag it to a little clearing and put it down such that it forms a little tent. I cut lengths off the rope and use some to tie down the Good Tent *Hope* so it won't rock about in the wind. I coil the rest neatly nearby. Shipboard habits die hard.

It is nearly dark now so I crawl into my new home and prepare for sleep. One bit of complete and total and almost sinful pleasure I have this night is in the taking off of that damned vest in which I had been crammed, corseted, and confined for a whole year.

I put the rolled-up vest under my head as a pillow and take stock of my situation. I have, besides my Immortal Soul, which is still thankfully tucked in my not-so-immortal body, the following:

> My clothes—drawers, vest, shirt, pants
> My shiv
> My whistle, with thong
> My Will
> The spyglass, with halter
> The Good Ship *Hope*
> Much rope

It's not much to ensure my survival in this strange land, but it will have to serve. I plan, on the morrow, to:

> Gather food and eat it
> Gather wood for signal fire
> Explore to determine danger if I light fire
> Light fire and await rescue

I always feel better with a plan.

It rains that first night like I have never seen rain before. It comes on in an instant and pours down in sheets instead of drops, and I know it is soaking every bit of wood beyond any hope of lighting as a signal fire. I reach my cupped hands out and they quickly fill with water, which I gratefully gulp down. It goes on for an hour, and then, just as suddenly, it stops.

Then there is silence. After the droplets stop dripping off the leaves, it gets so quiet I can hear my own heartbeat. I have never, in my whole life—with Mum and Dad and Penny, or on the streets of London with the gang, or on the *Dolphin*—ever been really *alone*. I curl up a little tighter. On the ship I was used to sleeping in a room full of sailors, a hundred or more in our hold, with their snores and grunts and other noises. All I hear now is the thump of my own heart and the sound in my ears that I know is the sound of my blood going through my veins, the rush of my own salt sea…

Then the jungle comes alive. It starts with an unholy shriek not ten feet from the tent, the sound of somethin' bein' ripped open and torn and eaten—or maybe it was the sound of the thing eatin' the other thing, I don't know—and then the rest of the fiends joins in with such a chorus of grunts and groans and chitterings and howls and screams that I spend the whole night with my eyes open and on the open end of the tent, my hand clutched around my shiv, and wondering what the snakes do after a rain.

I do fall asleep towards dawning and sleep away most of the morning. I figure there's no hurry; the fire's not going to light, anyway.

When I do get up, I head to the beach for breakfast. There's some of the plants that Tilly pointed out as all right to eat, and when I walk on the sand next to the water, things squirt water up so that will be clams. Very well. Clams and weeds it is.

I kneel down in the sand and commence to digging with my hands and my shiv right where I see a good strong squirt, and before too long I come up with a small round clam about the size of my thumb. I rinse it off and run my shiv between the shells and it gives up the fight. I pry off the top shell and see this disgusting lump of what looks like snot, but I must keep my strength up for the good of the Service and all so I lift it up and let it slide out of the shell, over my tongue, and down.

Not as bad as I would have thought. Sort of like salty nothing. I dig up a few more and do them, and then I try the weeds. Tilly called it pigweed when he was pointing out edible plants to us back on the island. Well, this is one little piggy what don't like it overmuch. It is stringy and not very good, but I force some of it down and it dawns on me that all of this would taste better if it were cooked. The problem is that I don't have a cook pot. Further thought is required.

The breakfast being less than hearty, I decide to explore to see if I can improve my condition in other ways.

The beach, which is about fifty yards wide at this tide, runs up to a line of low trees, and beyond them the land rises to a height of about a hundred feet. What's beyond that, I cannot see, and so I resolve to have a look.

I go back to my camp to pick up the glass and leave off some clothes 'cause it's getting terrible hot. I of course did not put the vest back on when I got up, just my white shirt, Charlie's old shirt, which is now as thin as gauze it's been washed so many times so it's nice and cool, and now I drop the underdrawers, too, and make do with my pants, which I roll up to my knees. *Poor Charlie,* I thinks, *your clothes have made it halfway around the world. And your shiv. And your Little Mary, too.*

Looking like a proper castaway, I head off and up.

The climb is not hard as there are plenty of vines and bushes to cling to, and after about fifteen minutes I make it to the top and look about. This is definitely *not* an island, at least not a little one. I put the glass to my eye and look from the south around to the north and I see nothing but a vast carpet of forest. No cities, no towns, no villages, no cooking fires, no nothing. Which is all right 'cause it might also mean no cannibals. 'Course they could be sneaky devils who've doused their fires and are creeping up on me right now with dinner on their minds.

Once, during that time back in the Mediterranean when that rotten Bliffil had been sent off with the prize ship, I snuck down into the midshipmen's berth and made off with a book called *Robinson Crusoe* that one of 'em had. I read it in a day, read parts of it out loud to the lads, and had it back before they knew it was gone. The boys, of course, really liked the part where the cannibals were about to roast poor Friday, the bloody-minded sods. Anyway, that's how I know all about cannibals.

Bringing myself back to where I am I reflect that the *Dolphin* don't need any towns or such—all she needs is good wood and it looks like there's plenty here. Next I train the glass westward towards where I last saw the island. Nothing, of course, not even a smudge. No matter. Time enough for that later.

Now I look down towards the beach and I see, off to

the left of my camp, a place where the water has come in and made a little lagoon, with many coconut palms about. I resolve to see what that offers when I climb down.

I come round the edge of the beach where the lagoon begins, and see the seawater streaming out with the tide. Quite fast it streams out. I wait, and at low tide there is only a small pool left and there are trees all around with roots sticking out of the water and oysters clinging to the roots, oysters like they sold in London, which we never could buy.

What really brings joy to my heart, though, is the small waterfall of fresh water pouring in at the far end. A big problem solved. After the tide rip has slowed, I wade through the shallow water and head for the other end. When I get there, I see that the waterfall actually empties into a small basin above the salt water, forming a little pond, and around the pond are flat rocks and grassy areas. I get the uneasy feeling that I'm being rewarded for something that I ain't earned. Maybe I earned it with my flight hanging under the *Hope*.

I stick my hand under the waterfall and drink from my palm. The water is fresh and good. It don't take much for me to decide that my camp is about to be moved.

After some thought, I decide that I'll make the signal fire down on the beach itself, between the tide lines 'cause that way the water will erase the ashes so there won't be any sign of it afterward for cannibals and such to see. If I build it on the ridge, I'd be getting a little more height, but it might attract the wrong eyes.

I take myself down to the beach at low tide—the sand is all smooth and level—and look out across the water to where I think the island is. I know that men with spyglasses were sent up to the tops of the highest coconut trees that day I was there and they couldn't see the tops of the cliffs behind me here. Given that the line of sight from a sailor standing in the mizzen top of the *Dolphin,* when she was sailing, to the horizon is about fifteen miles, I figure the island has to be at least twenty miles off. I don't think I was passed out for very long when I was up in the *Hope,* but I'll add another ten miles for it. Thirty miles, then. That means I'll have to get my column of smoke up three or four hundred feet.

It will have to be a very still day when I light it off.

So, after eating some of the oysters and still trying to think of ways to make a cook pot, I gather up a pile of sticks and branches near the beach and, while it is drying out some, I realize it could rain again tonight so I know I got to tie the Good Ship *Hope* over the top of the pile and fend for myself.

After I do that, I move my belongings over to the new camp. Climbing back up to the waterfall—which is more of a water trickle really, just a little stream coming down the hillside—I find some rocky outcroppings that I can crawl under for shelter tonight. It will serve till I can get the kite up here. Now for a fire and a bit of lunch.

I gather as dry a wood as I can find and spread it out on the rocks next to the pond. The pond is only about three feet deep in the middle and is about twenty feet across. The bottom is rock and it is slippery as I find when I wade in and slip and fall. I get out and add my clothes to the wood on the rocks to dry out and it occurs to me that I might have a bath. My first real one since my mum used to do me.

It's warm and in the heat of the day. The sun is almost directly overhead and there's a break in the trees so it shines nicely in on the pond and the rocks and the grass. I'm beginning to like my new kip in spite of my nagging fear that I could be left here alone forever. Old Crusoe had a problem with that, and I know that I would, too.

I go down to the lagoon by way of some stone ledges that make kind of a stairway and I dip into the water, but the bottom's sort of mucky so I go out to the beach and wade out beyond where the waves tumble over. Grabbing fistfuls of sand from the bottom, I scrub myself all pink and then dive into a wave to rinse it off. When I come up, another wave knocks me down again.

I snort the water from my nose. What marvelous fun. Being marooned has its good points. I resolve to learn to swim.

When I get back to my camp, I slip into my pond to rinse off the salt. As I float there on my back, I notice two turtles on the opposite bank, eyeing me with interest. *Careful, fellows,* I think, *Jacky's getting hungry again.*

I have learned to float, but I have not yet learned to swim, as I only got about three strokes in before I went under out in the salt water. I think the legs got to be made to help somehow. Further study is necessary.

The bits of wood and tinder I have gathered are dry now, I discover upon getting out, and I set about making a fire. My clothes are dry, too, but I don't bother putting them on. Why bother? It's hot and I'm all by myself.

There's a likely bunch of rocks for a sort of firepit over by the outcropping, so I build the fire there. Getting it all stacked up proper, as I have been taught by the ship's cook, I set about to light it. The big lens on the glass unscrews fairly easily and I hold it down to the tinder such that the sun shines through the lens and concentrates on a tiny point. Smoke arises. I blow on the spark and soon I have a blaze.

I gather as many oysters as my hands will bear and put them on a rock right close to the coals and go to gather more wood. When I get back they are sizzling nicely. Upon trying them I find that they are much better this way. It occurs to me that fish, too, could be cooked in such a manner. I nip back down to the beach to get some of the weeds, but even cooked they are still not very good. I eat them anyway 'cause Tilly said they are good for the digestion and prevent scurvy, and as a midshipman in His Majesty's Royal Navy my duty is to keep myself in good form for the good of the Service.

I lay back on the grass and put my hands behind my head and look up at the sky and smile about how poor Captain Locke is going to be repaid for his kindness in rating me midshipman, by being made the laughingstock of the Navy. Poor Captain Locke. I can see the broadsides now, tacked up on the printer's wall, with naughty verses and maybe a cartoon of the Captain looking all leering and lustful and me all spilling out of a midshipman's uniform and frolicking about the quarterdeck while the ship heads for the rocks. One of the rocks would be labeled

FOLLY, another DECEPTION, and another SHEER STUPIDITY. Poor Captain Locke.

Actually, that would make a pretty good sheet. I shall have to learn to draw.

I know, though, that I will never be inside the uniform of a midshipman and it makes me sort of sad. I would have been a good one.

Chapter 39

I passed the night in some fear, not even having the comfort of the *Hope* above me, but at least it did not rain. Before retiring for the night, I cut a good straight stick from a tree, split the end, inserted the hilt of my shiv, and wrapped it down tight with the thong from my whistle so now I at least have a spear for defense from any beast what might try me. How I will deal with serpents what slither up next to me, I shan't think about.

The night noise started again. In the daytime, there's plenty of noise from the birds I see darting about, and even some pretty loud and raucous cries from the bright blue and green and red parrots I see high in the treetops, but nothing compares to this. After I hear a particularly awful screech from nearby, followed by a nasty gurgle, I reach over and take my whistle and cover all the holes and take a deep breath and let out the highest, shrillest, longest blast of which the whistle is capable, and it rips through the night.

Silence.

Well, that stopped 'em. Perhaps they'd like a tune. So I roll over on me back and gives 'em "The Rocky Road to

Dublin" and it seems to help all of us get through the night.

For the signal fire to work, I will need a perfectly calm day, which this one ain't since a stiff onshore breeze is blowing that would take all the smoke and whip it away. No, it's got to be completely still so the column of smoke goes straight up high and stays there.

I gather more wood and this time I also gather some smelly wet seaweed that's tossed up on the shore, for making smoke when I do finally light it off.

I dive into the surf, manage to stay up for five strokes with my legs thrashing, then head back to camp. Breakfast is coconut milk. I can't get into the coconut proper yet, but I can shave the end of it with my shiv till I get down to these things that look like eyes and poke one of them open and then pour the juice inside down my throat.

I figure I'll walk down the beach to the south today to see what's there. I put on my shirt and pants 'cause if I'm taken by cannibals or other rascals, I'll not want to appear immodest. I take my spear in hand and put my whistle in my waistband. The Compleat Beachcomber.

I'm lazing along, poking in this pile of flotsam here, that pile of jetsam there, not finding much 'cept some dead fish that even I can't eat and some amazingly disgusting jellyfish when I come upon a real find. It's a large clamshell, about a foot across and three inches deep in the middle and it's good and thick. A cook pot, at last.

There's a lot of the same kind of shells at this spot and I pick up a couple of smaller ones. Spoons and cups.

Home for lunch.

A bunch of oysters and clams goes in the shell first, then I poke a hole in the eye of a coconut and pour in the juice. Then some pigweed and then on the fire in not too hot a place so the shell don't crack. I gather some smooth small rocks and wash them off and put them in the hottest part of the fire. When they get good and hot, I use a couple of palm frond stems as tongs to pick them and drop them in the pot to help things along. I got plenty of time to wait for it to cook.

Several hours later I'm lying back, patting my belly and thinking as how this was much more to my liking. Even the greens was good. I'm half dozing, looking up at the treetops, when I notice that they ain't moving. Not even a little bit. The wind has died and there's at least six hours of light left. Maybe it's time.

Down at the beach, the sea is calm as glass, with scarcely a ripple on its surface. The tide is down about halfway. I choose a spot just below the high tidemark and down the beach somewhat—I don't want someone to find traces of the fire and then find me and my camp right off. There I put an armful of the dry tinder I had tucked under the *Hope*. Next, bigger dry wood and then bigger yet till I have the whole rack laid out. One final check of the wind and I light it with the lens.

While it is catching, I drag the poor *Hope* down to the

shore and wet it down completely, then drag it back, much heavier now, to the edge of the fire. A column of white smoke is heading straight up.

I give it a while longer and then throw on more wood and then more, till the fire is forming some good coals. Then more, and this time the wood ain't dry at all and the smoke is darker now.

When things are really roaring, I toss on a bunch of the wet seaweed and it hisses and the smoke turns thick and black. Then I set the *Hope* up on its point next to the fire, and I let the black smoke get well up in the sky.

I let the *Hope* fall down over the fire, blocking the smoke, and I slowly count to ten before lifting it back up. The kite smokes a bit, but the wet fabric don't burn. I repeat the action three more times, leaving three puffs of smoke in the air. Then I take the kite back to the water and douse it again.

Looking up now, there's the first column of smoke, which is beginning to thin out and drift away, then the three puffs, then the next column building up again. It's got to be at least three hundred feet up there. I'll wait a few minutes and do it again.

I'm hoping Davy will remember the Brotherhood's secret number when he sees this. Tink'll probably still be in sick bay. Willy, well, forget it. And I know Jaimy'll be too deep in his grief over the death of his darlin' girl to notice anything.

He'd better be.

I go through the whole thing again and then put the glass back together to look seaward to where I think the island is.

Nothing.

I'll take a swim and then try again.

Again the puffs go up and again nothing. The tide comes in and puts the fire out. Tomorrow is another day. I pick up my things and head back to the kip.

There's a tall and wide tree that sits on the edge of my clearing, with its branches hanging out over the lagoon. Its trunk and branches are smooth and pink and have patches on them like peeling skin and there ain't many little branches and the leaves are mainly on the top canopy so it's real easy to climb. The branches are so wide and level that I can walk right along them, no hands.

There's a place right up top that looks out over the sea, where four branches come together, and so I get some rope and weave it back and forth, round and round the four branches, and make myself a little platform. I take another long length of rope and run it from there down to the ground where I pull it taut and tie it around a stout root that curls up from out of the ground. So I've got myself a foretop, like, and I can run up and down that rope just like it was a shroud on the ship. Keep myself ready for sea. I shall call it The Foretop.

I keep watch the rest of the afternoon and evening.

Nothing.

Dinner, and so to bed.

Chapter 40

It rained again last night, so all hope of another signal fire is gone for several days, at least. If I had not been so lazy I would have collected more wood and put it under the *Hope*, but no, I didn't. Conduct Unbecoming a Midshipman in His Majesty's Navy. I put myself on report.

I deny myself breakfast as punishment for my dereliction of duty and go right down to the beach to gather another stack of wood. I will regretfully put the *Hope* on top again tonight. I regret it 'cause I got drenched last night and didn't like it much. Even when it's as warm as this, sleeping wet ain't fun, and I really want to use the *Hope* as shelter again soon.

Oh, well, as Liam says, offer it up. I'll stretch out in the sun later just like my turtles and catch up on...

There.

Out on the sea, very low on the horizon. I'd have missed it if I hadn't been down here on the beach. A wisp of smoke. In puffs of three. Oh, my joy. My shipmates have answered and they will come for me. I figure it will take at least another week to finish the boat. Now all I have to do is wait.

The Good (and it *has* been good except for its initial treachery) Ship *Hope* is now suspended in the tree, securely lashed such that it gives shelter to the branches right below it. Between those branches I have made a rope hammock, more a bed, really, 'cause it's flatter than a hammock. It's a little coarse, but it's much better than sleeping on the ground. And, it's more secure from prowling beasts. And snakes.

With the help of several large rocks, I've managed to get into a ripe coconut and it's all white and delicious, both raw or cooked in my chowder. My chowder, which I keep warm by the fire all day and add to as I collect things for it and eat it as I need it, changes constantly depending on the day's catch. I noticed that schools of a certain flat-headed goggle-eyed fish swim in and out of the lagoon at times, and the next time they came in, I was ready for them with a spear, and two fell prey to my skill. After I cleaned them, I put one in the pot and I put one on a palm leaf and carefully roasted it, sprinkling it with sea salt. It is very good. I inform the turtles that I will not be eating them after all, as I have an ample supply of fish and will not be needing their services.

If this keeps up I shall grow quite fat.

My swimming is becoming acceptable, if not elegant, which the Navy would not like to hear, 'cause it doesn't like for its sailors to know how to swim, for fear they'll leave a sinking ship and swim for their lives rather than trying to save the ship. Or so I've heard.

I've got a real good game and that is to ride the rip out of the lagoon when it's really raging. I've taken another length of that dear rope and tied it to the end of a big branch of my tree that hangs out over the water. Now I can take the other end and go up on the bank and then swing out over the lagoon and drop in with a great whoop and splash and then be churned about and carried out by the ripping tide to the gentle sea. It's an awfully good game.

I haul myself out and stretch out on my rocks. I like to lie here and dream up little scenes about how it might have been with the lads back on the island after the loss of me and what they thought when they saw my signal later on. I picture Jaimy all white and wan with heaving great sighs and pining away over the death of his poor dear girl. He curses himself over and over for being a coward and untrue lover by not hanging on to the rope to the bitter end and joining me in my doom. He is praying that I'm happy up in heaven with all the other angels or maybe he's talking with Liam about taking holy orders and Liam's patting him on the shoulder in consolation when Davy runs up and says, "Hey, Jaimy! Remember that girl you used to like who is now lyin' dead and drownded at the bottom of the sea with sea slugs lickin' at her bare bones?" and before Jaimy can square around and belt him one, Davy points out to sea at my signal. Tears of joy pour from Jaimy's eyes as he clasps his hands together and falls to his knees in gratitude for my deliverance.

I have other versions of it, but I like that one the best. I think I'll run it by again.

And so, her brown legs hanging over the sides of her hammock, an opened coconut by her side, her spear within easy reach, Tonda-lay-o, Queen of the Jungle, plays her pennywhistle and dreams crazy dreams and awaits her Bold Rescuer.

And she wishes he would hurry.

Chapter 41

The water is wide, I cannot cross o'er,
Nor have I wings, nor can I fly,
But give me a boat that can carry two,
And both shall row,
My true love and I

I put down my whistle and look out over the sea. I certainly *can't* cross over, and it's going to take them at least another week to get the boat ready. If I'm right in my figuring of the distance being about thirty miles, they could make it across in around six hours, doing four knots in a moderate breeze. Less, with a good following wind. The waiting is hard, though, doubly so 'cause I don't know what's going to happen to me when they do come over. Did Jaimy, in his grief, tell about me? Has Davy let it all out? Does it matter?

The funny thing about this song, I thinks, putting the pennywhistle back up to my lips and breathing out the slow sad melody, is that it starts out like that with the two lovers all tight and true and then it goes to:

Love is gentle and love is kind,
The sweetest flower when first it's new,
But love grows old,
And waxes cold,
And fades away, like the morning dew

Pretty harsh, that. But is that what's really going to happen to me and Jaimy? Will he grow cold and fade away? He's in love with me now, I think, but then I'm the only girl on the ship, the only port in the storm, the only girl he's ever known. What's going to happen when he meets other girls, maybe girls prettier than me? I don't even know if I am even a little bit pretty at all. I look at my reflection in the pond when it's like glass, but I can't tell. I look down at myself and all I see is Small Girl with White Eyebrow and Tattoo, skin and bones, nothing more. I know the boys thought I was fetching when I was being a girl back in Kingston, but what do they know? If I was a female orangutan in a dress, I'd still have to watch myself with that randy Davy. I just don't know.

There is a ship, and she sails the sea,
She's loaded deep, as deep can be,
But not as deep as the love I'm in,
I know not whether I sink or swim

And whether he loves me or not, what's going to happen to me, anyway? The Deception is becoming a joke. Where will I be put off? When? What will I do?

The Captain, in his rage over being made a fool of in commissioning a girl, could leave me right here, marooned, if he wanted to.

I know they won't let Jaimy go now, wherever I'm dumped. But will he ever come back for me later, after he sails off and becomes an officer and meets proper fine ladies? Will he then find me common and cheap, as he said that time? *Am* I common? I suppose. I know I'm easy in my ways, but am I *cheap*? I've always tried to be good as I could be, even when I was a beggar and a thief, but is that good enough? Jaimy has talked about his family, how upright they are. What would they think of me? *Good afternoon, Ma'am, I am very pleased to meet you. Yes, I am the renowned Bloody Miss Mary "Jacky" Faber, Scourge of the High Seas, and I'm in love with your son James and he with me and we want to be married, and yes, I feel I know him quite well as we have been living together for the past two years...Right.*

I shake that song and all those thoughts out of my head. I'll take what comes. I look down at my little pond shimmering down below.

Ah, Jaimy, we could have had such a time here in my little paradise. I think you would like my camp and I think you would like your jungle girl in her new and golden tan. I would make some of my chowder for you. We would swim and I would show you the games and I would make up for all the times I could not go in the bowsprit netting with you when I wanted to so much. I hope you're feeling better now that you've seen my signal and I hope you didn't throw yourself in some volcano in sadness over the death o' my own sweet self, and wouldn't that be a proper Romeo-and-Juliet ending to my little story now? I'm always reaching up and touching my earring, which to me is my wedding ring forever and ever, and I think of you whenever I touch it.

Chapter 42

When I wake this morning, on the nineteenth day of my exile, it is very quiet. The birds are not singing. Something is wrong.

I hang the glass around my neck and go hand over hand up the line to the foretop. I scan up and down the beach but can see nothing. Maybe it's just the weather, like the calm before a storm when everything seems strange and still. I train the glass on the horizon and...

There! A sail! They've come!

I almost shriek with joy. They've got the wind behind them and they're roarin' in and prolly only a mile out, and I can see figures now and I've got to go down and put the vest and drawers on and...

Something to the south catches my eye and chills my joy. The leaves on the tops of the small trees at the edge of the beach shake every now and again, like someone or something is running into the trunks below. I see a flash of color and metal. I catch me breath.

Clothing! Men! Guns!

I go out on a long branch that stretches out in that direction and look down.

It's the pirates. They've come out into a clearing below and I slink back out of sight. They, too, must have seen the signal fires from wherever they were camped. They've brought along kegs and casks and chests, I guess, 'cause LeFievre didn't trust leavin' 'em, and he's there in his silks and he's placing his men with rifles along the embankment at the top of the tide line. All their eyes are on the incoming boat. I look out at the boat and see without even lifting the glass that they'll beach in a few minutes and there's the Captain and Jaimy and...

They are like ducks on a pond. It will be a massacre. I've got to warn them. They'll never see me up here, and if they did they'd think I mean for them to come in right there which, oh God, I don't.

I slides down my line and hits the bank running. I grabs me swing line and swings out over the lagoon and drops. The tide is out, which is good 'cause that'll give me some room on the beach, and so the water in the lagoon is only up to me knees and I splashes through it out to the beach and I runs out to the surf and waves me arms over me head and screams, "No, no! The pirates!" and I points south to where the pirates are and then points north and say, "Over there! Hard right! Over there! Hard right! Follow me!" and I runs in that direction and I keeps pointin' and yellin' and the boat starts to turn and there's the poppin' o' musket fire behind me and there's puffs in the sand around me feet and the Dolphins in the boat hear the gunfire and duck down and pull up guns of their own.

I'm poundin' on down the beach as fast as I can with me legs apumpin' and I hears somethin' comin' up behind me and I looks over me shoulder and it's one of the pirates and he's reachin' for me and I tries to run faster and I know I'm runnin' like a girl wi' me ankles flippin' out to the sides but I can't help it I can't help it and then he fetches me a blow to the back of me head and then I sees the sand comin' up t' me face and then I ain't seein' nothin'.

I wake up with me head throbbing and me hands tied behind me back. I'm lying next to a black keg and there are legs millin' all around me. LeFievre is standing next to me and is shouting something towards the beach. They are trying to parley their way out of this, I thinks through the fog in me head. I hear faint replies from down the beach.

Someone kicks me and I cry out.

"*Alors—elle s'est réveillé. Emmène-la ici.*"

Someone catches me under me arms and I am lifted up. I see a rope has been strung over a low branch, and at the end of the rope, over the keg and hanging down, is a noose. I am put on the keg.

At last, I thinks as I'm stood up wi' me legs all shakin' on the keg. The noose is put over me head and the knot is run down and the rough and hairy rope is pulled up tight against me neck. *At last.*

LeFievre says something in French to one of the men, and the man goes to the other end of the rope and takes the slack out of it so it's pulled taut, and I'm up on me tiptoes and weavin' back and forth and I'm startin' to gag already and, *Oh God, it's really going to happen to me I'm really going to—*

"Captain!" I hear LeFievre say through my terror. "Step away from the boat and the girl will not die. All we want is the boat. Step away or she hangs."

I force me eyes open and sees our men lined up.

The Captain crosses his arms and shakes his head and says, "A boat for a mere ship's boy? Or girl, as you say. Surely that's not an even trade for one such as you, LeFievre. We all know our duty. She will do hers."

Then there's pops and shouts from the woods behind us. The Captain has sent men to circle around to take the pirates from behind! Hope springs—

I hear LeFievre curse and I sees Jaimy running towards me with a sword in his hand. *Jaimy, oh…*

That's the last thing I sees, 'cause LeFievre sees his plan gone wrong and turns to run, but before he does he gives the keg a kick and over it goes.

And finally…for all me deceptions and all me lies and all me crimes…finally…

I swings.

Chapter 43

Blackness
Velvet Blackness
Blackness without End Amen
But in the Velvet Blackness a Point of Light
Which Grows Larger
And Larger
And Becomes
the
Sun

And the sun is in me eyes and I'm chokin' and coughin' and Liam is pumpin' up and down on me ribs t' make me breathe and *It hurts it hurts, Liam, please don't hurt me* and Jaimy is beside me and he's slappin' me face. I'm gaspin' and me throat is burnin' and the noose is still around me neck but it ain't so tight no more... *Oh so tight so tight I can't*... and so Jaimy stops the slappin' and just pets me head and cries, and I croaks out "Me hands, me hands," 'cause I can't move me hands and they hurt. *Oh God, the choke... the choking...* they turn me over and cut the rope and turn me again, and I throws me arms around Jaimy's neck and bawls away all snortin' and gaggin' and…

"Aye, we thought you was goners there, Jacky, a fair jig you was dancin' at the end o' that rope wi' you all twistin' and turnin' and all," and I see that it's Davy talkin' but I can't make no sense… "And when you went all limp at the end and just hung there, I thought sure you was done…" and then it's Jaimy sayin', "I thought the life had gone out of me again…" and he's lookin' all pitiful and tears are runnin' down his face and I thinks, *Whatcha cryin' for, Jaimy, what…* and all about me men are standin', and I put my face against Jaimy's neck and say, "Pick me up, Jaimy…" and I'm tryin' to hold me mind together but I can't… *Pick me up, Jaimy, and carry me, carry me away from this place, Jaimy, I want to show you my camp, and what's this on me neck,* "Oh God, get it off, get it off," and it's Liam what takes it off and I'm breathin' better for it. I feels myself picked up and… *It's not far, Jaimy, it's right over there. I know you'll like it. You'll like the pool, Jaimy, and the hammock and my wonderful tree, and Davy, you'll love me swing.* "Captain, would you care for some chowder it's really quite good…"

"Please don't mind her, Sir, she's off her mind."

Everyone come and have some, but please don't eat the turtles… and I points the way. I kiss the salty tears away from Jaimy's cheek but they keep on comin' and I rub my face on his and mix his tears and my tears together, and I say, "Don't cry, Jaimy, it's all right now, you'll see, we'll swim in the pool together and dry off on the rocks together and lie in the hammock together and be together forever and ever and ever and…"

Chapter 44

Well, we ain't together for ever and ever. In fact, we're never together on this ship again, at least not the way we were, at least not now.

I was hardly back in my camp at all when I was taken away from Jaimy and put into the boat and they don't let Jaimy come back with me, or even Davy. Liam is on the boat, though, and they let me cling to him for the five hours it takes to get back across the open sea to the island. We pull up next to the careened *Dolphin* and I'm taken to sick bay, which is still set up in tents on the beach, and slimy stuff is put on my throat to heal the rope burn. I'm still talking out of my head some, so they give me a bit of the sweet liquid and that shuts me up and I'm out for a day or so. When I awake, I'm quiet in my mind, well, almost—I still have the nightmares and wake up screaming—but my neck is getting better.

None of the men or boys are allowed near me—for my own protection, I am told. There's a Marine guard at the foot of my bed. Tink is in a bed across the way, but he is forbidden to talk to me so is not much company. He is getting better, though, which is good to hear. He will soon be out of bed. The Master, Mr. Greenshaw, is stumbling around getting used to his crutch. The stump of his leg hangs down with his pant leg neatly pinned up around it, but he is philosophical about it. He will get on with his life, he announces; he will still be a sailing Master. The rest of the men wounded in the sea battle with the pirates, except for those who died before the *Dolphin* limped to the island, recovered. None of ours were hurt in the final battle on the beach, 'cept maybe me.

Mr. Lawrence comes to sit with me for a bit and he tells me that the boat is making daily runs back and forth to my beach and hauling back fine lengths of good lumber. Looks like a right sawmill back there. The wood is immediately applied to the *Dolphin* when it arrives here. The hammers pound constantly.

He also tells me that Jaimy has been made Midshipman. The news fills my chest with happiness and I weep for joy. I wish only that we could be together to celebrate.

The Doctor examines me, which I don't like overmuch, and declares me fit enough to be taken to the ship and tossed in the brig. For my own protection. I get out of bed to follow my Marine escort, but before leaving the tent I dash over to Tink and plants a kiss on his forehead. He blushes mightily and the guard says, "'Ere, 'ere!" sternly, but I don't care as much for their rules as once I did.

When I get to the ship I protest that as Midshipman Faber I should be allowed a midshipman's berth, but Mr. Haywood will have none of it, and he is in command when the Captain is gone, so that is that. He actually laughs when I make the request, a strange sound I'd never before heard, and he says, "Midship*wench* Faber, I'll be damned." Some joke. The brig is not locked but the Marine stands outside, and he goes everywhere with me. I'm allowed to go topside during the day, but it's into the brig at night and the brig *is* locked then.

There are not many people left on the ship, as the list takes some real getting used to. Most stay on the beach and are actively engaged in either working or avoiding work. The only ones on board are the First Mate, Deacon Dunne and a few of his clerks, and a few Marines to guard the stores. And to guard me. I see the boat running back and forth carrying long planks of wood. Probably from my poor tree. I'm not getting much information on what's going on, but I do know they're keeping Jaimy over there on the mainland. I can guess why. I hope he gets to use my hammock. I like thinking of him in it.

With my red-coated escort in tow, I went down to my hidey-hole and got my dresses and other things, and I pass my days sitting on the quarterdeck sewing and playing my pennywhistle, which someone, probably Liam, found in my camp and sent over to me, and I spend my nights in reading and thought. I've given up planning, until I see which way the wind blows.

I have resolved that each morning when I wake up from now on, I will take three long breaths and think about each of them as I draw them in and let them out, and I will remember that time at the end of that rope when I could not draw such breaths. And then I will look at the blue veins in my wrists and will know that my blood is running through them, and for that I will be grateful. Amen.

The nightmares don't come every night now.

This day I get information.

During the morning I was doing my usual things and working on cracking the Marine's reserve. Actually, there're three Marines assigned to keep me from wreaking moral havoc on the crew. All three are young and good looking, quite splendid in their uniforms of scarlet and white with clay buttons and high collars and tight white breeches. They are not allowed to talk to me, but I talk to them as I sit and sew on the quarterdeck hatch and look out over the beach and try to figure out what is happening from all the fuss and scurrying about. "And I'm sure you have a young lass awaiting you at home, don't you, Johnny? Did she cry on the dock when you marched aboard? I know she did, Johnny, you're such a fine-looking lad, I know she did, and she couldn't stop, could she? She just kept on cryin' and cryin', I know, and it fair broke your heart to hear it. Here, let me play 'My Bonnie Light Horseman' for you, Johnny, because it's about a soldier just like you. It's ever so sad and beautiful..."

He still doesn't say anything when I'm finished, but I notice the tip of his bayonet shaking a bit and he's biting his lip. *Soon, Johnny, soon...*

There's Davy! The boat must be back over here! I go to the rail and call out and wave, but he just keeps going. He does wave, however, and taps his fist on his tattoo and points to the guard at the foot of the gangway leading up to the ship. I guess I'll have to wait.

"'Ere, 'ere, Miss Faber, you must come away from there! It's orders!"

Ah, so Johnny can *talk.*

I have not been put into female clothing yet, since they don't have any such thing aboard and they don't know about my two dresses, and they wouldn't let me wear the Kingston dress, anyway. I don't want them to know about my blue dress till I'm ready. Besides, I'm not likely to drive any of the men aboard mad with desire, so I'm told to just wear my ship's boy uniform in a modest manner and be good and don't flounce around.

What I do is get my Marine to take me to ship's store and I get a midshipman's black neckerchief, which I put right on. With my white shirt it looks quite dashing. I can't do anything about the rest of a middie's uniform, the black pants and black jacket, but they'll get the idea. I get a sea chest, too, and my first hairbrush. Deacon Dunne charges the items against my name and promises to come see me later in the day to continue my spiritual instruction. Praise be.

Johnny gallantly carries my sea chest back to the brig, and I put my things in it, which is satisfying. I resolve to get a carving tool and engrave the chest with my name.

The Deacon is as good as his word. Just after noon we sit at the table in the gun room and he assigns me more Bible verses, which I dutifully read and then try to explain, and then he assigns me more to read at night and then he goes into other topics such as my Immortal Soul, which we pray over quite vigorously. I find I have several other things in addition to my Immortal Soul that I did not know I had, one of which is my Sacred Honor and the other is my Precious Jewel, both of which seem to have something to do with the fact that Jaimy and I haven't done that baby-making thing yet.

Just before he leaves me to my studies, he leans back in his chair and fixes me with his gaze. Then he lobs the bomb. "You are to be enrolled in a girls' school in Boston, Massachusetts, in the United States. Mr. Tilden has connections there and will make the necessary arrangements. You are to receive a midshipman's share of the prize money, and that will be placed on your account at the school. Upon completion of your studies, you will receive the balance, if any. We all thought this would be best, and you should thank God for this opportunity to better yourself. Good day, Miss."

He leaves me with the wind knocked out of me and I just sit there for a while in thought. Then I get out one of the books that Mr. Lawrence has lent me and I go up on deck and before Johnny can say no I fly up to the mizzentop and Johnny says, "Please come down," and I put my head over the side of the top and says, "C'mon, Johnny, I'm right here, I can't get away and a girl needs some time to herself, like," and I put my back against the mast and let my mind race on.

Johnny stands guard below.

I take my dinners with Deacon Dunne in the gun room and they are pretty joyless affairs. The first time I tucked into my horse, he said, "Oh my, we'll have to do something about that," and so I'm being taught table manners and etiquette and how a fork is used and what goes where in setting a table and where to put my hands, which is all right because it gives us something to talk about. After dinner, I take a turn about the deck and then am taken to my kip and locked in. The Marine on night duty doesn't stand outside the door all night, as I'm not considered all *that* dangerous, but instead he beds down on a cot in the passageway.

I hear Henry Marine's snores coming through the bars not long after we have a bit of a talk and he goes off to turn in. Henry was the easiest of the Marines to crack, him having a mother and sisters at home and used to talking to females. I had him blubbering over "The Cruel Sister" in no time.

I light my candle and look over at my Bible but pick up instead *Moll Flanders,* which I borrowed from the midshipmen's berth and say to myself I'll only read a little and then I'll do the Bible assignment. The middies got some pretty interesting books, the naughty boys. I'm settling in but then I hear a tap on the bars of the little window. What…

It's Davy. I blow out the candle.

"Shushh…talk real low," I says, getting up and standing under the grating. "What's happened…how's Jaimy…what's—"

"Back in jail again, Jacky? My, my," says Davy, all full of himself for having snuck on the ship undetected and so full of news that he can barely contain himself. "Seems you've spent more time in here than any of us. It's proper, though, you bein' a connivin' deceiver and liar and all."

"Davy…," I hisses.

"All right, Jacky, calm yerself." He clears his throat. "Well, right after you got hung and we all charged up the beach, yellin' like banshees and swingin' our cutlasses and bangin' our guns with Jaimy in the lead—or I should say Mr. Fletcher, him bein' made midshipman about the same time you was but he didn't get to enjoy it none, you bein' dead and all—and anyways, Jaimy runs straight through the pirates' line and cuts you down with one swipe of his sword and you crumpled on down to the ground, all loose-jointed like you didn't have no bones, and you know the rest of that part, but you don't know that the pirates were all killed, LeFievre, too, except for a few who were real happy to tell us where their loot was stashed. There's tons and tons of it, Jacky, all gold and silver and jewels, and we're rich again, Jacky. The Captain is so happy, he's forgivin' you for bein' a girl and you're to get a full midshipman's share o' the plunder."

He pauses. "You did hear what they're gonna do with you?" I reply that I had.

"Sorry, Jack. Anyway there's more. After the pirates are buried—'cept for LeFievre's head, which we're goin' to hang from the bowsprit when we go into port as a warnin' to other pirates, neat, hey?—well, right after that, Jaimy goes up to Bliffil and slaps him across the face and calls him out! Right! He challenges him to a duel with swords to avenge the beatin' o' you. I guess the Captain's rule about no duelling amongst the midshipmen don't apply when the ship is far away and anyway he don't say nothin' against it. Calm *down*, Jacky, he's all right. Anyways, Bliffil weasels out and won't fight and ever'one sees that he won't and the Captain is going to put him off at the next port 'cause the Captain found out that Bliffil hung back by the boat when the fight was going on and he's to receive no share of the loot! How's that for justice!

"The fixin' o' the ship is goin' real fast, and they expect to be done in a few days. Everyone's comin' back now 'cause we've got enough wood, so Jaimy'll be here tomorrow, and Tink and I are now rated Ordinary, and didn't I have the best time in your camp!"

Chapter 45

So it is to be Boston. After all this time of wondering where I would finally be put off, it is to be there, the home of the bean and the cod. Well, it is a seafaring town and maybe I'll be able to find my little ship there, after I'm finished off at the finishing school, which is the Lawson Peabody School for Young Girls. So maybe I'll get to be one after all. A lady, that is.

Not that I have much say in the matter. When Tilly comes back on board, I go to see him and say, "Why do I have to go to this school? I have money now and I want to marry James Fletcher and he wants to marry me and why can't we?"

He says, "Because you're too young. The Doctor says you're probably about fifteen years old at the outside and therefore have not reached your majority and have no rights, and furthermore, you are female, which means you have even fewer rights. Besides, the Captain has obligations to Mr. Fletcher's parents and marriage to you is not in it."

"But Mr. Tilden, why can't I just be given my prize money and be put off? I've been looking after myself for my whole life now and I believe I'm qualified to continue doing it."

"I'm afraid the matter is settled, Miss," he says, primly. I think I make him nervous in my new femaleness. He looks over his spectacles at me. "The Schoolmistress is personally known to me. She is a fine upstanding Puritan lady. You and your money will be safe there. I will convey you to the school when we arrive in Boston."

End of matter.

Everyone came back aboard today. I will *not* be closeted away, and I browbeat the poor helpless George Marine and Johnny Marine to escort me down to the gangway. I have them stand on either side of me, all beautiful in their uniforms and me in the middle with my new black midshipman's kerchief and my dress whites. I have a Bo'sun's pipe, which I use to pipe everyone aboard, saluting smartly like a proper middie. There's Mr. Lawrence and Liam and the Master and…there's Jaimy.

He comes towards me and I go towards him, but the Marines step between us.

"Sorry, Miss Faber, but specific orders on this one."

The Captain is the last one to come on board. He returns my salute and orders me below. I think my midshipmanship is over.

It takes some doing, but the *Dolphin* is off on the tide.

Chapter 46

Bliffil was put off the ship without ceremony in Charleston. Before he left he laid his curse upon Jaimy and me and promised to see us both in Hell.

My poor dear Marines have been replaced with a trio of older men. Major Piggott, the commander of the Marine unit, apparently wasn't pleased with the level of discipline that the former dear boys were able to maintain in the force of my charms. No matter. I found that two of my new grizzled veterans have daughters of my age, so...

I am still entered on the books as a midshipman, since the senior officers consider it a great joke. When I had previously thought the Captain might be mad, I was mistaken. Mr. Lawrence tells me the Captain is the sort to quickly take offense and is a dead shot and has fought several duels already and left the other fellow the worse off for it, so no one is liable to be cheeky, to his face at least. "Plus," says Mr. Lawrence, "you've made him rich beyond all dreams of avarice, so he don't care."

I, however, do not consider my rank a joke. I wheedled Deacon Dunne into writing out my commission all fair and legal-like and he goes along with it, what could it hurt? The Deacon likes the idea of the prize money, too. It'll buy him a nice little parish up-country and he'll never have to go to sea again. I put the commission in my sea chest with my other things. Davy, on that first night when he brought his news, also brought me back my shiv and my other clothes, and so all I own is now in the trunk. Except for my share of the prize.

I get visited by the officers, but neither the midshipmen nor the sailors are allowed to see me. Especially not Jaimy. Or so they think.

Late at night, when the moon is bright and when the Marine is off to sleep, Jaimy creeps to my grating and through it we whisper. I have found chinks in the wall for handholds and toeholds, and I can climb up high enough so that I can leap up and grab the grating. Hanging there I slowly chin myself up, and through the bars we can bring our lips together for a moment till my arms start to quiver and weaken and I have to drop back down.

We left Charleston a week ago and the winds have been generally fair and so we're one day from Boston. I, who have been kept locked down for the entire time since we refloated the *Dolphin*, have finally been invited to dine with the officers and midshipmen. I suppose they figure I can't do too much damage now.

Now that I have a brush, I have experimented with my hair, which comes down to below my shoulders, and I believe that tonight, my last night on the *Dolphin*, I will wear it swept up, as that makes me look a little bit older. I have an old broken piece of comb to hold it in place.

There. Like that. And tonight I shall wear my blue dress for the first time. I start to make myself ready.

Outside my window, I hear the boys playing in the rigging and it fair breaks my heart to think of my younger self all carefree in the foretop and how I'll never be there again. It isn't the Brotherhood up there, now, though, it's new boys, brought on in Charleston. Some more will be picked up in Boston to fill our spaces. Good luck to them. I've certainly had my share of luck.

I hear other things from my window, too. Apparently, I have become Our Jacky, the Darling of the Ship, and Jaimy is in for some abuse... *"Lazing aroun' in the mizzentop wi' our little Jacky, 'e was, the dog..."* I can imagine the shaking of heads and the black looks from the suddenly pious bunch of scoundrels. *"And in the same hammock, mind you, for two years... Little hound, 'e is..."*

Liam has come by and given me a concertina, the one owned by Grant. "It's of no use to him now, Jacky, and I know he'd want you to have it. He loved the music and I know you do, too. You're a rare one, Jacky. I'll wave when you go off the ship tomorrow, lass, but I'll say good-bye now."

I put on the dress and look at myself in the mirror. My hair is up and my sandals are on my feet. I've tied my midshipman's neckerchief around my throat, and with the ends hanging down in back it covers up the welt across my neck and looks right elegant, and hey, I'm a middie, too.

The dress fits perfectly, as well it should, since I've had it on and off a dozen times adjusting the fit. The skirt hangs nicely, not too full, and the middle fits good and snug around my ribs, and my chest sits up all jaunty in the top part.

There's one bell in the second dog watch and a knock on the door. It's time for dinner.

I resolve to be merry.

They are all at table when I enter, and they all rise. I rather like that. Or most rise, anyway. Some of the midshipmen almost faint back into their seats. I can see they've already been into the wine as their faces are flushed. Mr. Lawrence casts his eyes to the ceiling and smiles slightly and pulls out a chair for me. I'm seated between him and Major Piggott. Always a Marine by my side.

Mr. Lawrence is the senior officer present. The First Mate is off dining with the Captain. It would be asking too much for them to be here.

I'm seated across from Jaimy. I hope he's pleased with how I look. I think he is. He does look a bit stunned, though, but then, they all do.

"Good evening, gentlemen," I purrs. "I thank you very much for your kind invitation." I have been coached by the Deacon.

"It is our pleasure, Miss Faber," says Mr. Lawrence. "Steward, a glass of wine for the lady. Oh, and a shawl for Miss Faber, too. There's one in my cabin."

The steward pours out the wine in a crystal goblet and I pick it up.

"Mr. Fletcher, will you give us the King?" says Mr. Lawrence.

They all stand and pick up their glasses and hold them out in front of them. I go to stand, too, but Mr. Lawrence very gently puts his fingertip on my shoulder to keep me down.

"The King!" Jaimy manages to get out and they all repeat, "The King!" Then they drink down their wine and sit and go back to staring at me.

Mr. Lawrence turns to me. "I perceive that you might be a bit chilly, my dear, as this is, after all, the coast of New England and not the sunny shores of the Caribbean. And I know that our midshipmen share my concern to the degree that they will be unable to speak or eat until you are made more comfortable. Isn't that true, gentlemen?"

Less than enthusiastic murmurs of assent, but the shawl is brought nonetheless and placed around my shoulders. It is a very nice shawl and I thank Mr. Lawrence for his kindness.

"It is a present for my wife. Do you think she will like it?"

I reply that I'm sure she will, Sir, but think to myself that he'd best not tell her that Bloody Jack Faber was first to wear it, or his homecoming might not be all he hopes it to be.

I lift my glass to my lips and gaze across the rim at Jaimy, and as he looks at me my eyes start brimming up 'cause I know the ship's leavin' right after they drop me off tomorrow and I thought maybe they'd stay around for at least a little while, but no, and everything else in the room falls away and...

But then they bring in the food and we fall to.

It is a most glorious dinner, and at the end there is laughter and talk and toasts all around, and when it is time for me to leave, I stand and lift my glass and say, "A toast to the newest member of your company, James Emerson Fletcher, by the grace of God, *Midshipman* of the Line of Battle, His Majesty's Royal Navy!"

Cries of *Hear, hear,* and the toast is drunk, and then my eyes start to fill up again and my lip starts quiverin', and Mr. Lawrence notices, so he stands and raises his glass and says, "To Jacky Faber, the fairest midshipman and saltiest sailor *ever* to grace the decks of the *Dolphin*!"

Cheers, and then my Marine leads me back to the brig.

Jaimy comes to me later, after all are asleep. I rise from my bed and go to the grating and reach up my hand and we whisper far into the night.

At last he must go on watch and there's nothing more to say.

"Good-bye, Jaimy."

"Good-bye, Jacky."

"Come back and find me, Jaimy, and take me away."

"I will, Jacky. I will."

Boston

My sea chest has been taken ashore. It will only be a few minutes now and I wait for my Marine to come fetch me.

I hear from the shouts and bustle and laughter outside that they are going to man the top for me and they'll all be lined up along the spars and in the tops and Jaimy'll be one of the sideboys on the quarterdeck and I'll have to go right by him and the word is that the fightin's started back up with France again and they're leavin' straightaway and they'll be right in the thick of it and *oh Lord*...And there'll be a coach on the dock and I'll have to get in it and it'll pull away from the dock....

Ah lads, I don' wan' to go.

No. No. Steady on. I've got to put on a good show and not start bawlin' and shame myself 'cause salty sea sailors don't cry and I knows right now from the constrictin' o' me throat that I ain't gonna be able to do it but I got to try.

Jacky. It's time.

Come on, girl. Up the ladder and out now. Head high, flags flyin', that's the way we does it, but I knows it ain't gonna wash 'cause I'm half blubberin' already and I knows that soon's I steps out they'll be hollerin' Hooray, Jacky, and Give 'em Hell, Jackeroe, and yes, Bloody Jack, too, and I'll see Tink and Davy and Willy and Liam, and they'll have to pry me off Jaimy whose face I may never see no more—*Dear God, please*—and I'll try to be brave but I never was really very brave...

Chatting with L. A. Meyer

Question: When did you begin writing? Did you always want to be a writer?

L. A. Meyer: While I've made a living most of my life through art of various sorts, I started putting words and illustrations on paper in my late twenties. In the early 1970s, I wrote and illustrated two children's books—one of them, *The Gypsy Bears,* was not bad, but the other one was totally forgettable. I was a graduate student at Boston University at the time, getting my master's degree in painting. About that same time, I wrote a long teen novel concerning the little French girl who posed for Edgar Degas' sculpture *The Little Dancer, Aged Fourteen.* Mercifully, that manuscript was not published, but the experience did teach me just what goes into constructing a novel.

Q: What sparked the idea for *Bloody Jack*?

L. A. M.: My wife, Annetje, and I have a small gallery in Bar Harbor, Maine. There we sell quite a few prints of my artwork, and each print has to be matted and framed... and I used to be the one that got to do it. While the work was gratifying—people were buying my artwork, after all—it was repetitive and my mind was free to wander. One day in late summer of 2000, I'm framing away in my workshop and listening to a program of British and Celtic music on our local community radio station when the host plays a long string of early nineteenth-century songs featuring young girls dressing up as boys and following their boyfriends out to sea. The best known of these songs are "Jackaroe" and "Canadee-i-o." These musical stories generally end up with the girl being found out quickly and happily marrying either the boy or the captain.

It occurred to me to wonder what it would be like if the girl, instead of seeking to be with her lover, connives to get on board a British warship just to eat regularly and have a place to stay—she being a starving orphan in the streets of London's slums in the late 1700s. What would she have to do to pull off this deception over a long period of time? How would she handle the "necessary things"? Further, what if she goes through puberty while on board and in the company of 408 rather rough men? Worse, what if she has no clue what is happening to her? And finally, what if the girl falls in love with one of the other ship's boys yet can never tell him of her female nature and her affection for him?

I started making notes, and seven months later *Bloody Jack* was done.

Q: The events in *Bloody Jack* take place primarily aboard an eighteenth-century British warship. Did you have to do any research to tell this story?

L. A. M.: Of course, I have read a lot of books concerning the British navy during the Napoleonic Wars—my favorites being the Horatio Hornblower series by C. S. Forester and Patrick O'Brian's Aubrey-Maturin series. I was a naval officer during the Vietnam War, and that helped, too—naval etiquette and rituals haven't changed all that much over the years. My lifelong love of traditional folk music also came to good use in Jacky's story.

Q: Was Jacky modeled after any real people?

L. A. M.: Not one person, really. I have two sons, no daughters—but I taught a lot of very fierce freshman girls during my seven years as a high school art teacher, so I got to know how girls of that age act. There is a lot of Annetje, my wife of thirty-seven years, in Jacky's character, too.

Q: In serving on HMS *Dolphin*, Jacky not only affects her own destiny, she makes a difference in the lives of the other sailors, too. In what ways do you hope your story will influence your readers?

L. A. M.: In developing the character of Jacky Faber, I wanted from the start to depict her as a regular kid, one that readers, as well as myself, could relate to. Many reviewers have described Jacky as brave and resourceful, but I don't see her that way. She is resourceful, yes, and clever and cunning, too, and bent on survival at almost any cost, but she is not a typical warrior princess, one with fearless eye and broad sword in hand. In fact, Jacky is not very brave at all—she is a peaceful sort of coward. In every instance she is *only* as brave as she needs to be in order to protect herself and her friends, and no more. In the concluding line of the book, "I'll try to be brave but I really was never very brave," she is not being disingenuous—she is speaking the truth.

In the next book, *Curse of the Blue Tattoo*, Amy, a well-bred schoolmate, says to Jacky, "When you hurt, Jacky, you cry. When you are unhappy, you whine. When you are mad, you curse" enumerating these and many other reasons why Jacky is not yet a lady. But don't we all do just those same things? When we are young, these very human traits are right out in the open, but as we grow older we learn to internalize those feelings, putting on the masks of adulthood and mature masculinity and femininity. But young or old, girl or boy, man or woman, the feelings are still there. Jacky has not yet learned to hide these things—because, as she says, "I warn't never meant to be a lady."

I hope readers will relate to these aspects of Jacky. As to how her story might influence them, I can only say that Jacky gets to where she is in each book by hard work, study, and her feeling that, no matter how mean the job, or how low her station, there's always something to be learned from it, and that learning may come in *very* handy some day. "There's a science to everything," she observes, from scrubbing pots to trimming sails to playing the pennywhistle to doing a proper bow and curtsy. This attitude certainly pays off for Jacky; a similar outlook may very well come in handy for readers.

Reader Chat Page

1. When Jacky first goes to sea, she doesn't care if she ever catches a pirate. Why, then, does she sign on to HMS *Dolphin*? What is her attraction to the sea?

2. Jacky worries that dancing and singing and playing and just showing off in general will ruin The Deception. Could this behavior really give her away? Why or why not?

3. Why does Jacky encourage Mr. Jenkins to fight Bliffil? What are the risks of her plan? What are the benefits? Why doesn't she think Jenkins needs to win the fight to accomplish her goal?

4. Admitting that she gets scared, Jacky calls herself a coward. Do you agree with her? What makes someone "a coward"? What makes them "brave"?

5. How did living on the streets of London prepare Jacky for her life on the *Dolphin*?

6. What do you think of the crew's reaction when they learn of The Deception?

Curse of the Blue Tattoo

Being the Misadventures of Jacky Faber, Midshipman and Fine Lady

"Bloody" Jacky Faber a proper Boston lady? Not if she can help it!

Found out as a girl, Jacky Faber is forced to leave HMS *Dolphin* and attend the elite Lawson Peabody School for Young Girls in Boston. For poor Jacky, survivor of the cruel streets of London and fights with bloodthirsty pirates, it's a fate worse than death.

Only now, floundering in land-bound misery, she faces her toughest battle yet: learning how to be a lady.

It seems that *everything* Jacky does is wrong. Her embroidery is deplorable, her French is atrocious, and her table manners—*disgusting!* And, of course, whenever she roams the city in search of adventure, she finds trouble instead. But even Jacky is surprised when her trouble turns out to be *murder....*

Turn the page to see Jacky two-steppin' right into trouble—again....

I don't want to leave the familiar sights and sounds of the port just yet and I figure I've got some time before High Tea and prolly wouldn't be missed, anyway, so I climbs up on a piling at the end of the pier and look about at the scene spread out before me, all flags and rope and pitch and tar and wooden ships and iron men, and I pull out my whistle and start to play.

I start out with "The Mountains of Morn," and then keepin' in the slow and sad mode, I does the "London-derry Air," that sad, sad song of a father sending his son off to war to the sound of the calling pipes. *Oh, Danny boy...*

"Luffly, Miss. Just luffly," I hears a voice say. "But could it be that you'll play sumthin' a bit more merry for poor John Thomas and 'is mates what had had enough of sadness and woe and hard times?"

I pops open me eyes and sees a group of sailors standin' in front of me. They look like they're just off the ship and heading for a bit of fun. A huge red-bearded brute seems to be the one what spoke, him grinnin' from ear to ear and flippin' a coin in an arc toward me.

The beggar in me reaches out and snatches the coin from the air without thinkin' and drops it down my front to free up my fingers and I hops off the piling and rips right into "New York Girls," a real rousin' tune that's sure to please this crowd.

It does. They whistle and stamp and some of 'em roar into the chorus of "*Oh, you New York girls, can't you dance the polka*" and John Thomas crosses his arms and starts in to dance, which causes his mates to cheer and shout, and so I starts into dancin', too, and that gets 'em cheerin' louder, and so I goes faster and faster and I had forgotten how much I love this singin' and dancin' and showin' off that I completely loses myself in it all, I love it so, and then John Thomas crows out with, "You can't match this step, girl!" and I taunts back, "Can, too!" and, though a part of me thinks that maybe I shouldn't be doin' this, I lifts up my skirts to show the steps and I does the step he did and then I tops it with one of my own and then...

And then I notice that they've all stopped dancin' and singin' and foolin' around and are slinkin' back and lookin' at somethin' over my shoulder. Then I feels a heavy hand on me shoulder and I hears a squeaky male voice that says, "Come with me."

I turns around and looks up into the sweaty face of a man with round, fat, pink jowls.

"Who are you?" I ask, all fearful and stupid and not likin' this turn of events at all.

His eyes are almost buried in the folds of his cheeks and they peer down at me with a feverish glint. He wears a black hat and a coat with a high collar that bites deep into the flesh of his neck. He carries a stout stick.

"I? Who am *I*, it asks? Well, I'll have it know that *I* am Constable John Wiggins, the High Sherwiiff of Boston." He smugly chuckles. "And *you,* my girl, are a dirty little twollop what's under arwest for Lewd and Lascsiwious Conduct!"